Praise for *Painting the Corners*

"With these stories, Bob Weintraub has executed a triple play: savvy baseball writing, unforgettable characters, and a home run ending for each tale. By all means, read this book."

—W. P. Kinsella, author of *Shoeless Joe* (the basis for the film *Field of Dreams*)

"Imaginative baseball stories for long rain delays and hot stove league nights."

—Darryl Brock, author of *If I Never Get Back* and *Two in the Field*

"Unique and wonderfully twisted."

—Ed Asner, actor

"Great storytelling for fans and nonfans alike. Bob Weintraub has big-league talent."

—Dan Shaughnessy, author of *The Curse of the Bambino* and columnist for the *Boston Globe*

"The prevailing trend seems to be to reduce baseball to numbers, to take out the adjectives and hyperbole, eliminating the descriptions of facial tics and personal travails and sunsets, to treat the game as some algebraic problem stretched across a blackboard in the basement of stats guru Bill James or some other math junkie. I myself prefer my baseball with the imagination left in, thank you very much. This collection of deft stories by Robert Weintraub takes us back to the bleachers and locker rooms, to the people who actually play and watch the game. Very nice. Very nice, indeed."

—Leigh Montville, *New York Times* bestselling author of *The Big Bam: The Life and Times of Babe Ruth* and *Ted Williams: The Biography of an American Hero*

"The world might have had its fill of good stories 'about' baseball, but I'm not sure it has had any that are 'like' baseball, until now. Bob Weintraub's sly, slippery tales carry within them something of baseball's very own cockeyed relationship to reality—the real game within a reality of artifice. They also convey, in a singular, accessible language, those acts of grace, coincidence, and improbable heroics that keep America tethered to its pastime. These stories are as faithful to the spirit of a baseball game as a box score, yet with all the color of a yarn told in a clubhouse during a rain delay."

—Michael Coffey, author of *27*

Painting the Corners

Painting the Corners

A Collection of
Off-Center Baseball Fiction

BOB WEINTRAUB

Skyhorse Publishing

Skyhorse Publishing books may be purchased in bulk at special discounts for sales promotion, corporate gifts, fund-raising, or educational purposes. Special editions can also be created to specifications. For details, contact the Special Sales Department, Skyhorse Publishing, 307 West 36th Street, 11th Floor, New York, NY 10018 or info@skyhorsepublishing.com.

Skyhorse® and Skyhorse Publishing® are registered trademarks of Skyhorse Publishing, Inc.®, a Delaware corporation.

"The Autograph" first appeared in *Spitball* (1995) and in *Fenway Fiction* by Rounder Books (2005).

"A Flare for Dan Nugent" first appeared in *Final Fenway Fiction* by Cornerstone Books (2012).

Visit our website at www.skyhorsepublishing.com.

10 9 8 7 6 5 4 3 2 1

Library of Congress Cataloging-in-Publication Data is available on file.

Cover design by Tom Lau
Cover photo credit: iStock.com/CSA Images

Print ISBN: 978-1-5107-2532-4
Ebook ISBN: 978-1-5107-2534-8

Printed in the United States of America

DEDICATION

For my wife, Sandra, who has given me more love and caring than I ever had a right to expect. For Rose and Ben Weintraub who devoted their lives to seeing their three kids get an education and move up in the world. For my son, Steve, with his wife, Sue, and for my daughter, Ellen, with her husband, Jim, who have given Sandra and me six wonderful grandchildren (Grace, Emma, Sarah Rose, Jack, Shayna and Alex) to keep us young. For my cousin, Maury Fisher, who bought me my first real baseball glove. And for Shelley, Lenny, Eddie, Moose, Don, Ritty, Paul and Billy, guys in the Iroquois, our Dorchester "gang," who played baseball together when we were young but who didn't make it this far.

CONTENTS

EIGHTY-THREE AND BUNTING

A Tribute to Johnny Pesky of the Boston Red Sox

"Don't look back. Something might be gaining on you."

—Satchel Paige

EVERYONE KNOWS HOW it started. All the media covering the team got word of it the same day the fax came in from the commissioner's office. *Nobody sits in the dugout during games*, it said, *unless he's a player, a trainer, one of the six designated coaches, or the manager, of course.* I don't know for sure but I'm guessing our Pirates' ball club was the only one affected in a meaningful way. What this new ruling did was ban Hank Cabot from our bench while the games were being played. Hank would have been on the field for a couple hours during practice, hitting fungoes or showing pitchers how to bunt or maybe just signing autographs for kids in the stands who snuck past the box seat ushers to get close to the field. Now, with this directive that came down, his choice, once it was time to play ball, was to sit in the clubhouse, use a player's reserved seat in the grandstand if one was available, or just go on home and watch the game on TV.

Keep in mind we're talking about a guy who played infield for this team for thirteen years, coached or managed three different teams in the Pirates' minor league system for another thirteen, managed the major-league club for four tough seasons when he had to send guys onto the field with a prayer, especially those masquerading as pitchers, and stayed connected with this organization in some way or another for most of the rest of his life. There wasn't another team in baseball that had a guy like Hank.

When I got the manager's job six years ago, Hank was doing the same stuff he always did before the games, and I remember finding out back then that the Pirates had a higher percentage of successful bunts year to year than any other team in both leagues. Anyway, unless he was under the weather, Hank always sat near me in the dugout, but he never butted into my job. If I asked him something about a player on another club or some strategy I had in mind, he'd tell me what he knew or what he thought, but he never said anything without me going to him first, never tried to show me up in front of our guys in any way.

We got that fax two days before the trading deadline at the end of July, and the new rule went into effect the first of August. I don't know who told Hank about it first — it wasn't me — but that look on his face when he found out was about the saddest thing I ever saw. The commissioner had just taken away the best part of Hank's life. During a ball game, the dugout was his home for the two and a half to three hours it usually took to play. Every game for Hank was like being dealt a new hand of bridge or poker, and he always had something different to look forward to. He loved the planning and thinking and sometimes the guessing that went into every inning; and he got the most satisfaction seeing one of the players do something on the field he'd spent time teaching him. So the new regulation was a real downer for Hank and for me too.

I had a lot of stuff to think about the next couple of days, every time the GM called me about a trade he had in mind and what did I think of it. At the time, we were on top of our division, five games up on the

Reds, and the ball club had looked pretty solid for the first four months of the season. But this thing with Hank was really bothering me, and then I saw an opening for an idea that must have crept into my head while I was sleeping. The trade that brought Jim McKenna to our club — to fill in for any of our outfielders when one of them needed a day off — was originally supposed to cost us Roy Deveaux and some cash. But I liked Deveaux for a lot of reasons, and I figured the Rangers would take a different relief pitcher with pretty much the same record if we threw in something extra. So I convinced Mike Graham, the GM, that we didn't have to keep carrying three catchers for the two months left in the season, and the Rangers were willing to take the pitcher/catcher deal we offered. That left us with an opening on the 25-man roster, and the next day I was up in Mike's office to tell him how I wanted to fill it.

"Are you crazy, MacGregor? Are you out of your mind? Do you think I'm about to sign an 83-year-old guy to a contract on this club? We'd be the laughing stock of baseball, and besides I'd bet the commissioner wouldn't allow it. You can guess what his staff and his lawyers would tell him: that it was a bad joke and wasn't in the best interests of the game. Tell me you are just kidding, Mac, and let me laugh it off."

That's about what I expected to hear Mike say, on my way up to see him, about my wanting to have Hank on the team. Actually, it could have been a lot worse, considering that what I was proposing was probably the most outrageous thing a manager ever went to his GM with. He never slammed his fist or anything else down on his desk or predicted he'd get fired on the spot if he went to the owner with my request. But after a while, when he saw I was serious, he agreed to sit back in his big chair and say nothing while I made my case for bringing Hank onto the team.

"Mike," I told him, "I know it's not your style to get too close to the players or the coaches, but you've spent enough time on the field with this club to watch Hank and see what he does every day. He's the best bunter out there, with no exception. When he played the game for the Pirates over 50 years ago, he was always one of the top three guys in the league for reaching on bunt hits. Half the time he was number one. He can lay the ball down anywhere he wants it to go, whether he's facing a righty or a southpaw. When he's teaching our pitchers how to move a runner along with a good bunt, he's not just talking to them, he's right there in the batting cage showing them how to do it. If you didn't know it was Hank in the cage, you'd tell yourself the guy in there bunting would make a hell of a number two hitter. Listen, Mike, I think the trade you just pulled off for McKenna was terrific. Now we can give the guys in the outfield a day or two off when they need it coming down the stretch. But I can still use someone on the bench to go to with confidence in a tight game when I want to move a runner over to second or third. Hank's the guy who can do it."

I knew I'd impressed Mike with what I said because he didn't start tearing me apart as soon as I finished. He kind of just stared straight ahead for a while, thinking about what I'd told him. "Could Hank drag a bunt down the first base line off a Roger Clemens fastball?" he asked me.

"No problem," I said.

"But he can't run. He'd never beat it out."

I knew that would be one of his main arguments. "I don't care about that, Mike," I told him, "I'm sending him up there to advance the runner. That's what's important."

He went into that cold stare again, sometimes looking straight ahead and sometimes up at the ceiling. I sat there eyeing a couple of bobble-head dolls on the table behind him, but I couldn't make out who they were supposed to be. Mike didn't say anything for a few minutes. Then he began tapping on his desk with his fingers for a while. "I really think the commissioner would have a hard time with it," he said, finally.

"I can't see it," I answered right away. "There's never been an age limit for a ballplayer in the big leagues. Minoso was 50 when he played in a game for the White Sox, and who knows how old Satchel Paige really was when the Indians brought him up. Besides, if Hank can do the job, there are age discrimination laws to protect him. The commissioner isn't going to use that 'best interests of baseball' clause if the lawyers tell him he'll be breaking the law. The baseball writers would tear him apart if they got the chance. He knows that, and he'd see this isn't anything like the midget Bill Veeck signed up for Cleveland. That was a freak show, but Hank is legitimate. That's why I'd bet he'd stay totally out of it. If anyone raised a question, he'd probably say the Pirates have every right to have Hank on their roster if they want."

"Okay, Mac, but it will have to wait until I speak to the owners. I've got to make sure both Mr. Egan and Mr. Stehlin understand we're not trying to make a farce out of this. Keep it to yourself just in case they don't go along. I'll get back to you in a couple of days."

Well, it took four days before Mike called me. That meant four days of having the writers speculate on who we were going to bring up from the minors to fill the spot. But I knew the owners were thinking this through pretty carefully and probably wanted some time to consult with their baseball friends. Anyway, Mike was able to convince them there was nothing wrong with what I wanted to do and that I was sure having Hank on the roster would help the team. They wanted to know what they'd have to pay him, and I said Hank would be happy as a pig in mud with the major-league minimum. And if the labor agreement with the union didn't call for a minimum, I said, he'd be happy with nothing, just to be in the dugout while the game's being played.

Mike had reached me late on Sunday morning, about three hours before we were to close out our series with the Rockies. He gave me the good news and said he was going to call a press conference for Monday, an off day for the team. He also let me know he was going to leak the story to Mel Jackson, his favorite baseball writer on the *Pittsburgh Gazette*. In his column on Monday morning, Jackson would tell the world what he heard the Pirates "were thinking of doing." Mike told me to meet with Hank at the park, tell him what our plans were and send him home right away so he wouldn't be letting the cat out of the bag. I also had to tell him to show up at the stadium at eleven o'clock the next morning to sign a player's contract and be ready to be the star attraction at the press conference at noon.

I couldn't take a chance on giving Hank the news in the clubhouse because he might have let out a scream of happiness to wake the dead. Since it was a Sunday and the traffic coming in from where he lived would be light, I figured he'd drive instead of taking the bus to the park as he often did. So I waited for Hank in the players' parking area and climbed into the passenger seat of his Toyota pickup as soon as he got there. "Relax," I told him, "it's nothing bad. But as soon as I let you know what's happening, you're going to go back home, keep it to yourself, and see Mr. Graham in the office tomorrow at eleven. Is that clear?"

It was, and when I told him our plans for him, he gave me the kind of hug you'd have wanted to give Marilyn Monroe, and then he let a few tears get loose. So I opened the door to get out, gave him my best wink, and watched him pull out of the lot.

There's no need my going into detail about what happened on Monday, except I found out the switchboard was totally lit up five minutes after the office opened for business. Every baseball writer in town was at the stadium hours before the press briefing was scheduled to start, and Hank was a big hit answering questions after Mike told the crowd in the press room the club expected to get more than its money's worth out of his performance the rest of the season. Some of the players had shown up that day for an optional practice, and when the media guys left the park, Hank put on his uniform, grabbed the fungo bat he kept in his locker and went out on the field. I'd have been shocked if he didn't.

Mike and I both figured we had to get Hank an at bat in a game as soon as we could. We didn't want him to get all nervous about that first one, and it was important to show the fans we hadn't gone off the deep end by signing him. The Dodgers came in on Tuesday for three games and there was a rush to buy up tickets for the first one that night. Wouldn't you know we went into our half of the ninth tied 3-3. We got the first hitter on and the pitcher was due up next. We couldn't have asked for a better situation. The crowd anticipated what was going to happen, and as soon as Hank stepped out of the dugout everyone was on their feet and the noise was as loud as it ever gets in the stadium. I could see Hank didn't want to tip his cap because he knew he hadn't done anything yet, so he just stood outside the left-hander's side of the batter's box and waited for the fans to settle down. The umpire was patient to a point, but then waved his hand for Hank to get in and hit. The bunt sign was on, of course, but the runner on first knew he couldn't go anywhere until he saw the ball on the ground. Hank took the first pitch for a strike, but I knew he wanted to see how the Dodgers were going to play it when the pitch was thrown. When Hank saw the pitcher's motion take him to the first base side of the field after his delivery, he knew where the opening was to put the bunt, and he put it right there on the next pitch. By the time the third baseman stopped rushing straight in and moved toward the mound to field the bunt, there was no play at second base. Hank was thrown out by a healthy margin as he jogged toward first, but the crowd was up and cheering again as he moved back to the dugout. All the guys came over to give him high fives, and a minute later our leadoff hitter singled to right to end the game. Hank had set up the winning run with a beautiful bunt, and everyone rooting for the Pirates, including the manager, went home happy.

Well, Hank's statistics for August and September made the papers a bunch of times, and there were more sellouts than had been expected, even in a pennant race. That's because the 65 and up generation filled the seats just to see an 83-year-old guy get in the batter's box, bunt the ball, and move as fast as he could down the first base line. Hank traveled with the club for all our away games and got standing O's whenever he made an appearance. The fans all over really appreciated who he was and what he was doing. I sent him up to pinch-hit fourteen times in that period and he laid down a successful bunt on thirteen of them. The only time the runner didn't move up was when Chico Hernandez was fooled by the pitcher's motion and was diving back into first while Hank was bunting. Hernandez had no chance to get up and run, and Hank was on the end of a double play. That's when he got serious about trying to get his legs in shape, and the team doctor gave him the OK to run laps as long as he didn't feel any kind of tightness in his chest. It was a laugh to watch him at the beginning, but little by little he began doing better and getting farther down the line before he was thrown out. I had to keep reminding myself that he'd be 84 in December, and that all I wanted out of him were those good bunts of his.

After we won the division, Hank played a big part in our series against Houston. Even though we swept them in three games, two of the games could have gone either way and put us in a hole. In the opener, he bunted Morgan to third after he led off the ninth with a double, and then Morgan scored the winning run on a sacrifice fly. And in the game that clinched the series for us, Hank moved two runners along in the seventh with a perfect bunt down the third base line and they both scored on a two-out error by the shortstop. Being two runs up instead of one when the Astros had their last at bat in the ninth changed the strategy in the inning, and we held on to win by a run.

We figured all along we'd have to go through the Mets to get to the World Series and we were right. What a series that was, huh! It was pretty much our hitting against their pitching and it was one of those rare times when the hitting won out. They went one up on us three times, but we came back each time to tie the series and send it to a seventh game. Hank batted only once in the first six games, and when the pitcher slipped and threw his bunt into right field, two runs scored and he moved that old body of his all the way to second. I had already used up most of our bench — that was the 13-10 game — but I pulled a pitcher out of the bullpen to come in and run for him. There was no way I was going to take a chance on Hank having to run some more on another play and have a heart attack out there. I told everyone on the bench to give him the silent treatment when he got back to the dugout, and Hank never even noticed. He just put on his jacket, got himself a Gatorade, and took a seat next to the bat rack.

In game seven we went up against Orman, their number three pitcher who had given us just two runs the first time around. But this time our hitting was strong right from the start. After seven innings we were up 9-5 and the fans were having a good time in the stands. In the eighth, though, our setup man didn't have it and the Mets scored three runs before I could bring in our closer to get us off the field. In our half of the eighth, Rudy Ruiz got to third with one out on a single and a two-base error by the center fielder who let the ball get under his glove and roll about 50 feet past him. It was Anderson's turn to hit, but I knew we could replace him at first base defensively and he hadn't been swinging a good bat the last couple of games. Besides, I was pretty sure the Mets would be looking for a suicide squeeze if I sent Hank up to bat, and I wanted to challenge them on it. We had the team's fastest runner on third and the league's best bunter at the plate.

As soon as Hank was announced over the PA system, Mal Nash came out of the Mets' dugout and took his time getting to the mound. The first thing he did was call his infielders together for a short conference. When it was over, they all moved in from their regular positions to no more than 40 feet from the plate. Then Nash signaled for his three outfielders to come in. He put his left fielder right on the third base bag, his right fielder on the base at first and his center fielder about ten feet behind the catcher. I guess that last move was in case there was a play at home and the ball got past the plate. If that happened, Nash didn't want Hank to be able to take an extra base.

I'll tell you, that was the first time in my career I'd ever seen that kind of shift on a baseball field, and I haven't heard from anyone yet who has seen it before. It meant, to me at least, that no other player who'd been sent up there to bunt, with everyone in the park knowing what was coming, had ever received the respect Hank was getting in that situation. Hank walked over to the rosin bag in the on-deck circle and rubbed up his hands. When he finished, he looked over at our dugout and gave me a wink with a little bit of a smile. I figured he knew what he was going to do and there was no sense in prolonging the suspense. I also felt sure that Nash expected me to have Hank take the first pitch so we'd see how close their infielders were going to come to the plate. As far as I was concerned, that all added up to a fastball looking for strike one, so I signaled for Ruiz to take off on the first pitch. I knew Tyson coaching at third would talk to Ruiz after he got my sign and tell him to get as big a lead as he could on the pitcher's stretch.

Well, you saw what happened. Hank showed bunt even before the pitcher threw the ball, which is almost always a "no, no," and all four infielders were about on top of him when the pitch reached the plate. But that's just what he wanted. It was a fastball, as I'd guessed, right down Broadway. When it got to him, Hank pulled the bat back a little, and instead of waiting for the ball to hit the bat, took a slight swing at it and looped it in the direction of the second baseman, but over his head. Walters — and he's been an All-Star for years — stopped in his tracks and tried to go back for it, but the ball fell on the infield grass before he could get there. He threw Hank out at first, but Ruiz scored standing up and gave us a two-run lead. Hank had pretty much done the impossible and the ballpark showed its appreciation by giving him a standing ovation as he walked back to the dugout. They wanted him to come out for a curtain call, but Hank's from the old school and doesn't believe in that stuff. The Mets got one back with a home run in the ninth, but that was all and then our guys were out there in a big pile — all except for old-man Hank — celebrating the National League Pennant we had just won and our chance to play the Detroit Tigers for the world championship.

When the World Series started that weekend, it was the kind of let-down you might expect after what we'd been through with the Mets. The National League had finally won an All-Star Game that summer, so we opened at home. The stadium looked beautiful with all the red, white, and blue bunting on the walls. They brought in that rock star to sing the

National Anthem, and the players loved being introduced individually and jogging out to the first base line. But we fell behind early and the fans never had much to cheer about. The team seemed to be playing at less than full speed, and deserved the loss the Tigers pinned on us.

I had a short meeting with the players before game two to try and light a fire under them. I told them they might never be in another World Series the rest of their careers, so they should focus on what they were doing and give everything they had on every play. The guys listened to what I said. We won easily at home that day, took two out of three from Detroit in their ballpark and came back to Pittsburgh hoping to wrap it up in six.

I gave the players the option of practicing or staying home to get some rest on the off day. Some of the writers thought that was a crazy move, but I knew they were upset because they wanted every chance to get personal interviews with the players for their papers. But most of the team showed up anyway, so that kept the grumbling to a minimum. Hank was all over the place, hitting fungoes to the outfielders, working on bunts with the pitchers and bench players who had to pinch-hit, and spending time out at second with our double play combination which had looked a little unsteady in the games at Detroit.

After practice, Hank came in to see me and thanked me again for putting him on the team. He said it was the best three-month period he'd ever had in the big leagues and he'd never forget it. I butted in to tell him we probably wouldn't be fighting for the championship if it weren't for him. He laughed at that and said it was because I sent him up there with the chance to be a hero every time and he'd been on a lucky streak. "That's bull," I told him, "it's because no one in baseball comes close to being able to bunt like you."

Hank got up from his chair then and said he wanted me to know he'd already decided to call it quits when the Series was over, that these were the last days he'd be spending on a big league ball field. Both of his daughters and two granddaughters lived in different towns around

Pennsylvania and they all wanted him to come and stay with them for weeks at a time. Carol, his wife, had passed away about two years earlier, and Hank felt those invitations were something he shouldn't turn down. "I'll be able to watch my great-grandkids grow up a little," he said, "maybe make a ballplayer out of one of the boys. And Lord willing, I'll still be able to get to some of the club's home games. The only difference is I'll be watching from the boxes, not the dugout." He went over to the door, said "See you tomorrow, Skip," and left.

Well, we lost game six 2-1, but I had nothing to complain about. Alex Ochoa gave us six terrific innings, a lot more than I'd counted on, and left with a 1-0 lead. The Tigers scored a run each in the seventh and eighth innings off our two best setup men. Holbrook allowed only four hits and one run in the eight frames he worked for Detroit, and that kid Macy showed us again why he was the best closer in the American League. My only regret was that I didn't have a chance to use Hank because I wanted to get him one more at bat before he hung up his spikes.

Before game seven the next day, I had the worst set of butterflies in my stomach I can remember, and they never went away. That may have been the best nine innings of baseball I ever saw, because even though the score was 4-4 after eight, both clubs could have been in double figures if not for some of the great plays you saw out there. Morgan should have had a grand slam for us in the fifth, and I still can't believe how high their left fielder got up there to snag it before it reached the stands.

But we're talking about Hank here, so let me go over what happened. We had shut the Tigers down in the ninth and were looking to score a run and end the Series right there. Everyone in the dugout was on the edge of their seat. Things looked great when Coffey swung late and flared one down the line in left for a double to lead off the inning. I could have sent Hank up right then to bunt him over to third, but Harris came out of the Detroit dugout to talk to his pitcher himself instead of sending his pitching coach, so I waited to see what he'd do. While they went at it, I decided to hold Hank back on a hunch, and it turned out to be a good move when Harris ordered an intentional pass to Mullins.

So we had first and second, no outs, and Trinidad, our shortstop, captain, and number eight hitter up next. I figured Harris was looking for a double play if Trinidad swung away, or at least a force-out at third on a bunt. That gave me another chance to call for Hank, but Trinidad was pretty good at laying one down so I decided to let him stay in the game. As soon as Trinidad was announced, Harris came back out of the Tigers' dugout and brought in Macy, his fireballing closer who had already saved two games in the Series. Trinidad bunted twice, but the ball rolled foul each time. I could have let him try again, but instead I took off the bunt sign and let him hit away. That hunch wasn't as good as my first one because he rolled it hard to the shortstop who started the double play.

That left us with Coffey on third, two outs, and Baldacci, our pitcher, due up. He had thrown two terrific innings of relief, six up, six down with a couple of strikeouts, and I felt he could give us at least one more strong frame. A suicide squeeze wasn't in the picture because Hank would get thrown out at first and the run wouldn't count. As I was thinking about what to do, Hank came over to me and said he thought he could get the run in if I let him bat. I could have asked him what he had in mind, but there was something about the way he said it and the look on his face that convinced me to just let him go. The fans started clapping and making noise when Hank stepped on the field, but you could tell everyone was wondering why he'd be batting in that situation.

All four infielders moved in toward the plate as the pitcher went into his stretch, and they inched in closer as the pitch was thrown. Hank didn't make any move to bunt and took the first fastball for a strike. The next two pitches were off the plate and he watched them both with the bat on his shoulder. On each delivery, both heaters, the infielders charged in even closer as soon as the ball was thrown. The next pitch from Macy was another fastball, this one showing a 98 on the radar gun.

Hank swung and missed, and you could almost hear the air going out of the crowd, like 52,000 balloons deflating at the same time. I didn't know what he was up to, but it was too late to be asking any questions.

Well, now you know Hank had been playing his own game with the Tigers and convinced them he wasn't up there to bunt. So with two strikes on him, they moved back to pretty much their normal positions. As Hank told me afterwards, with a big laugh, "They had me where I wanted them." The fifth straight fastball came in, Macy fell off to the right side of the mound as he did after every delivery, and Hank dragged one to the other side of the mound, right between the first and second basemen. Each of them thought it was his ball to field and went for it as Hank started down the line. Macy recovered quickly when he saw the play unfolding and ran to cover first base. The first baseman fielded the ball, and his only play was to throw it to the pitcher. With the crowd screaming, Hank ran as hard as he could and went into a headfirst slide to avoid a tag by Macy who was a little off balance when he took the throw. Hank recovered, got partway up and dove headfirst again, stretching his arm out to touch first base just before Macy stepped on the bag.

The fans roared when they saw the umpire give the "safe" sign and saw the winning run cross the plate. A chant of "Hank, Hank, Hank" began filling the stadium. Everyone ran out of the dugout to help him get up off the ground. They lifted Hank carefully on their shoulders and circled the bases with him as if he'd hit a home run and couldn't make it around without help. What a celebration that was! The Tigers were stunned and were slow to leave the field, but I never thought it was that hard for them to take because they knew they'd lost the World Series on a one-in-a-million play by a one-in-a-million ballplayer.

Later that week someone in the Pirates' organization sent a fax to the commissioner's office expressing the club's total agreement, albeit belatedly, with the rule that had kept Hank from sitting in the dugout during games without him having a position on the team.

THE AUTOGRAPH

"In retrospect, you are always looking back."
—Jimy Williams

I T WAS BY chance that I was walking down that street in Herkimer, New York — its name escapes me — and looked into the window of a store with the appearance of being a cross between a pawn shop and the unlikely resting place for an assortment of items I would have expected to find in a flea market. The shop's name, painted on the glass in faded gold lettering, was "The Treasure Chest."

Several electric guitars, some brass instruments, and an assortment of men's suits and women's dresses hung from two parallel wires that looked to be pieces of an old, orange-colored extension cord. In front, there were a number of china cup and saucer sets, a collection of foreign coins, and glassware of all types, some of it the opaque-green variety that was given away to movie house patrons during the depression. Farther back, several beat-up dolls joined a display of tin containers that once held tea or soap or crackers, and odd-shaped bottles that once were filled with unpasteurized milk, medicinal cure-alls, and Moxie. But what captured my attention was a baseball, sitting on a small square of red carpeting, near enough to the front of the window that I could read the signature, a name that for several moments I almost couldn't believe I was seeing again: Denton Heywood.

My daughter and I had left our home outside of Boston early that morning on a mission to visit five colleges in upstate New York over a period of three days. The first was already out of the way.

"I don't know. Don't ask me for all kinds of details," Tracy said, irritated by my persistent questioning after she had rated the latest one "about a 6" on a scale of 1 to 10. We had joined a group of other parents and high school seniors on a student-led tour of the campus, watched a film extolling the virtues of every academic department in the college, and sat through a welcoming presentation with one of the assistant deans of admission. He was prepared to take questions at that point, but despite the nervous glances that we mothers and fathers gave to the prospective members of the Class of '87, they indicated by their detached silence that they were not there to take risks but only to be entertained.

On the thruway heading toward Syracuse — our first stop the next morning — we saw signs for the General Herkimer Inn. The name seemed to amuse Tracy, and she suggested we stay there. I had no reason to disagree. Tracy wanted to rest after we checked in, so I changed into some comfortable clothes, put on my factory-discount New Balance sneakers, and began exploring downtown Herkimer.

I turned twelve years old on October 2, 1945. It was a Sunday, and the last day of the Major League Baseball season. Baseball had entered my life for the first time that summer when I became friendly with some boys who spent the better part of each day playing ball at the huge field in our neighborhood.

My father, who worked a grocery store owner's typical fifteen-hour day, had responded to my plea for a baseball glove — "I need my own mitt" — by purchasing what looked more like an extra large leather mitten. It had very little padding, and there was no webbing at all between the thumb and fourth finger. I never fully considered the words "mitt" and "mitten" until years later when my father said he thought he bought me exactly what I wanted; that he understood a "mitt" to be a training glove that one used before being ready to play with a regular one. But the glove served me well that summer as I learned how to play the game.

Sunday was my father's only day of rest, and he normally slept until noon. But on that particular morning he had washed and dressed and was at the breakfast table before ten o'clock. My mother made apple pancakes for my two sisters and me because she knew what would please me the most. For it was my birthday.

"We haven't had a chance to buy you anything," my father said, pausing for some theatrical effect, "but maybe you'd like to see the Red Sox with me today."

I was thrilled. "Yes," I said, almost shouting my response. My father could see the huge smile breaking out on my face. My mother told me years later that it was the happiest she'd ever seen me.

"Can we come too?" my sisters asked, almost in unison.

"Not this time," my father told them. "Another time we'll all go together, but today it's just the men." He waited a few seconds before turning back to me and winking.

Our trip to Fenway Park that afternoon was one of the rare occasions when — for the first time in both their lives — a father and son got to experience the thrill of emerging from the dark entrance ramp into the sunshine of the field and were momentarily spellbound by the lush green carpet of grass filling the ballpark. I was overwhelmed by the noise of the crowd, the shouts of the vendors moving up and down the aisles with their peanuts, soft drinks, and hot dogs, and the smack of baseballs hitting leather as players from both teams loosened up in the area between the dugouts and the foul lines. I wanted to get as close to the field as I could, but the ushers in their red blazers and blue pants allowed only box seat ticket holders into those sections. As game time approached and the lineups were announced, we moved away from the action and out to our seats in the right field bleachers.

The competitive season had ended for the Red Sox weeks earlier when they were eliminated from the pennant race; but they were playing their last series of the year against their hated rivals, the Yankees. I spent much of that cool, sunny afternoon teaching my father the rules of the game and sharing with him the accomplishments of the Boston hitters as they came to bat. He wondered why the players left their gloves out on the field when they returned to the dugout each inning, and seemed disappointed that no one on either team had made his prediction come true by stumbling over one while running to make a catch.

There was drama in the game we saw, right to the very end. The Red Sox were down by one in the ninth inning and had runners on second and third base with two outs. The public address announcer informed the cheering crowd that Denton Heywood was being sent up to pinch-hit for the pitcher. Heywood, a left-handed batter, would face the Yankees right-handed pitcher.

"They'll walk him," I told my father, anticipating my being able to explain the strategy to him as soon as the intentional pass began. The Yankees manager ran out to the mound to talk to his pitcher.

Most of the major-league players who had gone off to war in the early '40s did not return to their teams in 1945, after the Japanese surrender in August. They were content to go home to their families and take a long rest before getting their bodies ready for spring training and a new season of baseball the following year. The teams competing for the championship that year were stocked with minor league players who wouldn't have been there if the real "big leaguers" hadn't had to interrupt their careers.

Denton Heywood was born and raised in Dorchester, about nine miles from Fenway Park and a dozen blocks from where I lived. I discovered years later — while looking through a biography of wartime ballplayers — that he had just passed his twenty-second birthday when he batted in the first game I ever saw. The Red Sox had promoted Heywood to their Triple-A farm team in Louisville that summer when injuries forced them to bring several players from that club to Boston. Then, as soon as Louisville was eliminated from its playoffs in September, he was called up for the last few weeks of the season so that everyone in management could get a look at him.

Heywood had asthmatic problems that kept him out of the military, and the Boston sportswriters — skilled at impugning any rookie's ability upon his arrival into town — were almost unanimous in telling their readers that he lacked the talent to play the game at the highest level. He had made their stories about him in the city's four major newspapers appear accurate by failing to reach base in the dozen pinch-hitting appearances he'd had since coming to Fenway Park.

To the surprise of the crowd — and to my embarrassment — the Yankees manager decided to go after Heywood instead of loading the bases for the leadoff hitter. "I knew it," my father said, when he saw what was happening. The count went to 1 and 2, and then Heywood barely managed to stay alive by foul tipping the next three pitches. He looked completely outmatched.

"Hit one out," I begged, in desperation, and was rewarded an instant later with a fly ball that rose on a glorious arc and carried over the visitors' bullpen into the right field bleachers — a game-winning home run. Rising to my feet along with everyone else, I watched the flight of the ball, certain for most of its ten-second journey that it was heading directly at me. And then, in the most jealous moment of my life, I saw it come down into the glove of Billy Killian, a boy who was two grades ahead of me in the same junior high school back in Dorchester.

On the following day, I got the chance to hold the baseball at school and listen to Billy exaggerate the difficulty of his catch. I heard him tell everyone around him during morning recess how he waited at the players' gate for Denton Heywood to leave Fenway Park and asked him to autograph the ball. On the side opposite his name, Heywood had — for whatever reason — also inscribed the date, "10/2/45."

The store where I discovered the baseball was located on Herkimer's main street, which included several blocks of rather seedy-looking establishments. Next to it on one side was a movie theater; it must have been long since abandoned because there was a poster for a Steve McQueen/Ali McGraw picture still encased in plastic on a wall just beyond the iron grillwork erected to close off the entrance. The two sides of the triangular marquee that pushed out high above the sidewalk carried a complete message between them in foot-high black letters, "CLO" on the left and "SED" on the right. A jewelry store, with a display of Timex watches that moved around in the front window on an oval-shaped conveyor belt, was situated on the other side.

When I entered "The Treasure Chest," the proprietor came out of the back room to help me. He was a man about my own age whose heavy black mustache struck me almost as a stage prop that was there to try and distract attention from what otherwise was the most outstanding feature of his head — a crew cut that wouldn't have been any shorter had he just finished his first day of Marine Corps training. He nodded at me, offered that it was a nice day and asked if there was something he could help me with.

"Believe it or not," I said, pointing at the baseball in the window, "I remember the guy who signed that. He played for the Red Sox when I was a kid."

"Is that right?" he answered, and hesitated a few moments. "Well, I'm not much of a fan myself, beyond Pete Rose or Joe DiMaggio or a few others. You know, the great ones. But no one who's been in here has ever heard of this fellow. What's his name again?"

"Denton Heywood," I told him. "He had one hit in his whole major-league career. But it was a home run on the last day of the season. He won the ball game with it."

He watched me looking down at the ball and probably sensed that I would be the only person coming into his store who'd have an interest in buying it for whatever added value it received from the autograph. He encouraged me to pick up the ball and hold it. "Have a feel of it," he said.

I did. The signature was written so clearly, as if Heywood had wanted to be certain that everyone would be able to read it. I flipped the ball in the air, not more than a foot above my hand, and when I caught it I saw the writing on the other side for the first time. Just numbers: "10/2/45." A shiver moved through my whole body.

Denton Heywood reported to the Red Sox camp in Sarasota, Florida for spring training in 1946. By that time, Bobby Doerr was back playing second base, and Heywood realized that his only chance of staying with the team was as a utility infielder. He played in about fifteen exhibition games, splitting his time in the field between second, third, and shortstop, but didn't impress Sox Manager Joe Cronin. About a week before the team headed north for the start of the season, Heywood was assigned to Louisville.

On the Saturday after Thanksgiving, in 1945, Heywood had married Patty Ann Shea, his high school sweetheart. She didn't accompany him to Florida when he left in February, not wanting to distract him in any way from the goal he hoped to achieve; but she packed up their few belongings and joined him in Louisville a few days after he rented an apartment within walking distance of the ballpark.

The club installed Heywood at third base, grooming him to play that position in a year or two in Boston, and he responded by having an excellent season both at bat and in the field. He was ticketed for a return trip to the Red Sox in September, as soon as the team was allowed to expand its roster for the final month of the season. With Ted Williams leading the way, the ball club had overpowered everyone that year and was able to coast to the pennant. Heywood's only concern was that his wife, who was pregnant, was due in the latter part of September.

On August 29th, while the Louisville team was playing a three game series in Utica, Patty Ann was in an automobile accident just a few blocks from their apartment. She was rushed to Memorial Hospital by ambulance and spent the next four hours on an operating table. Word reached Heywood in the middle of the game, and he was driven to the airport by the police. By the time he arrived at the hospital, Patty Ann had given birth, by Caesarean section, to a baby girl. Heywood was told that his wife was dying and that a priest had already prayed with her. He spent the last 30 minutes of Patty Ann's life at her bedside, watching her cradle the daughter she wanted to be named Christina. By the time the funeral took place back in Dorchester several days later, Heywood realized that he would probably never wear a professional baseball uniform again.

"Where did you get this ball?" I asked the owner.

"A woman brought it in about two weeks ago," he told me. "Lives a couple of towns over. Said it belonged to her husband and asked me to try and sell it. He's the one that got hit last month out on the thruway, just a little west of here. Said she needed to raise whatever she could." As he spoke, he walked over to the counter where the cash register was located and stepped behind it. "The paper said he was changing a tire in the rain — a nasty night out there — and got killed by some hit-and-run driver they haven't found yet. You might've read about it."

I told him I was from Massachusetts and just passing through the area. "Do you know her name?" I asked.

"Not offhand," he answered, "but I got it written down in the back with her phone number. I'll go get it if you're interested."

I said I was, and asked how much he wanted for the ball. He answered right away, telling me he thought $30 was a fair price, especially since I'd known Denton Heywood. He turned a key in the register, took it with him as he headed toward the rear of the store, and returned a few minutes later with a small spiral notebook.

"Her name's Ruth Killian," he informed me, "and she gets half if you buy it."

I told him I would take it, and said that I wanted to leave a note for Mrs. Killian. "Do you have a piece of paper I can use, and an envelope?" I took three $10 bills out of my wallet and handed them to him. He tore a page from the back of the notebook and gave it to me.

It took me a couple of minutes to think about what I wanted to say. At home, I would have written the note out on a scrap piece of paper and edited it until I was satisfied that it expressed all my thoughts. But as I leaned over the counter the words didn't come easily.

By the time the owner returned, I had finished, telling Ruth Killian that I had seen her husband make a spectacular catch of the ball that Heywood had hit for a home run. The owner had wrapped the ball in tissue paper and put it in a plastic bag. I turned around, folded two $20 bills inside the note to Killian's wife and put them in the envelope he had handed me. I sealed it and wrote her name on the front. "Be sure she gets this," I told him. "It's very personal."

The next two days passed quickly as Tracy and I visited the other four colleges. The baseball I'd purchased seemed to have me thinking about my own diamond heroes a lot of the time. Heading back, I contemplated a third night on the road and a visit to the Hall of Fame in Cooperstown the next day, but my daughter wouldn't hear of it. Still, I resolved to try and find out what had happened to Denton Heywood. Perhaps he still lived in Dorchester. Maybe the Red Sox would know. I might even have the chance to show him the ball, I thought.

We got off the highway in Albany and stopped for dinner at a Chinese restaurant. We talked about the schools we had seen, Tracy's feelings about possible career choices, and her strong desire to backpack by herself around Europe during the upcoming summer. The fortune cookies we opened relieved some of the tension and were good for a laugh because the messages inside would have been perfectly appropriate if only she had picked mine and I'd gotten hers. I had already found my true love and Tracy wasn't in any position to receive a big promotion. Then I told her about the baseball and Billy Killian. "That's weird, Dad; it's really weird," she said.

Shortly after we crossed back into Massachusetts, Tracy rested her head on a pillow against the passenger door and closed her eyes. A few minutes later I turned on the radio, looking for some soft music, and picked up a New York station that was doing the news at the top of the hour. Before I could turn the dial, the announcer began reporting that a Massachusetts man had come forward in the hit-and-run death of William Killian on the New York Thruway 26 days earlier. He said that the individual was a regional distributor for Eastman Kodak in Boston who had driven home from the company's Rochester plant the night of the accident and couldn't account for a dent in the right fender of his automobile when he discovered it the following day. But on his next trip to Rochester, he read a story about the ongoing search for the hit-and-run driver and suddenly recalled the thump he felt against his car that night during a heavy rainstorm near the Herkimer exit. Police inspected the man's Buick LeSabre and determined that it was the car that struck Killian. The driver — against whom no charges had yet been filed — was identified as a 59-year-old, one-time professional baseball player for the Boston Red Sox, named Denton Heywood.

Unbelieving, I looked over at Tracy, but she was already asleep. I spent the rest of the night wondering about the ways that fate had of entangling the lives of total strangers. Surely, I told myself, Ruth Killian had to be thinking about the same thing if she read my note. Somehow, I felt better knowing that she would never have to see that baseball again. And I was suddenly glad that it wasn't me who had caught Denton Heywood's home run.

KNUCKLEBALL

"There are two theories on hitting the knuckleball.
Unfortunately, neither of them work."

—Charlie Lau

THERE IS AMPLE testimony to the fact that a major-league manager can move from a state of blissful dreams to near insomnia, almost overnight, so to speak, by the sudden loss of one of his starting pitchers. Even more so is that proposition true when his team has been picked by all the self-anointed "experts" to win the pennant, and the standings in the middle of July show that the second place team — eleven games behind a month earlier — now trails his own by just a game and a half.

Moose Carlson, watching every move on the field from one end of the St. Louis dugout, felt sick to his stomach in a matter of seconds when he saw Art Whitlock drop his glove and grab his right elbow with his left hand after releasing a pitch to the plate. The ball was seven or eight feet outside the strike zone when it flew past the three people at home who were intent on its arrival. Minutes later, as he stood on the Sportsman's Park mound awaiting the arrival of a relief pitcher, Carlson was certain that Whitlock would not be seeing his name in another box score that season. When the game ended, the Browns manager was distraught that the four run lead they held just before Whitlock's final pitch had completely evaporated over the final three innings. The team went to sleep — all except Carlson, that is — a mere half game ahead of Detroit.

At five-thirty the next morning, Johnny Abbott was roused out of a deep slumber by the harsh ring of the telephone in his hotel room. He reached over to the night table for it, and listened to Carlson's high-pitched voice directing him to be downstairs in the coffee shop in half an hour. By the time he hung up, Abbott was unable to remember the events that had transpired in his dream before it was interrupted; but he smiled at the sudden recollection that everyone else in his nocturnal escapade was female. As he headed for the bathroom, the agitated tone of Carlson's jarring wakeup call was still fresh in his ear. Abbott had no doubt that his job of pitching coach for the Browns was about to enter a time of turmoil.

Carlson was the only customer in the coffee shop when Abbott pushed open the glass door leading from the lobby and walked in. The Browns skipper had chosen to sit in the booth farthest from the entrance, facing the far wall. He hadn't shaved, and his puffed eyes told of little sleep. Abbott understood his long-time friend's anxiety about finding a reliable pitcher as soon as possible. He watched as Carlson nervously moved his hand through his full head of white hair, busily scratching it.

"Sit down, Johnny, and tell me what in blazes we're gonna do for another pitcher."

Abbott lowered his long, wiry frame onto the red, vinyl seat sacross from Carlson. Years of use and abuse had produced cracks in the faded covering on both sides of the booth, and strips of duct tape had been applied to hold the material together. He saw that the silver-colored, tin ashtray on the table already held six or seven cigarette butts, each one smoked down to its very end. The package of Lucky Strikes was visible through the pocket of Carlson's short-sleeved white shirt. Abbott was surprised to see him wearing a pair of metal-framed glasses, something he never did at the ballpark, even when the two of them were alone in the manager's small office. The frames were resting near the tip of his nose, and he lowered his head so that he could look out over them.

"Couldn't we be having this conversation about two hours from now, Moose?" is what Abbott wanted to say. He knew that Carlson had given himself that nickname years earlier, rebelling against his parents' choice of having him go through life as Morton, or even Mort. It had nothing to do with the enormous size of his shoulders or the girth of his waist that forced him to the racks carrying the size 46 when he had to buy a new pair of pants.

But Abbott was too smart to speak those words. The last six baseball seasons sitting next to Carlson in the dugout had taught him how the manager would react.

"Two hours from now?" he would say, his voice rising. "Why the hell not two days from now? Better yet, let's wait a couple of weeks." By that point Carlson would be rapidly approaching a full bellow. "Maybe by then we'll be five or six games out of first and pissing away the whole pennant race." He would stop then, take a deep breath and let out a long sigh. His next words, released as if the shouting had been an uncontrollable aberration they should both ignore, would be spoken in a normal tone, but reeking of sarcasm. "You're right, Johnny, what's the hurry? It's no big deal."

Instead, Abbott said, "You look like shit this morning, you know that?"

"I feel good, too," Carlson countered quickly. "So how come you can sleep like a baby with the problems we've got?"

"That's easy," Abbott answered. "Because if I stayed up all night and looked like you do now, you'd think I was after your job." He pointed at Carlson's coffee cup. "Did you have to make that yourself, or what?"

"Nah, the blonde waitress is here. Helen, or Helene, whatever her name is. She's making me some French toast. Probably be out in a minute."

Abbott reached over and took a sugar cube from the small ceramic bowl sitting next to the salt and pepper shakers. He unwrapped it and held the end in his mouth for a few seconds, then broke a piece off with his teeth.

"I don't know who we can use for another starter," he said. "There's definitely no one in Tulsa ready to make the jump up here yet. Bobby Reynolds is the best of them, but some days he can't find the plate with a map, and he's got a bad habit of throwing too many gopher balls." Abbott folded his arms and pushed his shoulders against the thinly padded back of the booth. "It's a shame that Whitlock waited until after the trading deadline to break down. If it happened sooner, we'd have had a choice of two or three guys on other clubs who could help us out. Seems like all we can do is watch who gets put on waivers and hope no one else grabs them before it's our turn." He waited a few seconds but Carlson didn't say anything. "You got a better idea, Moose?"

Before Carlson could answer, the waitress came over and put his dish on the table. The nametag fastened to the breast pocket of her green-and-white uniform informed her customers that she was "Eleanor."

"Coffee?" she asked Abbott.

"Yeah, and a couple pieces of white toast."

"You take it regular?"

"With cream, no sugar." She started to turn away. Abbott spoke again. "Wait a second, Eleanor. Mind my asking if you're married?"

She looked at him carefully before answering, as if trying to decide what she'd say to this man, at least fifteen years older than her, rapidly turning bald, and not wearing a wedding band, if he asked her out.

"The answer is nope and nope."

Abbott didn't hesitate. "Are you looking for someone?"

Again, she took her time before responding, and prefaced her words with a nervous smile. "I've been looking for fourteen years, ever since my seventeenth birthday." She didn't see any sign of doubt in their eyes about the numbers she had given them to add together. They didn't have to know she had turned 35 a month earlier.

"So what do you do until the right one comes along?" he asked.

"Just keep praying, I guess." She smiled again at both of them, sensing that Abbott's questions weren't leading to any kind of proposal that they get together. "Let me go put in your order," she told him.

"What the hell was that all about?" Carlson asked as soon as Eleanor had moved several booths away from them. "Are you thinking of getting married at your age?"

"You know me better than that. But she just gave you the answer to your problem."

The manager put down the bottle of maple syrup he'd been applying too generously to his French toast. He looked at Abbott, waiting to be enlightened. "What do you mean?" he asked.

"Start praying for a pitcher, and keep at it 'til we find one."

Johnny Abbott was allergic to tobacco smoke. When he was forced to breathe enough of it, he would get a rash on his body — like hives — starting on his neck and moving down his chest and back to his belt line. It had been an occupational hazard over the years as he traveled with baseball teams by rail from city to city. Very few trains reserved either a passenger or dining car for non-smokers. There just weren't enough people like him to warrant it. He avoided the dilemma on some occasions by driving alone in his car between cities when the team was playing a series close to St. Louis and returning for a home stand when it was over. Abbott did it all the time when Chicago was the only destination, and occasionally when it was the first stop on a road trip that included Cleveland or Detroit, or both.

The Browns were scheduled to play a weekend series in Chicago at the end of July, beginning on a Friday afternoon. In the ten days since Whitlock's injury, they had been overtaken by Detroit and had fallen into second place — two games behind. Carlson's face had taken on a wasted appearance, like a man in the first hours of recovery from major surgery.

On Thursday, a scheduled travel day, Abbott left St. Louis after breakfast for the roughly 300-mile trip to the home of the White Sox on the shores of Lake Michigan. About halfway there — as he approached Peoria where he always stopped for lunch — his three-year-old Chevrolet sedan began losing power periodically and making some popping sounds he was certain he hadn't heard before. Abbott slowed down to no more than twenty miles an hour and coaxed the Chevy to a Mobil station located on the main road into town.

While the mechanic was filling the gas tank, he listened to Abbott describe the symptoms. He checked under the hood and then had Abbott move the car inside — above the oil pit — so he could examine it from underneath. A few minutes later he informed him that the problem was with the muffler. He assured Abbott that he could fix it, but that he wouldn't be able to finish the job until sometime the following morning.

"But I'm supposed to be in Chicago at noon tomorrow. We're playing the Sox at one-thirty."

The mechanic didn't say anything. Abbott could see that he didn't understand. "I'm a coach with the St. Louis Browns. We've got a weekend series with the White Sox, starting tomorrow afternoon, and I've got to be there."

"I getcha," the mechanic answered. That explained the deep tan on the man's leathery face, he thought. "Ordinarily, I'd be able to get this done before dark, but one of my boys is playing a ball game himself today, starting about four. I'm going to have to close a little early to go help him out. I'd send you someplace else but none of the other stations do any work after five." He watched Abbott's facial expression turn to one of disappointment and uncertainty. "Tell you what I can do, though," he said. "I'll get in here early tomorrow, finish up, and have you on the road by nine at the latest. With a little luck, it could be eight-thirty."

Abbott didn't understand what this man had to do to help his son during a baseball game, but he was afraid the boy might be crippled in some way, so he didn't ask. He nodded his head. "Okay, I'll leave it here."

"There's a few places in town you can stay at," the mechanic said, "but I'd recommend the Morgan Hotel. The rooms are good, it's a fair price, and it sits right across the street from Rose's Diner, where you can order the best pies you'll ever taste."

Abbott liked this mechanic. "My name's Johnny Abbott," he said, holding out his hand. "I'll take your word for it that I can be on my way to Chicago tomorrow morning. What'll it cost me?"

"I'd say probably about eighteen dollars. Most of it's the parts." He shook the hand extended to him. "I'm Galen Morrison. And if you're short of cash, don't worry about it. I'll give you an address where you can send a money order."

"I'll be okay," Abbott said, "unless I eat too much pie over at Rose's before I leave town. The hotel's about ten blocks or so from here, right?"

"Just about," Morrison told him, "but I'll have my helper drive you over." He walked outside and around the corner of the building before calling for someone named Lloyd. A young boy appeared a minute later, dressed in the same kind of green shirt and pants as Morrison, and wearing a pair of high-top, black sneakers. He just nodded when he was told to take the red Ford and drop Abbott off at the Morgan Hotel. Abbott figured the helper was no more than fifteen, and learned on the short ride to the hotel that he had overestimated by almost a year. The boy, when asked, bragged that he had been driving since he was eleven.

"Who's playing in that game you told me about, and where's the field at?" he asked Morrison, while getting in the Ford.

"It's the guys from a couple of the factory teams around here. They'll show you some good baseball. Some of them played in a semi-pro league, and there's two or three with a little minor league ball under their belts. Game's at Lindbergh Park. They renamed it just a few months ago. It used to be Harlow Field, after Jetson Harlow, a lawyer downtown. He contributed the most when they fixed the place up and put in a grandstand about ten years ago. But Ray Beazley, the mayor, convinced the folks it ought to have the name of someone well known." Morrison laughed. "Of course, Harlow gave a lot of money to the mayor's opponent in last year's election." He hesitated, to let the point sink in. "It's no more than a seven or eight-minute walk from the hotel. Just ask anyone how to get there."

Just after three-thirty Abbott took a second row seat in the wooden stands on the third base side of the field. A quick look around told him that there was room for about a thousand people to sit down and watch the action. He was the first spectator to arrive, and was one of only a handful there watching the teams take fielding practice until about ten minutes before the game began. Then, suddenly, cars were coming from all directions, and both grandstands began filling up.

The crowd, mostly men, seemed to know all the players warming up. They shouted words of encouragement to some of them or began heckling those on the other team. But it was all in fun, and every few minutes one of the players being razzed would stop and, with a big smile on his face, point a finger toward the person in the stands baiting him.

Everyone on both teams wore a uniform, but Abbott couldn't find two alike. He realized that each player probably had on the shirt and pants he'd been given by some club or league he'd played for in the past. Looking around, Abbott spotted the shirts of the Cincinnati Reds and Philadelphia Athletics on two of the players. He learned from an attractive girl in blue jeans who sat down near him that the team on their side of the field was from Gibson Filters, a company that made automobile filters. The group on the first base side worked at Peoria Packing, where farm vegetables were cleaned, cooked, and canned for shipment all over the Midwest.

It took less than an inning of play for Abbott to shake off the indifference he'd brought with him to the game. The pitcher for Gibson Filters was throwing a knuckleball on almost every delivery, and Abbott could see it dip and move around from where he sat. The Peoria Packing hitters weren't coming close to making contact with it, but the catcher had the same difficulty trying to get the ball into his glove. At least one of every three pitches went to the big wire backstop. The pitcher's occasional changeup was a fastball that overpowered the batters when it crossed the plate, catching them off balance as they tried to time their swings to the next fluttering move of the knuckler. But it was a welcome relief to the catcher who knew where it was going and didn't have to hurl his body in one direction or another to stop it.

"What's the pitcher's name?" Abbott asked the same girl. He had listened to her root for each of the packing company hitters flailing away at the plate and wondered why she hadn't taken a seat on the other side of the field.

"That's Tommy Morrison," she answered. A few moments later she added, "He thinks he's so good."

"He is good," Abbott said to her. "From what I can see, he's damn good."

Peoria Packing scored two runs in its long first inning, without the benefit of a hit. Morrison walked one batter and struck out five, but three of his victims reached first base when the third strike eluded the frustrated catcher's grasp.

When Morrison went back out for the second inning, leading 4-2 on the runs his team had just answered with, Abbott went to watch the action from behind the wire backstop. The first three batters went down swinging and became official strikeouts, but all of them reached base on passed balls. At that point Abbott was convinced that he had never seen as good a knuckleball in his life.

The team manager went to the mound along with the catcher and spoke to Morrison. When the conference ended, the young pitcher began throwing mostly fastballs. The Packers, realizing that they no longer had to worry about looking foolish in the batter's box, got a couple of hits in the inning and regained the lead by two runs. Abbott saw that the first two innings had taken an hour and a half to play and figured that the teams would be lucky to squeeze in three more. Tired of standing, he returned to his seat in the grandstand.

But he was wrong about the time. Gibson Filters tied the game with two runs in their half of the second and had a new catcher behind the plate when Morrison returned to the mound. He threw twelve pitches, nine of which were knuckleballs. All but one were handled cleanly by his battery-mate, and he struck out the side.

Abbott's female neighbor was clearly upset. "Ringer!" she had begun shouting toward the field after the second out. "Take out the ringer!"

He could see that her resentment was being directed toward the catcher who had come into the game. The man looked vaguely familiar but Abbott couldn't see his face. "Who's catching for them now?" he asked her.

"That's Tommy's father," she said. "He worked for Gibson before he opened a garage. All the teams let him play when Tommy's pitching because he's the only one who can catch a knuckleball. We'll never win now."

And she was right. Gibson scored three runs in the next four innings while Morrison allowed only one more hit the rest of the game. Incredibly, Abbott's running total showed that the kid had struck out nineteen batters in seven innings.

That night, after a most satisfying dinner at Rose's, topped off with a huge slice of cherry pie, Abbott called Carlson at the team's hotel in Chicago. He explained why he had to stay in Peoria until the following morning and told Carlson about the game he had watched.

"This kid's unbelievable, Moose. I'm telling you he's got a major-league knuckleball."

"How old is he?"

"Nineteen."

"Nineteen, for Chrissake. Johnny, I'm worried about winning this year, not three years from now."

"What I'm saying is that he can do it right now." Abbott realized that he was yelling into the phone. He stopped and took a deep breath. "Tell me, Moose, how many times in your career did you hit against Stitch Walters? Best knuckleball you ever saw, right? Could pitch every other day, right? Believe me, this Morrison's better right now. I saw it with my own eyes."

"How can you say that, Johnny? You told me they were guys from a factory down there hitting off him. We play in the big leagues, remember?"

"That don't matter. No one's gonna hit him. The ball dances like it's on strings. You've got to see him pitch for yourself."

Abbott could hear Carlson exhaling loudly and guessed that he was smoking a cigarette. Several more seconds passed before the manager spoke. "And even if he's as good as you say, who's gonna catch him? Sheroff's too old and worn down to start fighting a knuckler behind the plate, and Holmes probably never saw one before. I know the three years he's been up here no one's ever thrown a knuckleball on this staff. So what's the use?"

"There's a guy here who can catch him. Handles him like every pitch is straight down the pike. Only one ball got by him in five innings last night. And the kid had twelve strikeouts in those frames. We could sign them both." Abbott waited for an answer. When he heard nothing, he said, "The least you can do is take a look. Either that or just keep praying."

Carlson sighed heavily into the phone. It was clear that he wasn't convinced. "Okay, bring them with you tomorrow. And if they're not everything you say, I'm gonna let you drive them straight back to Peoria."

It wasn't easy for Abbott to convince the Morrisons to make the trip to Chicago with him. Galen Morrison was standing in the oil pit, hard at work on the Chevrolet when Abbott got to the garage just after seven-thirty the next morning. He had walked there from the hotel, stopping first at Rose's for coffee and a couple of her homemade chocolate donuts.

When Morrison saw him peering down from around the front end of the car, he hollered, "What are you doing here so early?" and said that he still had a good hour's work or more ahead of him. Abbott told him to take a break, that he had to speak to him for a few minutes. Morrison climbed the four iron steps from the oil pit, wiping grease from his hands onto a dirty blue towel.

"I saw you and your boy in that game last night. I think he's gonna be a real fine big league pitcher," Abbott said.

"Yeah," Morrison answered, nodding his head up and down, "he's got a knuckler that sure moves around. There's no ballplayer in town that wants to hit against him. You can pull your back out trying to do something with what he throws up there." Morrison laughed at what he had said. "He's got all the makings. But he's also got a good job, a souped-up Dodge, and a girlfriend right here in town. I don't know that baseball's so important to him that he'll stay with it and try and catch on professionally."

"Listen, Mr. Morrison…"

"Call me Galen. You're a customer."

"Okay, Galen. Let me tell you first off that I've been around pitching all my life. I've seen the best of them, the worst, and all the ones in between. Unless I'm crazy, your kid's ready for the Majors right now, and I want him to tryout with the Browns as soon as we can get him to Chicago. If he makes it, I'd say he can earn himself $1000 a month. And I'm sure we could get the front office to pay you half that for catching for him."

Morrison was speechless, as Abbott guessed he would be. "You heard me right, Galen. I told Moose Carlson, the manager, how you were probably the only one who could hold on to those knucklers, and he said to bring you along. Tommy pitches and you catch him. In the Big Leagues. How does that sound?"

As soon as the work on Abbott's car was finished, he and Morrison drove over to the Gibson Filters plant. Someone brought Tommy to a room in the large office area that was empty except for a big oak desk and two chairs. Abbott closed the door.

"What's up?" Tommy asked his father. "Someone get hurt? Is mom okay?"

"Everyone's fine," the senior Morrison assured him, raising his hands, palms out, for emphasis. "It's nothing like that." He and Abbott had agreed on the way over that it would be better for him to raise the matter with his son. He sat down on a corner of the desk. "How much you making here, a month, right now?"

"With overtime, about 350 or so, why?"

"How'd you like to make three times that much and not have to work as hard?"

"What are you talking about, Pop?"

"Tommy, this here's Johnny Abbott. He's the pitching coach for the St. Louis Browns. He saw what you did last night out at the park and thinks you can pitch for the Browns right now. Is that right, Johnny?"

Abbott jumped right in. "I'd bet anything on it, Tommy. You're a natural with that knuckleball. And right now my club's desperate for a starting pitcher to replace Art Whitlock. He tore out his elbow a couple of weeks ago, in case you didn't read about it." The blank stare on the younger Morrison's face told Abbott that he probably didn't even know who Whitlock was. He decided not to push it. "If you can do the job, it's a thousand a month for August and September and probably a full share out of the pot if we get into the World Series. You get to be on the field with the best ballplayers in the game and you've got a chance to be a real hero. What do you think?"

Tommy Morrison's answers made it clear that he wasn't overwhelmed at all by what Abbott told him. He didn't want to be away from his girl-friend for two months, he said. He'd visited St. Louis once with his parents and younger brother and didn't like it at all. "Much too hot," he said. And he figured it would be hard to make friends with players who were at least three or four years older than he was. "Besides," he asked, "how could I be sure that Gibson would take me back when the season was over?" Before either Abbott or Galen Morrison could begin to reply, Tommy had made up his mind.

"No, I want to stay right here. Pitching's fun when you know every-body in the stands who's watching and you can have a few beers with the guys on the other team afterwards, but not when it's so important to win.

Playing for Gibson is good enough for me. I don't need more money to do what I like and I'm not sure I want to be anyone's hero."

And that would have been the end of it if the Browns already had someone on their team who could catch a knuckleball. But they didn't, and when Tommy found out that his father would go up to the big leagues with him and be behind the plate whenever he took the mound, that changed things around. Almost two hours later, Galen Morrison had communicated the sudden turn of events to his dazed wife and unbelieving younger son, and Tommy had comforted his girlfriend on the telephone as best he could. Father and son — suitcases packed — were in Abbott's car, with its new muffler, heading north to Chicago. Abbott drove faster than usual, reassured by the knowledge that he had a mechanic with him in case of any other trouble. He hoped that he wouldn't be on this same road, returning to Peoria, the next day.

The Browns lost to the White Sox that afternoon by a score of 10-5. It was a laugher for the Sox who were ahead by eight runs most of the game, giving up three meaningless tallies in the ninth inning. Abbott and the Morrisons got to Comiskey Park about a half hour after the game started, in time for the coach to put on his uniform and be in the dugout when Carlson had to pull his starter out of the game in the bottom of the third. It would have been Whitlock's turn again to pitch in the rotation if he hadn't been injured. Carlson was especially agitated that day, watching his team get beat again and thinking about what might have been.

As the Browns were batting in the ninth, Abbott asked whether Carlson wanted to see the new pitcher and catcher work out after the game or wait until Saturday morning.

"Let's get it over with today," the manager hissed. "A few of our guys look like they can use a little extra batting practice."

"Okay, Moose, but remember that this kid pitched seven innings last night. He could be a little tired."

"Just get this phenom of yours in a suit and out on the field. I don't want to hear any excuses. What about the catcher, is he here too?"

"Yeah, he's here."

"Okay, have them both ready to go at four-thirty."

By five o'clock, Carlson had seen enough. Tommy Morrison had thrown his knuckleball to six of the Browns' regulars and not one of them had made solid contact. Every so often he mixed in a hard curve or a fastball to keep them off stride. Even though Carlson had hoped to see his hitters pick up some confidence in the batting cage, he let the young pitcher serve up whatever he wanted and show what he had. By the time he sent someone else out to take over for Morrison, Carlson was exuberant.

"Great pitching, kid. Johnny here was right. You got an amazing knuckler. Thing just doesn't want to be touched. Congratulations, you just made the St. Louis Browns, and you'll be on the hill for us Monday when we get to Detroit."

Morrison showed no sign of excitement. "My dad's on the team, too, right?"

Carlson didn't understand. "Your dad? What the hell's this got to do with your dad?"

Abbott dreaded the moment. He spoke up quickly. "His old man's the catcher. Name's Galen Morrison. Handles that knuckleball like a charm, doesn't he, Moose?"

Carlson looked over at the elder Morrison, still behind the plate in the batting cage. "His father? How old is he for Chrissake?" he shouted at his pitching coach.

"Forty-two. But look at him work. You'd think he was ten years younger."

"Goddammit, Johnny. Why didn't you tell me on the phone you were talking about the kid's old man? The writers would crucify me for bringing in someone his age and letting one of the younger guys go back down. I can't do it."

Abbott saw the expression on Tommy Morrison's face. He knew the young pitcher was only seconds away from telling Carlson to shove the job, that nothing could ever get him to take the mound for St. Louis. He moved over to Carlson and pulled him aside, leading him a few steps toward the outfield.

"They're a team, Moose. If you want the kid, you take his old man. If you don't, Tommy goes back to Peoria with him. But don't feel like you'd be hurting the club by signing them both. You saw how he handles his kid's knuckler, and we don't have another catcher in the whole organization who can do it. So I think you'd better put down the welcome mat for these guys in the next half minute or you'll be trying to figure out who else can pitch for us against the Tigers on Monday."

Carlson looked glum. He felt he had a tiger by the tail. "Bring him over," he said reluctantly, nodding his head toward Galen Morrison. "I guess I got no choice. And tell Rollins to write up the contracts tonight for whatever you promised them. Let's hope these guys are the answer."

It was a crisp, sunny October afternoon in New York. The Polo Grounds was filling up with its rabid Giants fans, all of them grateful for having been able to get tickets to the game. The lush grass that stretched all the way from home plate to the clubhouses in deep center field was resplendent. Banners could be seen hanging in every part of the ballpark. Dozens of writers and photographers roamed the area near the two dugouts looking for interviews. The constant sound of "thwack" echoed in the stands as players — taking turns in the batting cage — teed off at the soft offerings being thrown to them.

"You know, Johnny, we never would have gotten here if it wasn't for that heap of yours breaking down in Peoria and you going to that ball game. And you wouldn't have been driving through there at all if you didn't have that damn thing about cigarette smoke. It's hard to figure how some things happen."

Carlson and Abbott were sitting in the dugout, watching their team take batting practice before the first game of the World Series. Tommy Morrison would pitch the opener for the Browns. He was being counted on, not only to start game four, but to be on the mound for the seventh game if the Series went that far. In the last two months of the season he had been fantastic, beating one team after another. He won eleven of his twelve starts, with an ERA of 1.96. His only loss came on a score of 1-0 when his father, on a whim, called for a fastball instead of a knuckler on the first pitch of the game. He regretted it moments later when the ball was hit over the left field fence. Morrison's extraordinary performance was even more meaningful in light of the fact that the rest of the pitching staff lost a game for every one they won in the August and September stretch drive.

"Just dumb luck, Moose," Abbott replied. He was sure the Browns would win the Series, and had already begun worrying about the next season. He knew that Galen Morrison was going to call it quits for his short career in baseball and stay in Peoria. Morrison didn't want to be away from his family for such long periods of time, he had said, and he missed his work in the garage. Abbott knew that the team would have to trade for a catcher who wouldn't panic on the receiving end of a knuckleball. But even if it did, he wouldn't bet that Tommy Morrison would be willing to stay in the Big Leagues without his father. He kept telling himself to enjoy the moment; that it was his great scouting discovery that had gotten the team into the World Series, but it was difficult to do.

The New York crowd was screaming at fever pitch when their heroes batted in the first inning, intensifying the nervousness Tommy Morrison took with him to the mound. He couldn't control the knuckleball and walked the first two batters. Galen ran out to talk to his son. Abbott got up from his seat next to the bat rack, but Carlson told him to stay in the dugout. The runners moved up a base on a slowly hit ground ball to the second baseman, and the only run of the inning scored when the cleanup hitter checked his swing on a knuckler and rolled it down the first base line for the second out. Morrison closed out the inning by throwing three straight knuckleballs past the powerful Giants center fielder.

For the next eight innings Carlson exhorted his players to get some runs, but it was in vain. The Browns had several good chances, twice putting a runner on third base with only one out, but the Giants got out of the jam each time. The final score was 1-0, the second time Morrison had been victimized that way, and Moose Carlson had to be concerned about the fact that his team lost with its best pitcher.

In the second game the next day, Warren Potter gave the Giants twelve hits and five runs, enough to lose most games. But the New York pitcher had to watch in despair as his teammates made three costly errors in the field. The miscues gave the Browns four unearned runs to go along with the three very legitimate ones that scored on third baseman George Wacker's long home run. The 7-5 final tied the Series at one game each, and the teams had that night and part of the next morning to ride the Century Limited to St. Louis. Abbott bought a deck of cards and spent all of his non-sleeping time in the last seat of the last car, playing solitaire. It wasn't entirely free of smoke, but the rash he got was more like goose bumps than the large, itchy hives.

It had been a while since Sportsman's Park had seen the red, white, and blue bunting of World Series flags. They hung from the facade of the upper deck all around the field, no more than five feet apart at any location. Still others were draped over the railing of the box seats situated down the line from home to the first and third base bags. The crowd was in a festive mood from the time the gates opened two and a half hours before the game's one o'clock starting time. They cheered loudly at the conclusion of the singing of the National Anthem by Kate Smith. The Governor of Missouri threw out the first ball and probably should have guessed from the loud chorus of boos responding to the announcement of his name over the public address system that his bid for re-election in exactly 29 days was doomed.

But all the fun and excitement ended for the Browns fans when the Giants knocked out the starting pitcher in the first inning, scoring six runs. A box seat customer told an inquiring reporter after the game that it was like seeing a brand new car come off the assembly line and get driven into a brick wall. St. Louis tried hard to catch up and was behind by only three runs after a rally in the sixth, but the Giants weren't to be denied and won 9-5.

It was unseasonably cool in St. Louis the next day. When Tommy Morrison finished warming up and walked alongside his father from the bullpen to the Browns' dugout before the start of game four, Carlson asked him how he felt.

"Like winning a World Series game, in case I don't get another chance," he answered.

Carlson smiled, showing Morrison the big gap on the right side of his mouth where two lower teeth had been knocked out in a fight with one of his own ballplayers several years earlier. "You'll have plenty of chances, kid, for at least the next ten years."

Whatever Morrison thought of Carlson's reply, he took advantage of the opportunity he had that day and pitched the Browns to a 3-1 victory. It was the seventh time in the season that he had at least ten strikeouts, falling one short of his personal high of fourteen. The Giants scored their only run in the eighth inning when a knuckler snuck through Galen Morrison's legs after dropping sharply and bouncing in the dirt in front of him. He felt bad that he had cost Tommy the shutout and told him so after the game. The Series now belonged to whichever team could win two of the remaining three contests.

The Giants and Browns both scored two runs in the second inning of game five, and the score remained that way until each team duplicated its feat in the eighth. Both clubs blew at least one good scoring chance in the next three innings. In the twelfth, the Giants pushed across an unanswered run on three seeing-eye singles through the infield. Browns fans — emotionally exhausted — filed out of the park quietly, wondering how their heroes would respond with their backs to the wall.

The team from New York had good reason to celebrate on the long train ride back to the east coast. They were ready to clinch the championship in their own park, in front of their own fans. Carlson and Abbott spent most of the trip exchanging ideas about who would do the pitching for them in the next game. All they wanted was the opportunity to get to game seven and another chance for Tommy Morrison.

Everyone agreed afterwards that the game in which St. Louis tied the Giants at three victories apiece may have been the most exciting World Series contest ever played. It featured five home runs — two by the Giants, including a grand slam by a rookie pinch hitter named Dawson Douglas in his first at bat of the series. The Browns' shortstop pulled off an unassisted triple play just when it appeared that the home team wasn't satisfied with rallying from a five-run deficit but was ready to blow the game wide open. There were two incredible outfield catches on balls about to clear the fence that saved another home run by each team. And at the end, the disappointed crowd witnessed five consecutive strikeouts by Tommy Morrison who was brought into the game in desperation by Carlson when the Giants loaded the bases with one out in the eighth inning of an 8-8 tie.

The winning run for St. Louis was scored by Galen Morrison who had entered the game at the same time as his son. He walked to lead off the ninth and scored from second on a single after a hard collision at home with the Giants catcher. In the last of the ninth, the elder Morrison found that it became increasingly more difficult for him to throw the ball back to the mound. On the first two strikes to the final batter of the game, he was forced to run out to the mound, as if he had to converse with the pitcher, to hand Tommy the ball.

Carlson and Abbott both saw that Galen Morrison had a problem, even though he claimed to feel just stiffness, not pain. An hour later, X-rays confirmed that he had seriously injured his shoulder and wouldn't be able to play in the final game. That meant that it would be futile to pitch Tommy Morrison, even if his knuckleball was as good as it had been that afternoon. The Browns had no one else who could catch it. The manager and his pitching coach had seen too many baseball games in their long careers to ever concede defeat, but they were realistic enough to know that they'd be the heavy underdog without Morrison on the mound.

The two of them were consoling each other in Carlson's office long after the game. They were trying to work out the order in which they might best use their other pitchers the next day, when Galen Morrison knocked on the door and opened it. His right arm was in a sling, tucked in close to his stomach. He assured them that he felt all right and reported the doctor's prognosis that he'd be as good as new in a couple of months.

"You'd like to find a way to pitch Tommy tomorrow, wouldn't you?" It was more of a statement than a question.

They looked at him, but said nothing. They had already concluded that circumstances had taken that choice out of their hands, and couldn't imagine what Morrison had in mind.

He realized what they were thinking. "Well, you can still do it," he said. He saw each of their heads move slightly, as if asking him to let them in on his secret. But their eyes were blank and their silence continued. Finally, Carlson spoke, unable to restrain the sarcasm in his voice.

"Oh yeah? How? Please, don't be bashful."

"Listen," Morrison answered matter-of-factly, "there's one other guy back in Peoria who can catch Tommy as good as me. Caught him a lot while Tommy was in high school when he was learning the knuckler out of a pitching manual and finding out what he could do with it. If I get hold of him right away, I can have him here tomorrow by game time. I already checked the train schedule and we can do it if you want."

Carlson and Abbott were flabbergasted. The questions suddenly flew out of their mouths. "What's his name?" "How do you know he's in shape?" "Are you sure he'd come?" "When's the last time Tommy pitched to him?" They were both standing very close to their injured catcher by the time they exhausted their inquiries.

Morrison answered everything they asked, assuring them that Lee Carteret could do the job. "But he's gonna have to catch a train to Chicago pretty quick to make connections if you want him here. You've gotta fish or cut bait."

Carlson and Abbott looked at each other and communicated without saying a word. "Call him," Abbott said, pointing his finger at Morrison. "Get him here," Carlson shouted. "Hurry up, find a telephone."

Morrison left the office. Carlson went back to his chair and fell into it with a loud sigh. Abbott kept standing, rubbing the back of his neck with his hand.

"What do you think?" Carlson asked. "Is this guy gonna be for real?"

"I don't know, Moose." Abbott shook his head. "I'm afraid to think about it. Did we do something to deserve two miracles in one season?"

The cab bringing Galen Morrison and Lee Carteret from Grand Central Station to the Polo Grounds arrived at the ballpark about 30 minutes before game time. Carteret already had on the size 32 Browns uniform that Morrison had picked up from the equipment manager that morning, along with the brown team cap that bore the city's initials in front and was quartered off with narrow orange lines running down in four different directions from the button on top. He brought his own spikes and would use Morrison's catcher's glove. Abbott gave Carteret a handshake with a fast "Glad to see ya." He hustled him out to the bullpen so he could watch him in action as Tommy Morrison warmed up. Twenty minutes later the coach returned to the dugout with a big smile on his face.

"It looks good, Moose. Morrison's knuckler is doing everything but a disappearing act and Carteret can handle it. He's a real silent type, though, doesn't say a word. Tommy told me that's the way he always is. Has to concentrate every second. It suits me, as long as he catches what the kid throws up there. Only thing is he's on the short side and his arm doesn't seem all that strong. It could be a problem if Tommy lets them get on."

As crucial and deciding games go, the last game of the World Series between the Browns and Giants was just average, one that would have bored many observers if played during the regular season. There were no home runs and not a single outstanding defensive play. It was a major letdown for both teams from the day before and could only be called exciting because the score stayed close for all nine innings.

The fans who jammed into the park that afternoon were pumped up. Their anticipation rose whenever one of the Giants got on base, and their hopes were dashed each time Morrison recorded another strikeout to end a rally. In the end, St. Louis took a 3-2 lead into the bottom of the ninth. Then, despite a one out opposite field triple by the Giants' shortstop, it held on for the victory. With the crowd on its feet and shouting encouragement, the second out was recorded when Morrison's knuckleball dipped past the hitter trying to squeeze the run in from third. Dawson Douglas, a hero a day earlier and New York's last hope, took three desperate swings at Morrison's servings, all in vain.

When Carteret caught the final strike, the Browns players rushed out to the mound from the dugout and the bullpen. They grabbed and hugged each other as the disheartened fans watched in silence from the stands. The team's celebration on the field lasted fifteen minutes and then continued in the locker room when several cases of iced champagne were brought in.

About an hour after the last pitch had been thrown, while the revelry was still going on, Johnny Abbott discovered that Lee Carteret was nowhere to be found. He wanted to congratulate him again for the game he caught and talk about the coming season. Abbott pushed his way through several members of the press who were still interviewing Tommy Morrison about the game, trying to squeeze more quotes out of him. He interrupted and asked if the pitcher knew Carteret's whereabouts.

"Yeah, Johnny, my dad took him to the train station. He had to get back to Peoria right away for something special happening there tomorrow. I heard him say there was no way he could miss it."

"That's too bad. I wanted to talk to him about catching you next year."

Morrison smiled. "Forget it, coach. Lee would never do that. Lee's the stay-at-home type, just wants to hang around Peoria all the time."

They had asked the driver to stop at a Mobil station on the way to Grand Central. While Carteret took off the Browns uniform and got into street clothes in the washroom, Galen Morrison chatted with the station owner about business and invited him to stop by for a visit if he was ever in Peoria.

When they reached the terminal, they had to wait 40 minutes for the train to Chicago. Morrison bought a cup of coffee for each of them and purchased an assortment of fruit for Carteret to take on the overnight trip back to Illinois. He found two seats in the crowded waiting room and they sat down.

"I've got to tell you, Lee, that was one heck of a game you caught."

Carteret smiled. "Thank goodness none of their base runners tried to steal. If they did, I probably would have just held on to the ball instead of showing them I couldn't throw that far."

"Now you've got to own up that you're glad I got you to learn how to catch Tommy's knuckler when I couldn't be there."

"Yes, you were right, but who'd have thought it would ever come to this? I still don't believe it."

"And if word ever gets out, no one else will either. Listen, I understand the team's going back to St. Louis tomorrow and then there'll be a parade downtown on Wednesday or Thursday. So me and Tommy should be getting back to Peoria one of those nights."

"That's okay. You guys know where to find me."

"We sure do," he answered.

Two months later, as winter was beginning to send ominous warnings of its rapid approach, and as the hot stove league began to heat up in baseball towns from the Hudson River to the Mississippi, the Browns notified the local press that both Galen and Tommy Morrison had sent back the contracts tendered to them. They informed the team that they would not return to Major League Baseball under any circumstances. The last part of the statement indicated that the Browns still had some interest in bringing Lee Carteret to spring training, but had been unable to make contact with him.

Shortly after New Year's Day, Dean Haller, the baseball reporter for the *St. Louis Dispatch* decided to do a story on "The Boys From Peoria," as he called them. Haller wanted to find out what made the Morrisons tick; why they were willing to give up the opportunity to play ball in the Big Leagues and make the "easy bucks" ballplayers could earn. He wrote in his column that every red-blooded American boy he had ever known would give his right arm (if he was a southpaw) to trade places with Tommy Morrison. He also hoped to meet with Carteret, learn more about him, and see whether he intended to return for a tryout with the team.

When interviewed at his garage, Galen Morrison told Haller the same thing he'd said to Johnny Abbott. "At my age I want to be home with my family during the long summer, not riding trains back and forth to the east coast. It's when I enjoy going fishing or on camping trips. Besides, there's a lot of people in Peoria who rely on me to take good care of their automobiles." No, he said, when Haller was leaving, he hadn't seen Lee Carteret in a while and didn't know how to get in touch with him.

Tommy Morrison had his girlfriend with him when he met the reporter at a drugstore counter just a block from the Gibson Filters plant. He'd received a promotion at work, he said, and his face lit up when he mentioned that they were thinking about getting married later that year. Morrison said that he enjoyed fooling hitters with his knuckleball, but that sitting and watching baseball every day, as he had to do with the Browns, wasn't fun for him. He'd rather be working in the filter plant with his friends and pitching for their team once or twice a week. He told Haller that the money Gibson paid him was enough for what he needed, and said he was sure he'd be doing a lot better in a few years when they promoted him to supervisor.

"Yeah, pitching in the World Series was a thrill, but I've already done it once," he said. "I don't figure it would be any different the next time." Smiling at his girlfriend, he told Haller he was sure he wouldn't miss the heat in St. Louis, or packing and unpacking a suitcase all the time, or trying to sleep on a train while it click-clacked along at night, blaring its loud whistle at railroad crossings every few minutes.

Haller wanted to know where he could find Lee Carteret so he could ask how he felt about getting a last-minute call to catch the deciding game of the World Series. Morrison said he couldn't help, that Carteret seemed to have dropped out of sight for some reason. He was sure the Browns had seen the last of him.

Haller checked the local telephone book but there were no Carterets listed. He drove over to the storefront offices of the *Peoria Gazette* on Main Street and spoke to the editor, but the man was not even aware that someone named Carteret from that town had played in the World Series. "We don't tend to follow baseball all that closely here," he said, "and if there's a story on it, it'll usually be about the White Sox or the Cubs. Those are the teams folks around here would be more interested in."

Leaving Peoria, Haller decided to make one last try at City Hall. The information clerk directed him to the elections department where he learned that there was no Lee Carteret registered to vote. He then walked down the long corridor, with its white tile floor and mahogany walls, to the tax assessor's office. There he was told that there wasn't any property in town in Carteret's name.

"Well, does anyone by the name of Carteret show up on your records?" he asked, indicating his impatience by speaking in too loud a voice. His frustration was getting the better of him.

The clerk behind the counter wet his forefinger with the tip of his tongue and began slowly turning the pages of the large cloth-covered book in front of him. "Yes," he said, a short while later, "Amos and Helen Carteret."

"Good," Haller said, confident that the mystery was about to be solved. "Where do they live?" He knew he asked the question in an overly demanding way, but didn't apologize for it. Instead, he quickly took a small spiral notebook out of his jacket pocket and got ready to make a note.

"My best recollection is they're somewhere in Texas now. They moved away from here about five years ago because Amos needed the dry heat." The clerk turned around toward a heavy woman with jet-black hair who was occupying one of the two desks in the office. "You remember the Carterets, Frances? Where'd they move off to?"

Frances looked up and stared at both men for several moments. When she answered, she spoke hurriedly, as if annoyed at being interrupted. "New Mexico, I think. Maybe Santa Fe. I just don't know."

Haller stood there. He craned his neck toward the high ceiling above them, drumming the fingers of his left hand on the countertop. "Tell me this much," he said finally, turning back to the clerk and again showing his irritation when he spoke, "did they have a son named Lee?"

The clerk turned around to look at his buxom co-worker again. They locked eyes for several seconds, as if that was the only way either one could find an answer. "No, they sure didn't," he told Haller as he faced him again, shaking his head from side to side. "Had two daughters, was all."

The reporter gave up. It was going to be a long drive back to St. Louis and he decided to get started. His disappointment at not locating Carteret for his story was obvious. "Thanks for nothing," he said, and left.

Frances got out of her chair and walked slowly over to the counter. "What was that all about, Earl? I knew something was going on when you asked if I remembered the Carterets."

"I just didn't like anything about that fellow," Earl said. "He never told me who he was or what he wanted to know for, and he sure didn't talk with any respect. If he didn't know Amos Carteret was mayor here for four terms, I wasn't about to tell him. And I didn't want him bothering Amos down in Phoenix on my account."

"That's what I figured when you asked," Frances said. "And how do you think he got Lee Carteret mixed up that way?"

"I don't know. Beats me. But if he's got some crazy idea about Lee, it's not up to me to straighten him out. I didn't see any reason to let him know she married Galen Morrison and has been Lee Morrison for some twenty years now. No, sir, not that rude knucklehead."

THE LEAST MISERABLE CHOICE

"When a pitcher's throwing a spitball, don't worry and don't complain, just hit the dry side like I do."

—Stan Musial

THE AFTERNOON BEFORE Opening Day should have been a pleasurable time for Paul Remy. The sound of bat against ball had begun to fill the park late in the morning as the two divisional rivals that would do battle the next day went through their hitting and fielding drills. Media representatives swarmed around the batting cage, their notebooks and microphones at the ready for any interviews they could coax from the players. Maintenance men wiped down the seats throughout the park while others hung red, white, and blue banners on the short wall in front of the field boxes. Food and souvenir vendors moved their products from a line of trucks on the crowded street to the booths that had been set up for them behind the grandstand and bleachers. Remy had been in the middle of it all, smiling unabashedly at everything involved in the start of a new season of baseball. It was everything he had been anticipating for weeks. It was what he lived for.

But just before noon he had to break away from the commotion around him and return to his office in the executive suite. When he arrived, he found Rick Keenan waiting for him. Keenan was an agent known for his high-priced stable of ballplayers commanding annual salaries in excess of ten million dollars. The item on that day's agenda that Remy hadn't been looking forward to was the negotiation of a contract extension for Jamal Orlando, the team's superstar left fielder. The club's three-year pact with Orlando would expire at the end of this season.

Remy had dealt with Keenan on a number of occasions in a twelve-year career as general manager for three major-league teams. He always felt a certain nervous tension whenever a session with the agent was scheduled. There was something unsettling about the man who came to every meeting totally prepared, disdained small talk, and refused to waste time listening to long speeches about why his client's employer couldn't afford to pay him market price.

"I'm not interested in your small ballpark or your low TV revenues or anything else," Keenan had said moments earlier, just fifteen minutes into the meeting. The words conveyed a tone of annoyance, as if to a student who hadn't yet learned an obvious lesson. Keenan wore a navy blue blazer over a black turtleneck sweater. His curly black hair had a purposely disheveled look and the lenses of his glasses were the kind that adjusted to the light around him. He didn't apologize for interrupting Remy's discourse as to why Orlando's salary demands were overwhelming. "You know what the going rate is for a player who hits 38 home runs and averages a 120 RBI's every year. We're not asking you for any more than what the Braves just agreed to give Wilfred Perez. Like I said, three more years will cost you 33 million dollars."

Remy leaned back in his swivel chair and was silent. He was a tall man with brown hair, deep brown eyes, and a tendency to dress inform-ally in clothes of that same color. His left knee ached from all the walking he had done that morning. He was grateful that the date for the arth-roscopic surgery it required had been moved up and was only nine days away. That meant he would have to spend his forty-fifth birthday on crutches and that the long weekend in Las Vegas his wife had given him as a present had to be postponed.

Remy took off his glasses, held them up to the fluorescent light in the office, and saw that they needed cleaning. He reached into the pocket of his short-sleeved beige shirt for the package of Redi-Wipes, couldn't find them, and then remembered he had used the last one just after arriving at work that morning. The weather forecast for the next day, which by late morning was suddenly warning about possibly heavy rains at game time, was beginning to affect his mood. He knew he had no answer that would make Keenan reconsider his position. Months of trying to convince him that Orlando wouldn't do as well in another city, that the team's ballpark was the perfect place for his hitting style, had achieved nothing. "Take him out of here and his stats will suffer," he argued each time they met. "You know it and I know it. This park's made for him." That was his best pitch toward persuading Orlando's agent to let him sign for less, to agree to a "hometown discount," as the media called it.

But Keenan rejected it every time, without even legitimizing the proposal through any discussion of its pros and cons. He knew from past encounters that Remy's goal — his disposition in fact — was to pay as little as possible in every situation. "Reasonableness," he recognized, was just another term the general manager used in trying to bring the price down. "No bargain-basement rates," Keenan said. "No hometown discounts. Pay him what he's worth today because it's only going to be more tomorrow."

Once Remy came to grips with what it would cost to sign Orlando for another three years, he considered his options. Conceding the player's value and agreeing to Keenan's terms would make life a lot easier. It would resolve the matter at once and keep any pressure from building up as the schedule progressed. Every heroic at bat Orlando had that helped the team win games could make it more costly to sign him when the season was over. The problem was that the agent's uncompromising demands would push player payroll for the following year right up to the line already drawn by the club's ownership.

Remy realized that factor wasn't a complete stumbling block. He'd still have the chance to reduce payroll through trades or by not picking up the team's options on certain players. But his experience wouldn't let him rest comfortably with that sort of planning. Players with options on them had a strange way of suddenly producing results, turning their salaries for the next season into irresistible bargains. And potential trades might come along that would cost the team more money, but significantly improve its chances for a championship.

His second choice was to treat the negotiations as ongoing and to stress for public consumption his continued desire to sign Orlando, but be ready to move him to another team before the trading deadline in July. Remy had actually been leaning in that direction for a while, having become disenchanted with his superstar over the winter for several reasons. It began when Orlando caused a stir while being interviewed on a local radio station during the World Series. He complained that the team hadn't done enough during the season to bring in players who could win the big games. "We'd have had a shot at the Series ourselves with just a little more help," he had said. "Sometimes you wonder how much management really cares about winning."

The sports talk show hosts had been all over Remy to respond, but he refused. He disliked almost every one of them and knew that appearing on any of their shows might only make matters worse. Instead, he instructed the club's publicist to issue a statement pointing out that the team's payroll was the sixth highest in all of baseball, demonstrating its commitment to putting a winner on the field.

About a month after the interview, Orlando was arrested in California and charged with being present at a party where illegal drugs were confiscated. He pleaded innocent, and a public relations firm hired by Keenan took the offensive on his behalf. The charges against him were ultimately dropped when the district attorney couldn't prove that he had any prior relationship with the men who supplied the drugs or that he knew they were being passed around that night. On the advice of the team's general counsel, Remy had taken a "wait-and-see" attitude about it when the story first broke. Later, he was belittled by Orlando in the sports pages for not supporting him publicly from the outset.

Remy was also disturbed by Orlando's physical appearance at the Baseball Writers' dinner in the middle of January. He guessed that his left fielder was at least twenty pounds overweight and in the worst shape he'd ever seen him. Watching him slowly move to the stage to receive an award, Remy began to fear that Orlando's weight, if not kept in check, would quickly shorten his productive career. At a photographer's insistence, the two of them posed for a picture together, but their mutual greeting had been cold when they first met that evening and there was no other conversation between them. Remy felt he was owed an apology and saw no reason to be cordial toward the player if one wasn't forthcoming.

Those incidents had forced Remy to think about whether it would be wise to sign Orlando for three more years. On a personal level, he didn't appreciate criticism from anyone on the team regarding his efforts at putting together a contender, least of all from the player who commanded the most media attention. His position was that they should play the game, as they were paid to do, and keep their mouths shut about things that weren't their business. He worried about Orlando's statements causing a rift between himself and the owner who thus far had confined himself to the numbers side of the ball club he purchased three years earlier.

But that aside, Remy also knew he had a limited amount of time to put together a team that could play its way into the World Series. Money purchased talent, and he wanted to be sure he didn't waste a lot of it on Orlando if his superstar had peaked and was on the way down.

Remy had spent more time than usual with the team during spring training. (It was while shagging flies in the outfield one afternoon that he slipped on some wet grass and tore the meniscus in his knee.) He wanted to get a close look at several players he hoped were ready to move up from the minor leagues, as well as the low-cost free agents he had signed over the winter. At first he was pleased to see that Orlando had been working on his own to get himself in condition. Some of the excess weight had disappeared and he was usually in the middle of the pack when the team was running wind sprints.

As the players got ready to break camp and move north, Remy evaluated the team's chances. He concluded that it was probably good for a third-place finish, still two years away from being a World Series contender. He also felt that signing Orlando to an expensive extension wouldn't get them there any sooner. Although he suspected that most fans would be upset if he traded his left fielder during the season, Remy was sure he could get excellent prospects in return from a team that saw itself in the race for the playoffs. The idea appealed to him. His job was to bring a championship to the city, and he'd have to do what he thought best, whether or not it was a popular move.

Remy's third option that April day, as he heard Keenan extol his client's valued presence in the clubhouse, was to let his left fielder play out his contract. He could then decide whether the team would bid for Orlando's services before he filed for free agency, or even after he did. Remy recognized the gamble he'd be taking if Orlando had another good year. His price tag would go up even further and the club would be in danger of losing him to another team without getting any compensation in return.

Keenan had finished talking. He sat almost motionless, his hands resting on the table, fingers intertwined. For once, it didn't seem that he was negotiating while a cab waited for him outside, its meter ticking away.

"Let's break for lunch," Remy said.

"Sure. That's fine," Keenan answered. "But just 30 minutes, okay? I've got to get a plane out this afternoon." The cab was back in the picture.

Remy presented the three options to the team owner, Karl Vance, and solicited his input. Vance sat behind a large oak desk, arranged so that his chair was in a corner of the office. The shades in the room were drawn, the only light coming from the Tiffany-style desk lamp in front of him. His face was well tanned, almost to the point of having a cowboy's leathered look, and he kept his hair short so that the gray moving in rapidly at his temples was less obvious. Vance was a no-nonsense kind of guy. He had made his fortune in software, and the millions he spent to acquire the team had come from the industry giant that purchased his company seven years earlier. At 55, he cared more about celebrity status than power. Remy had come to understand that the owner said what he meant and meant what he said.

Vance put the ball right back in his general manager's court. "You know what I did whenever I was faced with several lousy options, Paul?" he said. "I always tried to figure out the least miserable choice and then went with it. In my opinion, signing him now would be that choice." But then he hurried to add, "That's what I'd do, but you're the baseball man and I count on you to make the right decisions."

Remy barely had time to finish the sandwich and orange he'd brought from home that morning before Keenan returned. While eating, he decided to rely on what he had seen in Florida and not press to negotiate a contract extension for his left fielder with Keenan. Orlando had hit only two home runs in the exhibition games and was still overweight with the season ready to get underway. At the end of spring training, Remy comforted himself with the fact that he could trade him before the deadline if the right deal came along. It would be easier to justify the move to the media and fans if Orlando's performance was below average during the season, as he suspected it would be. But if a trade didn't materialize, Remy felt he could persuade Vance to pay Keenan's price for the player's services when the season was over, either before or after Orlando became a free agent.

"It's your call," Keenan told him as Remy balked at Orlando's price tag and their meeting came to an abrupt end. He picked up his papers, put them in his Coach portfolio and walked to the door. "I think you're going to regret it," he said, and left. "Asshole," he mumbled, going down the stairway.

When he drove out of the ballpark on July 4th, an hour after his team had scored four runs in its half of the ninth to steal a victory, Paul Remy found himself in a quandary. Much to everyone's surprise, his club was leading the division by two games. Several players were having breakout years. The team's batting average was third in the league and it had already banged out 24 more home runs than on the same date a year earlier. To complement the slugging, several members of the pitching staff were consistently giving the club six or seven good innings, lowering its earned run average to the fourth best in baseball. The come-from-behind win that holiday afternoon was, incredibly, its eighteenth of the half-completed season. There was a lot to feel good about.

Remy's concern, however, centered on Jamal Orlando. He had been both right and wrong in predicting the kind of year the left fielder would have. Orlando was batting 30 points below his average and striking out more often. His playing weight remained a problem. He was slow fielding his position and was seldom waved home from second on a sharp single to the outfield.

But his clutch hitting had been outstanding. He led the league in runs batted in — fourteen ahead of his closest pursuer — and was third in home runs. He was the player everyone wanted to see at bat in the late innings when the tying or winning runs were on base. On three occasions he had been walked intentionally even though first base was already occupied. Opposing managers were more willing to move the potential tying run to second base and pitch to someone else than risk being beaten by one swing of Orlando's bat.

With the trade deadline just weeks away, Remy knew that Orlando's name would come up in discussions with other clubs. His experience and gut told him that the time was right to part company with his star outfielder. There was the certainty of getting some good prospects in return versus the increasing likelihood of losing Orlando to free agency later on with nothing to show for it. He was certain that Keenan would have Orlando test the free agency market and that the asking price for his client could increase dramatically from what it had been in April if he continued having success at the plate. Trading Orlando would incense the fans if it affected the team and derailed its pennant hopes, but it was a gamble he might have to take. Still, a sense of panic attached itself to his thoughts on the matter. As much as he wanted to see the team continue to do well, he hoped that if a long slump were in the offing, it would start right away.

But the baseball gods weren't smiling at him. While the ball club began to lose as many games as it won, the same held true for the other teams in the division that were chasing it. With two days remaining to consummate any trades, Remy's club was still holding on to its slim lead.

That afternoon, the Rangers offered him his pick of three out of five minor league prospects in exchange for Orlando. Remy did his statistical research and made several telephone calls to scouts who would have seen the players in action. The reports were all favorable, with two of those on the list projected to be star-quality major-league players. The proposed trade was a winner, he felt, assuring future talent for the team and saving it millions of dollars in the short term. He could try to find another left fielder with power in the next 36 hours or replace Orlando with a less expensive free agent after the season.

Remy was certain that his club's worst days that season were still ahead of it. He brought the deal to Vance and recommended it. But this time the owner wasn't letting his general manager make the call.

"We can't do it, Paul." Vance pointed a finger toward the computer spreadsheet showing on his monitor. "We've sold more tickets in July than we ever hoped for. The fans think we're in the race all the way. They're buying up all the seats for the games in September. If we let

Orlando go, we'd break their hearts. In fact, they'd probably want to run us out of town. I say we have to keep him, even if you're right and we don't make the playoffs."

"But that could mean losing him in free agency and coming up empty," Remy warned. "The fans wouldn't like that too much and the media would have a field day over it."

Vance's reply didn't conceal his impatience as he turned back to the monitor. "We'll have to worry about that when the time comes, Paul. Right now, considering the options, our least miserable choice is to do nothing."

Remy returned to his office and called the Rangers. "It would have been a good deal for both clubs," he said, "but there's a problem here and I can't pull the trigger." He wanted the Texas GM to know that the cold feet belonged to someone else.

On August 16th, Remy's team went to sleep in first place for the last time. The following evening it blew the lead and the game in San Francisco on a walk-off home run by the Giants catcher. That was the start of a nine-game losing streak, the last two of which were played in front of a frustrated and ill-tempered home crowd. After making a final surge by winning five of its next six, the club went into permanent cruise control, playing consistently at the .500 level. At season's end, just as Remy had predicted, it finished third in the division, seven games behind the leader. Orlando had slacked off some in the last two months, not having as many runners on base for him to deliver, but still led the league in RBI's and cracked the 40 home run mark again.

Remy met with Rick Keenan on the afternoon of the third playoff game between the Mets and the Dodgers. He'd had little sleep the night before, trying to script a firm but friendly approach for himself the next day. Keenan's portfolio lay unopened on the table in front of him. He seemed to be sending a message that he didn't expect the negotiations to go anywhere.

"We want Jamal to stay with us," Remy said. "I think we can give you a contract you'll like without his having to test the market. Even though his average was off by 32 points, we recognize that he won a lot of games for us and carried the team the first half of the season."

Keenan chuckled to himself. He knew that the reference to Orlando's batting average was the only negative Remy could raise about his client. It would have been meaningless to also make reference to the player's weight problem or the step or two he had lost on the base paths. Orlando's run production was all that mattered, and he had shown again that he was one of the best. Keenan saw no reason to argue statistics. He knew he was in the driver's seat and his attitude confirmed it.

"In April we wanted 33 million for three years," the agent said. "Now the price is 50 million for four. I don't think Orlando will have any trouble getting that as a free agent. In fact, if a number of other signings go higher than what I've figured them at, we may be asking for even more."

Remy kept his poise but was stunned by the numbers. He had figured on a maximum commitment of 36 million for three years and had convinced Vance to authorize it. He considered it a bad risk to sign a player for any longer than that, especially one who had already been through ten big league seasons. "That would be almost fifteen percent of our payroll for one player," he said, falling back on an old argument. "Where do we get the revenue out of this ballpark to pay for the other 24?"

"I can't tell you how to run your business," Keenan answered. "If you'd listened to me in April, you wouldn't have had this problem. I figure you were betting on my client having a bad year. Sorry to disappoint you, but that's a bet you lost. Meanwhile, Orlando sold a lot of tickets for this club. You were pretty much out of the race for most of September but you had sellouts every day, whether or not they showed up to watch you play. Now Vance has got to show his gratitude for all that money he took in." Keenan smiled.

Remy had nowhere to go. He could see that Keenan was prepared to reject anything less than the numbers he had put on the table. He was beginning to dread his next session with Vance even though he had warned him about the predicament they were now in. "I'll bring your proposal to the owner and see what he says. If we put something together, I'll fax it to you within a week."

Keenan was unhappy with Remy's emphasis on the word "proposal." He finished the can of Diet Coke he had been nursing and got up to leave. "Let's not have any misunderstanding," he said. "As of right now, you can keep him here for 50 million over four years. Only the amount of the signing bonus is negotiable. Don't bother offering anything less. If you pass on that deal, he'll be on the free agent list the first day it comes out."

That left Remy with just one loose end to tie down. "If that happens, I assume you'll give us the chance to match any offer," he said.

"That'll be up to Orlando. I understand you didn't have much to say to him all season. He may prefer a change of scenery…and I'm not talking about the ballpark." Keenan smiled again as he walked toward the door.

The financial commitment was more than Vance was willing to make. "If he can get that money as a free agent, good luck to him," he said. "If he can't, maybe you'll still have a chance to sign him for the 36 million we talked about. But that's as high as I'll go, Paul. If we lose him, we lose him. Again, I'd say our least miserable choice is to do nothing."

The hometown media began to press Remy about the status of negotiations with Orlando. He found the words to save face for the club and avoid an outright lie, without revealing the sad circumstances. "We've been in talks with his agent," he said, "and there are proposals being discussed."

Orlando opted for free agency as soon as he was eligible. He was considered one of the most desirable players on the market. The print media found space every day in which to speculate on which clubs wanted him and could afford him. When questioned, Remy was reduced to saying that the team hadn't been able to satisfy Orlando's present contract demands, but that it still hoped to sign him. He telephoned one sports writer and claimed to be frustrated by the negotiations, indicating that Orlando's asking price kept going up whenever he talked to the player's agent. Unrevealed, of course, was that only two conversations with Keenan had taken place between April and October.

Early in December, Keenan called. "I'm pretty sure you have no intention of signing my client, but I don't want you badmouthing him to the press and saying he went elsewhere without giving you the chance to match the offer. The Indians have 48 million on the table for four years with a club option for a fifth year at twelve more. If they don't pick up the option, it's a two-million-dollar buyout. We'll give you 24 hours to match it, and I'm going to confirm that with a fax in the next few minutes. If you're not in the picture, at least you won't have to worry about him hurting you all the time, playing in the other league."

Remy knew there would be other meetings over other players with Keenan. There was no sense being anything but cordial. "Thanks for the call," he replied. "If you don't hear from us, tell Jamal I wish him well."

One week later, Remy had his new left fielder. Oscar Johnson had been with three other teams in the past seven years and had never been signed for more than one season at a time. He was a lifetime .262 hitter whose bat seemed unable to generate the long ball two years in a row. Coming off an unproductive campaign, he was almost a steal in the free agent market. Remy had studied Johnson's statistics very carefully and felt confident about taking a chance on him for the upcoming campaign. But the media didn't share his enthusiasm, and the talk show callers ridiculed him repeatedly for losing Orlando without getting some players in return. The off-season was a major disappointment to them thus far and they weren't accepting it quietly.

Karl Vance had been away most of December, vacationing in the Caribbean. He returned to his office on the Tuesday after Christmas and spent the next several days catching up with all the baseball news he had missed. Vance was especially interested in what the local sports columnists had been writing about his team.

The staff had already been notified that there would be no work on Friday, the day before New Year's Eve. Late on Thursday afternoon Vance invited Remy to his office. He was sitting on a corner of his desk, flipping an old baseball in the air, when the general manager came in. He had removed his tie and unbuttoned the top two buttons of his shirt, revealing a gold chain Remy hadn't seen before.

"Have you been watching ticket sales for next year?" the owner inquired.

"Yes," Remy said, "I've asked Isaacs to update me on it every week."

"As of right now, we're down about twenty percent from a year ago."

"I know. I'm sure some of it has to do with Orlando."

"And the fact that we haven't signed anyone exciting to replace him," Vance replied quickly. "If we finished third with him, where will we be without him? That's what the writers are asking."

Remy wanted to remind him whose decision it had been to forego trading Orlando back in July. He knew that if Vance had listened to him then, the fans and the media wouldn't be complaining now. Instead, they'd be looking forward to how the players obtained for Orlando would help the team. But he realized that the urge to put the blame where it belonged was self-destructive, and he controlled it. "I think Johnson will have a good year," Remy answered. "He won't give us Orlando's numbers but he'll help win some games."

"Games that we may end up playing in front of a half-empty park in August and September," Vance said

"I'm doing what I can, Karl." He tried to score some quick points. "And remember that Johnson's going to cost you just a fraction of what Orlando wanted." He gave the words a second to sink in before adding,

"What's out there right now is either overpriced or what probably won't help us next year. I don't want to spend money that we can put to better use in June or July when some teams give up on the race. When they're ready to unload some good players, we'll have more to choose from. Besides, we've got a couple of rookies coming up that should excite the fans. Timmy Boland stole 82 bases in Triple-A last year and — "

Vance interrupted. "I've got a decision to make, Paul. You know how quickly we use up our TV and advertising revenue. What we take in there isn't anything close to what some of the other clubs get. The bottom line for us is filling as many seats as we can 81 games a year. That means the fans have to have something to get them excited during the winter, good hot stove league stuff. They need it long before we go to spring training. Otherwise, attendance will be down when the season begins and will stay that way or even get worse if the team's off to a bad start. We've got to give them something to talk about now, to stir up interest."

"Do you have any particular players in mind?" Remy asked.

"No, that's still my general manager's job," Vance said. He got up from where he was sitting and moved around the desk to his chair. He dropped the baseball into an open drawer and pushed it closed. "As I see it," he continued, "I've got three options right now. The first is to terminate your services. The writers and fans are all blaming you for losing Orlando to free agency with nothing to show for it. If you were gone and a new GM came in, they'd expect to see some changes. I think the anticipation would get a lot of them fired up and remind them where our ticket office is located. The second option is to do nothing. We can just hope the fans wake up and catch baseball fever one of these days. The last one is to authorize you to spend whatever it takes to sign some big name free agent right away. He may not be what the team needs to win more games next year, but that would also get the town talking baseball now, when it's important. Those are all lousy options, but I had to consider each of them and I've decided that letting you go is my least miserable choice. You can understand that, can't you, Paul?"

ALL THE SIGNS SPELLED VICTORY

Dedicated to Roger S. Driben

"Why do I have to be an example for your kid? You be an example for your own kid."

—Bob Gibson

FINALLY, ON A miserably cold October afternoon in Montreal, the baseball curtain was about to come down on the end of the season. It rained lightly most of the morning, but on several occasions the sun had surprised and delighted those walking in the crowded city streets by slipping through the slightest opening in the heavy, gray clouds, like a slowly hit ground ball somehow finding its way through the infield.

Everyone knew what kind of weather Quebec's largest city could expect when playoff games had to follow the completion of the long regular season. Fans streamed into the ballpark wearing leather jackets and heavy woolen coats, with colorful scarves wrapped around their necks. Many of the men had on hats that could cover their ears and that normally sat on a closet shelf until it was time to be taken down for a football game in autumn. Gloved hands held on to thermoses of hot coffee as devoted supporters of the two baseball teams found the way to their seats. And on this day, with the series coming to a close and the championship resting in the balance, the Expos and Yankees were facing the reality of playing in temperatures that were in the mid-30s when the first pitch was thrown and would drop to below freezing by the fifth inning.

The players danced around at their positions on the field, holding still only while the next pitch was on its way to the plate. They smoothed the infield dirt in front of them, occasionally picking up pebbles that they flipped beyond the first or third base foul lines. They pounded their red fists into the well-oiled pockets of their oversized gloves and kept up a constant stream of chatter toward the pitcher on the mound. There was no way to ignore the cold. They could only try to fight it off by moving back and forth between pitches, keeping their faces turned away from the wind, whenever possible, and making a lot of noise.

"Strike the bum out, Vic." The words of encouragement were shouted in from center field. "No hitter, no hitter, Vic, just up there for a walk."

"Come on, Victor, one-two-three, one-two-three," the shortstop and second baseman said almost in unison.

"Hum Vic baby," the catcher hollered as he set the target behind the plate, "put it over, he'll never see it." They engaged in the baseball banter they had grown up with and that they hoped would pump up the player most responsible for their fortunes that day.

On the benches, the players wore windbreakers under their team jackets, zipped to the very top. They sat hunched forward, their arms folded tightly across their chests, their feet stamping the ground. The ones whose teammates were at bat tried to stay warm by calling out more of the timeworn banalities of the game to whoever was in the batter's box.

"Good eye, good eye, Joe." "He's wild, Joe, can't find the plate." "Get a hold of one, Joe boy, park it baby." Each side seemed to bring its own rhythm to the words of encouragement it offered both on the field and from the bench.

Everyone dreaded taking his turn at the plate that day. The players knew that if the ball made contact with the bat near where they gripped the handle or down at the very end, beyond the sweet spot, it would send a sudden resonating sensation — an awful stinging, almost like an electric shock — racing through their fingers and wrists and into their forearms. Batting gloves or wristbands were useless to stave off the painful numbness that would settle temporarily in their hands, bringing tears to their eyes. Many players refused to swing as hard as they normally would, trying to cut down on the degree of discomfort they expected to have if they didn't get good wood on the ball.

The two managers were hardly oblivious of their players' feelings about going to bat in such circumstances, having experienced the same distress in their own days on the field. As a result, each team attempted an unusual number of bunts during the game. The strategy anticipated that the hitter's speed — even though slowed somewhat by the cutting wind — would still get him to first base before the fielder could move in, pick up the ball cleanly with his cold, partially numbed hand and make an accurate throw in time. After several innings, each side changed its defensive alignment, having both the first and third basemen stationed on the infield grass, ready to charge the plate at the first sign of the hitter's intention to try to bunt his way on. And recognizing that the harsh weather conditions were forcing the game to be played this way, the managers did not always signal the infielders to return to their normal positions at the corners, even when the count on the batter reached two strikes and the likelihood of another bunt attempt was greatly reduced.

The result, as any terribly uncomfortable spectator at the game could have foreseen from a combination of such elements and strategy, was that hits and runs were scarce. From the stands, it appeared that the players on both sides were more concerned about getting the game over with as quickly as possible and avoiding injury than with which team would leave the field as champions. And an impartial observer sharing the bench with either of the two clubs would have seen that the only players exhibiting any emotional concern with the outcome were those who already knew that they wouldn't be returning the following season for another chance at the baseball jackpot.

The Yankees took a two-run lead in the second inning on three well-placed bunts and two consecutive errors on ground balls hit to Guy Crawford, the Expos' tall and talented shortstop who, other than for that very uncharacteristic lapse, played a brilliant game.

"I can't believe it. I've never screwed up twice in a row like that before," was all Crawford could say to Jack Martineau, his manager, when he returned to the bench.

At first, Martineau's response was just a major-league scowl, conveying his great displeasure with one of his team's best players. But then, realizing how that show of disapproval might have looked to others observing the scene, he put his arm around Crawford's shoulder and offered a stream of moral support. "Don't let it bother you, kid. Just play your game out there. You'll get a chance to make up for it."

The Expos got one of the runs back in the fourth inning when the Yankee third baseman was charged with two errors on the same bunt. After dropping the ball when he first picked it up, losing whatever chance he had to throw out the batter at first, he grabbed for it again and fired it wildly down the right field line. That gave the Expos runner time to race around to third. The next hitter followed with a chopping infield single over the head of the pitcher, on which everyone close to the action could hear him cry out in pain when his bat met the ball. It allowed the run to score and immediately brought the Expos fans — quite subdued up to that point — back into the game. Most of them took the opportunity to stand up and move around while cheering, twisting their bodies back and forth in an effort to shrug off the penetrating effects of the raw afternoon.

They had to wait two more innings, however, before the tying run came home on a walk that was followed by a clutch two-out double to the gap in right center field. Kelly LaBarr, the Expos catcher, stood on second with a big grin on his face. He knew he had made the right decision in ignoring the third base coach, who had been frantically waving his arms and shouting at him to try and stretch the hit into a triple. Time was called while one of the Yankees' infielders retrieved LaBarr's batting helmet that he had lost after rounding first. Putting it back on, he asked the umpire for more time while he bent over, hands on his knees, and tried to catch his breath. A poor hitter, and notoriously overweight, LaBarr was not used to running fast over any distance.

When play resumed, and the crowd — which had treated the delay as another welcome occasion to twist and turn in place — sat down, a change of pitchers by the Yankees brought the Expos' rally to a halt.

The seventh and eighth innings gave neither team the opportunity for resorting to strategy on the base paths or cause for raising any excitement in the stands. The baseball gods — paying rapt attention to what was going on, and having to choose from all the cries of encouragement coming from both players and fans — had clearly become temporarily enamored with each side's "Hey babe, hey babe, let's get 'em one-two-three" chant that drifted upwards from a number of different locations on this very cold field of dreams.

But something had to give. Light snow had begun falling an inning earlier and was making the baseball slippery to grasp. Before the start of the ninth inning, the umpiring crew met with the two managers at home and informed them that the game would be called on account of the weather if the score remained deadlocked after each team's at bat. In that case, it would have to be replayed in its entirety. "And I hope I can hold off this terrible piss I have to take," the plate umpire told them, grinning as he said it.

The Expos pitcher, their third of the game, responded poorly to the official ultimatum by walking the Yankees' curiously named leadoff hitter, Dee Dijon, on four consecutive balls. The first sacrifice bunt moved him into scoring position. The next one caught the infielders flat-footed, despite the defensive strategy that had prevailed throughout the game. And the play put the Yankees ahead when the speedy Dijon rounded third and never hesitated on his successful dash to the plate while the ball was unwisely being thrown to first. High fives abounded when he returned to his Yankee teammates, and the feat was rewarded with loud applause from those sitting in the seats behind the visitors' dugout.

Before the Expos batted in the last half of the inning, Martineau spoke to the first three scheduled hitters and reminded them to watch carefully for signs from the third base coach before every pitch. "We've got to get at least one run home or there are going to be a lot of unhappy people in this ballpark," he told them.

Raul Bauer, the team's center fielder, led off and watched the first two balls cross the plate wide of the strike zone. Martineau clapped his hands and flashed the "take" sign across the diamond to Andy Simone, the coach at third. He didn't want Bauer swinging at anything until the new Yankees reliever showed he could get the ball over the plate. Simone promptly relayed the manager's call, communicating through the quick movement of his hands over different parts of his face and body. Bauer waited for the coach to finish, stepped back into the batter's box, and hit the next pitch sharply down the left field line.

"Why the heck did he swing?" Martineau mumbled under his breath, pleased, nonetheless, with the result. Meanwhile, the Expos' bench shouted its support to Bauer as he ran to first, made the turn, and coasted into second base with a double.

Danny Orr, the Yankees manager, who had twice been voted to the All-Star team years earlier, was on his feet, waving at his infielders to move in close for the expected sacrifice bunt. He rested a finger on the left side of his nose for several seconds, signaling the shortstop to move towards third on the pitch and cover that base for a play on Bauer when the ball was bunted. "Look alive; be alert out there," Orr shouted to his infielders. At the same time, he picked up a bat, wrapped both fists around the handle, and began squeezing hard in an effort to relieve the tension coursing through his body.

On the Expos' bench, Martineau sensed the defensive strategy Orr would be employing and decided to have his next batter swing away. It was the left-handed hitting LaBarr, whose double had tied the game in the sixth inning. Martineau flashed the sign to Simone and then groaned out loud when LaBarr waved his bat timidly at the first pitch after it had already exploded into the catcher's glove. Although concerned by what he had just seen, Martineau stayed with the same strategy. When Simone looked over to him from third, the manager indicated by a total lack of movement on his part that the "hit" sign was still on. Simone went through his motions and passed it along.

The Yankees pitcher, Ken Montaigne, took a lot of time getting ready. It was his third year on the team and he knew how to play the psychological game with an anxious hitter. He stepped off the mound, wet several fingers on his throwing hand, wiped them on his uniform shirt, and smacked the baseball into his glove a few times before turning his attention back to LaBarr.

At the corners, the infielders were beginning to creep in even closer to the plate. Martineau felt they were playing right into his strategy and was sure they'd be totally handcuffed by any ball hit hard in their direction. It was up to his catcher to get a piece of it. Then, as Montaigne started to pitch, even before the next delivery left his hand, LaBarr suddenly squared around and showed bunt.

"What are you doing?" Martineau yelled, but it was too late. LaBarr was holding his bat out over the plate, and as soon as the ball made contact, it went to the onrushing first baseman on two easy bounces. He picked it up and in one fluid motion fired it to third. The shortstop, getting there quickly and straddling the base, dug the low throw out of the dirt and had the ball waiting for the sliding Bauer. The umpire pumped his fist down toward the ground and called the runner out.

The Yankees fans, and a few of the more discriminating Expos supporters who risked verbal abuse from those around them, rose to their feet and applauded the defensive skill shown on both ends of the play.

Pacing in front of his players, Martineau silently fumed at the costly mistake that now left his team with one out and a runner on first. He couldn't understand why the hitters were suddenly ignoring what they were told to do. If it weren't the end of the season, he thought, he'd spend as long as it took at the next practice making sure everyone on the club had each and every sign down pat.

The Yankees infielders backed up to their normal positions, prepared to try and turn any ground ball into a game-ending double play. They were confident that Guy Crawford, the Expos' leading hitter would be swinging away, not bunting. For his part, Crawford was looking to atone for the earlier errors he'd made that had given the Yankees their first two runs. He felt confident at the plate, certain of getting the hit that would turn the game around.

When the count reached a ball and a strike, Martineau saw a chance to catch his opponents off guard and signaled for a bunt on the next pitch. Simone did his job in the coach's box, whistling for Crawford's attention before the fingers of both hands began touching his cheeks, nose, chin, elbows, and the bill of his cap. Crawford nodded, resumed his stance at the plate and proceeded to take a vicious swing at the fastball Montaigne threw over the outside corner. A moment later he began howling in agony as he dropped his bat while the ball blooped behind first base, down the right field line.

"I don't believe it," Martineau hissed, getting up quickly and slamming his hand against his thigh as several Yankees ran hard to try and make the catch. "What are these guys trying to pull?" he asked, spitting the words out slowly as the players on the bench turned their heads away from him. The ball, a classic "Texas Leaguer," landed fair by inches when no one could reach it in time. Only the speed of the right fielder in retrieving it in foul territory and throwing it home kept the tying run, in the person of the slow LaBarr, from attempting to score. But the Expos had men on second and third, and their fans were up again, screaming for victory.

Danny Orr came off the Yankees' bench and ran out to the mound. As soon as he got there, joining Montaigne and Ricky Sanderson, the catcher, he had his infielders come over as well. He had something to say to each of them, and was still talking and pointing to the different bases when the home plate umpire came out to break up the conference.

"Come on, Danny," he said impatiently, "I'm ready to piss my pants. Let's play ball and get this over with."

Orr patted his pitcher on the backside and started off the field. "Maybe you guys ought to wear a catheter and a bag on days like this," he hollered to the umpire who was already halfway back to the plate. Suddenly, as the thought began to work up an unwanted result, he wished he had one on himself.

The Expos anticipated that their next hitter, Bobby Dumart, would be given an intentional walk. Martineau figured that the Yankees would then be looking to go for a force play at home or be willing to try for a double play in the right situation.

But Orr decided on a different strategy. He was prepared to accept a tie, instead of risking defeat at that point, knowing that the ace of his staff would be able to pitch for them the following day or whenever the deciding game was scheduled to be replayed. He didn't want to walk Dumart, not known for an ability to come through in the clutch, and then have to face Lou Thornton, the Expos' power-hitting third baseman, with the bases loaded. Instead, Orr preferred to go after Dumart, even if it meant giving up the tying run on the play. If that happened, he would walk Thornton intentionally and hope to get the last out from the hitter who followed.

Unlike his opponent on the opposite side of the field, Martineau was going for a win, not a tie. He had already used his best pitchers in the last two games and wanted to see the Series end now, even if it meant a dangerous gamble on his part. He knew that a successful squeeze play would tie the score at three, but realized that there would be only one more chance to get the hit that would bring them the coveted crown. Besides, a poorly executed bunt could result in the tying run failing to score. If that happened, he thought, it would put tremendous pressure on Thornton, his third baseman, to deliver a hit with two outs.

Martineau decided to have Dumart swing away and hope that he could knock in at least one run. He figured that a hit to the outfield would win the game, but that even if the ball were caught, LaBarr would have a chance to tag up at third and score after the catch. Suddenly, he realized that he should have already had a runner in for LaBarr, whose defensive skills were no longer needed, and scolded himself for the mental error. He called down the bench to Phil Arlette, a rookie with the Expos who had a lot of speed, and sent him in to run at third. The stage was now set, and Martineau, feeling the adrenaline, knew that this was why he loved doing what he did and being a part of baseball.

Although both managers were aware that the game was riding on every pitch, neither one ever expected the sudden ending they were about to witness. Dumart watched Simone carefully from the batter's box as the signs were flashed to him, and then touched the buckle of his uniform belt with his left hand to show that he understood what he was supposed to do. That move, never one that Martineau insisted upon from his players, gave the fifth-year skipper a strong sense of confidence in his right fielder and convinced him that he had settled on the right strategy.

But all that good feeling evaporated in seconds. As soon as Montaigne kicked his leg in the air and threw to the plate, Dumart turned to bunt and dropped the ball down the third base line. Unable to restrain himself, Martineau yanked the Expos cap off his head and began shouting "No, no, no," even as he saw the play beginning to unfold. Moments earlier, Arlette had listened as Simone whispered in his ear at third that he should be ready to tag up on a fly ball or try to score on anything hit to the infield. He was totally unprepared for a bunt and got a late start toward home.

Gene Gabriel, the Yankees third baseman, was playing on the edge of the grass as he'd been instructed, and started in to field the ball, about a step ahead of Arlette. From the stands, the two of them appeared to be racing side by side. Gabriel picked up the ball barehanded as he was running and dove to his right in an effort to tag the base runner instead of trying to throw the ball home. But Arlette had put on a burst of speed in the last few strides and was past the sprawling third baseman before Gabriel could reach out and touch him with the baseball.

Gabriel knew he had missed the tag when he hit the ground, landing heavily on his stomach. He turned over quickly and tried to throw the ball to his catcher from a prone position. But he was unable to put much on it, and the Yankees' bench, seeing the play develop in front of it, watched in shocked disbelief as the ball landed in the dirt, several feet to the left of Sanderson, and skipped past him to the backstop. Crawford followed Arlette across the plate and the game was over.

In his mind's eye, even as he sought to come up with a reason for the series of botched plays by his hitters that inning, Martineau could see and hear the play-by-play announcer shouting into his microphone, "The Expos win the Series. The Expos win the Series." He couldn't keep the huge grin from spreading across his face. After all, he had just reached the pinnacle of his managerial career. He looked toward the stands, waved to his wife, and put up two fingers in a victory salute. She returned the greeting and blew him a kiss.

Cheering fans stood and clapped their hands as the winners ran to embrace each other. They watched with pleasure as the jubilant teammates soon become an ecstatic pile of players on the infield grass. Then, as if permission to do so had been broadcast over the public address system, they quickly started moving out of the stands to get as close to their young heroes as they could before exiting the park for the warmth of their car heaters.

In an interview he gave after the game to *Le Jour*, a local newspaper, Martineau was asked to discuss the strategy he employed with each of his players in the last of the ninth inning. Not wanting the fans to know that every hitter in the inning had apparently missed or misunderstood the signs while they were at bat and had failed to execute his strategy, he sidestepped the question. Instead, after reflecting a few seconds, he told the reporter that as a manager he had to know what his players did best, and call on them to do it at the right moment. "They just did what I asked them to do, and we were fortunate that most of it worked out."

The reporter smiled. "Well, Jack," he answered, "in the end, all those signs you gave them spelled victory. Congratulations."

Martineau thanked him. He liked the way the reporter had put it. But it wasn't quite that simple. He knew that the victory his players had just attained, coming the way it did, could only happen in the kind of games he managed. Boys would be boys. And as he went over to join his wife, he told himself how lucky he was to have his own team in the Montreal Intracity Little League.

BLOWING BUBBLES

"If Satch (Paige) and I were pitching on the same team, we would clinch the pennant by July fourth and go fishing until World Series time."

—Dizzy Dean

Robert Lee Harrison, Jr. was two years old when his father took an afternoon off from work on the farm, drove the 40 miles into Knoxville where his draft board was located, and signed up for duty in the United States Marines. It was barely nine months after the Sunday morning on which angels of death, emerging from a cloudy sky disguised as Japanese fighter-bombers, wrapped their arms around the sleeping American fleet at Pearl Harbor.

Chances are that Bobby Lee's dad wouldn't have been called to serve for quite a while, if at all. He was the sole support of his wife and child, and had mortgage payments to meet on a farm that he and Roselynn purchased just three years earlier. They had put whatever savings they had into buying the land shortly after finding out that she got pregnant on their honeymoon.

But Robert Harrison, the great-grandson of a man who served the Tennessee legislature for twelve years and vigorously supported the course of conduct that led to secession, the Civil War, and his own death at Antietam, wanted to fight for his country. At 25, his good fortune was in having a wife who understood how he felt, and two younger brothers, both with medical deferments, who were willing to live on the farm and take care of it until he returned. His bad luck was in being among the first wave of troops to assault the beach at Munda in the Solomon Islands. Bobby Lee was still a month shy of his third birthday when his father's body was returned to Plainfield for burial among his ancestors.

Robert Harrison met Roselynn Spark in the summer of 1938. He was 21 years old and playing minor league baseball for the Cincinnati Reds' farm team in Memphis, the lowest level of the Club's organization. The players knew that they either had to be good enough to move up a notch, to Double-A ball, after two years there, or "go on back where you came from."

Bob was an infielder with a lot of potential. He had been spotted earlier that same summer by "Horse" Mabry, a Reds scout well known for his annual pilgrimage through the farm country of Georgia, Alabama, and Tennessee, looking for raw, emerging talent in American Legion or pickup games on Saturday and Sunday afternoons.

Mabry liked what he saw of the agile, muscular shortstop who played his game confidently, but quietly. He offered him 75 dollars a month to sign with the Memphis Gulls. Bob's father, himself a farmer, wasn't pleased about losing his son's help, but didn't try to talk him out of it. It was his way of showing appreciation to the boy who had eagerly taken on an ever-increasing number of chores and responsibilities from the time he turned six. And as far as Bob Harrison was concerned, going back to the farm, if that's what life had in store for him, was almost as enjoyable as playing baseball.

On one of the Gulls' rare days off, Bob stopped to watch some girls playing fast pitch softball at a local playground. Each team had its own matching caps and T-shirts, and brought an abundance of spirit and a fair amount of skill to the game. He was attracted by the red-headed pitcher of the Robins. She wore the number "0," chewed gum continuously, and occasionally blew large bubbles while overpowering the batters on the other side. She had a nice figure, and her short white skirt called attention to a suntanned pair of long, slim legs. Bob smiled every time she celebrated another strikeout by pumping her fist in the air.

He probably wouldn't have had enough nerve to speak to her, despite an immediate desire to do so, except that one of Roselynn's teammates recognized him as a Gulls player. Several of them at a time began drifting over to where he stood near the high-wire backstop. To them, the tall, good-looking boy with the wavy blond hair, deep-set brown eyes, and shy smile had "most eligible bachelor" written all over him. When Roselynn asked for his autograph on a page she ripped out of the team's scorebook, Bob asked her to tear it in half and let him have hers also. She blushed but did it, correctly suspecting that he would also want her telephone number.

Bob called her a few days later and they went to a movie that Sunday, after his game. They stopped at a drugstore on the way home and talked for hours over hamburgers and cherry cokes. He learned that she was eighteen, had graduated from high school that spring, and had never lost a softball game she pitched.

"Do you always chew that much bubble gum?" he asked, watching her remove some from the package for the third time since they left the theater.

Roselynn blushed. "Only when I'm a little tense," she said, "like when I'm playing ball or working hard." She hesitated a moment. "And sometimes when I'm out on a date." She smiled on the last words, and he smiled back.

During the rest of the summer, Roselynn went to all the Gulls' home games that didn't conflict with her own softball schedule. She worked as a secretary for a trucking company, and her early quitting time made it easy for her to prepare dinner each evening for her father, a widower, before going off to play ball or watch Bob's games. The Gulls owner, aware of the relationship, had given Roselynn a pass. When the games were over, she waited for Bob outside the park and he would take her home.

By the time his season ended and he had to return to Plainfield, at the other end of the state, they knew they were in love. Bob's playing had earned him an invitation to the Reds' spring training camp the following February and a place on the Gulls' roster for a second year.

They agreed that they wouldn't get married until Bob had been assured by the Cincinnati organization that he had the talent to make it to the Major Leagues, or if he quit baseball and returned to farming full time. Roselynn understood that the first option might require her to wait several years while Bob's progress was charted and measured in hits, runs, and errors.

But it didn't work out that way. After burning up the league for the first two months of the new season, Bob was involved in a violent collision at home plate and suffered some badly torn cartilage in his left knee. He was sent to Cincinnati for an operation and remained there during the early stages of his rehabilitation. But he soon learned that his knee would never be able to hold up to the constant stress it would have to take in the Majors, and the Reds released him.

Bob returned to Memphis and broke the news to Roselynn. "I guess that means I'll never find a Bob Harrison card in my bubble gum packages," she said, teasingly, and then embraced him quickly so she could hide her own tears. "But now I can have the real thing to myself a lot sooner," she whispered, kissing the side of his neck.

They began planning their small wedding right away, and were married nine weeks later. Roselynn knew that her move to Plainfield as Bob's wife would probably end her competitive softball days. Playing with a vengeance, she pitched twelve more winning games for her team and was also its leading hitter.

On their short honeymoon, she told Bob that with the athletic ability they shared, she was certain they'd have a son who would play baseball in the Major Leagues. He smiled at her. "Rosie, honey," he said — he was the only one who called her "Rosie," and he did it all the time — "if they ever have a big league for gals, there's no reason we shouldn't have both a son and a daughter playing up there."

Bob's brothers stayed on to work the farm after his death, and his father came by often to make sure everything was okay. The Harrison family loved Roselynn and had no doubt that a girl with her beauty would find another husband in time. They hoped it would be someone who lived near Knoxville so they'd be able to see her and Bobby Lee as often as they liked.

Roselynn grieved for her husband, but cried only when she was alone. For several months she was afraid to let Bobby Lee out of her sight, and insisted that he play inside the house when she had to be there alone. As tenderly as they could, Bob's family helped her get over the feeling that harm would come to her son also.

About a year after Bob's death, as spring slowly moved in on what had been a severely cold winter, Roselynn received a letter from Etta Miller, her closest friend on the Memphis softball team and maid of honor at her wedding. Etta informed her that a southern league for women baseball players was being formed, to play within a five-state area, and that Memphis was going to have a franchise. She had already learned, she wrote, that home games were being scheduled for the city's minor league park whenever the Gulls were playing on the road. The players would be chaperoned while outside of Memphis, she added, and wouldn't have to travel for more than a week at a time. Etta intended to go to the team tryouts during the third week in April and urged Roselynn to join her there.

Bob's parents were enthusiastic about Roselynn being part of the team if she was still good enough to make it. Bobby Lee, almost four, could stay with them for the summer. Bob's mother was certain that she could find plenty of things to keep her grandson busy. She had even gone to an old toy chest and taken out the small baseball glove they had given Bob when he was just a little older than Bobby Lee. Roselynn's father said she was welcome to use her old room back in Memphis and kidded her about his being able to get a good meal for a change. For the next few weeks, she did a lot of hard running each day and threw hundreds of pitches to Bob's brothers.

The tryouts were long and difficult, but Roselynn knew before the end of the eight days of workouts that she would be playing for the Memphis Mudders. She was one of the better hitters among the group of over a hundred women who checked in on the first day in full or partial uniforms of every description. Some wore spikes, while others were content to perform in sneakers instead of making a risky purchase that might not pay dividends. Roselynn's strong desire to play communicated itself to the surly four-man coaching staff that seemed to take pleasure in gloating over the lack of ability so many players showed during practice games. At the end of each workout, a group of aspiring players were thanked for their interest and told that they would no longer be needed.

On the final day of practice, Etta was one of the last ones chosen for the team. She had been concerned that her "pleasingly plump" body and general lack of speed would be her undoing, but her ability to scoop balls out of the dirt at first base worked in her favor. She ran over to Roselynn after the final cuts and gave her a big hug. "Now you've got someone you can share all that bubble gum with," she said. They both laughed, happy to have each other's company.

The Memphis Mudders were good, and Roselynn enjoyed the competition with the other teams in the league. The season began on May 15th and ended on the first Sunday in September. Roselynn played the outfield and pitched every fourth or fifth game. The Mudders finished second in their division the first year, then ran away with the division championship the following season and swept the playoff series with the Charlotte Wonders. Roselynn easily captured the league's Most Valuable Player award that year and had a feature article written about her in the country's most popular sports magazine. The accompanying picture showed her standing in the outfield in a typical pose, another bubble she had blown threatening to burst.

During the off-season that followed her team's championship performance, Roselynn met Sam Whitman, an insurance agent who had his own office in Tileston, a small town about halfway between Plainfield and Knoxville. The bank holding Roselynn's mortgage had suggested that she increase the coverage on the farmhouse, which Bob's brothers had expanded, and recommended Whitman to her.

Roselynn made an appointment to see him the following Monday morning. She arrived a few minutes early and was pleased that Whitman didn't keep her waiting. When he got up from behind his desk to shake hands with her, Roselynn could see that he was about an inch shorter than her and heavier around the waist than she liked a man to be. He had the soft look of someone who handled paperwork easily and hired others for whatever physical work had to be done. But Whitman was a pleasant-looking man whose best feature was the inviting twinkle in his blue eyes. Although his sandy-colored hair was obviously thinning, it was doing so evenly. No attention-getting bald spot had yet emerged. Roselynn found out later that he was 45 years old.

Whitman had lost his wife to tuberculosis almost five years earlier — just a week before Christmas, he told Roselynn sadly — and had been raising his children alone since then. Sarah was twelve and Neal had just turned nine.

Sam liked Roselynn from the start, and once he became familiar with her own situation, began courting her eagerly. He took her and Bobby Lee on drives with his own children on Sundays, and occasionally dropped by the farm on a weekday evening to have coffee and talk with her. Roselynn could see, from the size and location of his brick home and the new DeSoto he drove, that Sam was a wealthy man.

On a Sunday in February, Sam and Roselynn were able to be alone together and enjoyed the luncheon buffet in the dining room of the new Roosevelt Hotel in Knoxville. Despite the fact that the room was crowded most of the time, he reached over and held her hand in his on several occasions. It was the first time he had shown his affection for her in public. During the ride home, after Sam described the business boom he expected the end of the war to bring, Roselynn told him that she would be leaving for Memphis in the middle of April to start preparing for the new baseball season.

Several days later, Sam drove out to the Harrison farm in the middle of the afternoon and asked Roselynn to marry him. He wanted her to give up baseball and move into his Tileston home. Although she had suspected that the proposal would come at some time, Roselynn hadn't allowed herself to think about what her answer would be. She felt that the spontaneity of the moment would guide her, but found instead that all she could do was promise Sam an answer by the weekend.

It was a difficult decision to make. Roselynn knew how much she would miss Bobby Lee if she were away again, but had to admit that he did wonderfully during those months in the care of his uncles and grandparents. She had a strong desire to play another season and prove again that she belonged on the list of female all-stars, but was concerned about the future of the league. Roselynn figured that the return of the major-league veterans from military service would affect the turnout of fans in the women's league significantly, hurting all the players whose earnings were based entirely on attendance at the games. She was afraid that the chain of events could ruin the team owners financially and force them to shut down operations long before the season was over. Her foremost concern, however, was Bobby Lee's opportunity to continue his education after high school. Roselynn knew that Sam could provide that security. She convinced herself that she felt good enough about him to accept his proposal.

Roselynn wrote to Etta, giving her the news, and asked her to be maid of honor again at the wedding in June. At first, Etta said she'd be there if the Mudders gave her the time off. But when its general manager refused to let her go even though Memphis had become one of the two worst clubs in the division, she quit.

"The season's been no fun at all without you around," she told Roselynn when she got off the train in Knoxville. "I'm just as happy they gave me a reason to quit. Now I can stay home, find myself a husband, and make babies." They hugged each other a long time.

Roselynn didn't sell the farm after the wedding. Instead, she gave it to Bob's brothers, who wanted to stay on, with the condition that there would always be room there for Bobby Lee if that's what he chose.

The first ten years of Roselynn's marriage to Sam went by quickly. His business success continued, with the establishment of a second and larger office in Knoxville. She assumed the role of the gracious hostess at the parties that Sam liked to throw for the wealthy Tennessee businessmen whose insurance matters he was handling. Sarah went off to the state university in Chattanooga, joined eighteen other debutantes at a ball in their honor just after graduating, and settled into her father's Knoxville office with the promise of being put in charge after two years of training.

Neal, paunchy like his father, had no athletic ability. The beard he had grown made his face look gaunt and gave him a stern appearance that belied his real personality. At home, he had a favorite leather wing-chair in the den, and spent most of his spare time reading history. He was mainly interested in the biographies of famous world leaders.

Roselynn told Sam that she was sure Neal would go on to teach history in high school or college, and probably would have been right if

Sam had been content to continue accumulating his wealth on a steady basis. But he invested heavily in several real estate deals put together by some of his newer, brassier acquaintances, and found himself overextended when the ventures collapsed. A month after Neal completed his sophomore year at Ohio State University and returned home for a lazy summer, he left Roselynn at the country club one afternoon to pick up a book at home. The sound of a car engine inside the garage led him to his father, lying down in the back seat of the Cadillac, dead from carbon monoxide poisoning.

Bobby Lee had one year left in high school when Sam took his own life. By then, he could look back on eight years of having played baseball whenever he could find anyone who would pitch or hit ground balls to him, or just play catch with him. Roselynn had instructed him from the time he showed an interest in the game, and she made certain that he learned how to do everything right. Often, when his friends begged off or didn't want to be on a ball field under a hot sun, Bobby Lee got his mother to play with him.

When her son was twelve, Roselynn gave him the glove his father had used when he played for the Gulls. She had kept it in perfect condition with an annual application of neat's-foot oil, wrapping it tightly around a baseball the rest of the time. That same year she showed Bobby Lee the scrapbook that recorded the highlights of her husband's short minor league career, and the ones she put together about herself, long after leaving the Mudders. She had spent many nostalgic evenings sorting through a number of large envelopes of newspaper stories, pictures, and box scores she clipped and saved during her two seasons in the league. That was the year, of course, that Bobby Lee decided he wanted to be a major-league ballplayer.

Sam's will was read to the family about three weeks after his death. By then, Roselynn was aware of the extent of the financial reversals that had virtually wiped out their entire savings. Still, she was unprepared for the final decisions Sam had made just days before killing himself. He knew the business would be able to survive, and left it to Sarah and Neal as equal partners. The house was willed to Roselynn, Sarah, and Neal, with the provision that each had a lifetime interest in it while they were all alive. However, he stipulated that as soon as one of the three passed away, the survivors would own the house in two equal shares. Roselynn realized that the will assured her of a roof over her head in Tileston the rest of her life, if she wanted it. She also understood that in all probability she would have no financial interest in the house to pass along to Bobby Lee when she died.

Sam also left the Cadillac to Neal and Sarah, and gave the five-year-old Chevrolet to his wife. Bobby Lee's name was mentioned only once in the will, granted the right by his stepfather to live in the house as long as Roselynn was there. When the lawyer finished reading the document and looked up, he was momentarily nonplussed at seeing the large bubble Roselynn had blown and was about to pull back into her mouth. She said nothing to anyone that conveyed either the pain or disappointment she felt over what Sam had done.

Roselynn used Sam's business contacts to find herself another secretarial position, this time in a plant that produced cardboard boxes. She easily recaptured her old skills, and her good looks and personality were well received in the office.

Bobby Lee completed his final year of high school, working most afternoons and weekends in a hardware store. He was the captain on the baseball team, leading it to an 18-3 record and into the semi-finals of the State tournament. Despite the fact that Tileston was eliminated at that point, Bobby Lee showed enough talent to have scouts for three major-league teams approach him.

During his senior year, Bobby Lee had taken all the steps necessary to go on with his education, and had been accepted at two colleges. Each had an excellent baseball program and offered athletic scholarships. But shortly before his high school's graduation exercises in June, he told his mother that he wanted to defer his studies for a while and start playing minor league baseball right away. Roselynn knew that he was good enough to make it. When Bobby Lee promised that he would work for a degree by taking courses in the off-season, she gave him her blessing.

Roselynn always did everything she could to be both a friend and a mother to Sarah and Neal, even though she was only 26 when she married their father. Her first two years in the Tileston house were the most difficult as she tried to overcome the hostility that the children, especially Sarah, showed toward her. Roselynn understood that their conduct simply reflected the feeling they had that she could never replace their real mother. She recalled how jealous and resentful she had been herself, as a teenager, when her father occasionally dated another woman. It was a time when she hoped that he wouldn't marry again and force her to have to share his affection with someone else.

Eventually, Sarah and Neal saw that Sam's happiness had been rekindled. They also found that Roselynn could be trusted to keep their secrets and relied upon to support them in disagreements with Sam when she felt they were right. Roselynn never expected them to call her by anything but her name, and that's what she got. Still, she knew she had gained their respect, and succeeded to some degree — enough to please her — in getting them to think of her as their mother.

But although Roselynn derived a good deal of pleasure from her relationship with Sam's children, she could see that Sarah and Neal refused to accept Bobby Lee in the same familial way. It bothered her that Neal, who was only three years older than her son, ignored him most of the time and preferred being alone to joining him in some leisure activity. It didn't seem to matter that Neal had few other friends. Roselynn knew that Bobby Lee wasn't cut out for the insurance business, in the event he didn't succeed in baseball, but it disturbed her to realize that Sarah and Neal wouldn't welcome him into the office.

Bobby Lee's first three years of minor league experience were good ones. He received a small bonus to sign with the Pittsburgh Pirates, and was making steady progress in that organization. He played shortstop for the club's Single-A team in Marriott, Georgia, but the decision was made to try and convert him to an outfielder when he was moved up to Double-A the following year and assigned to Wheeling, West Virginia. The experiment was a success, and Bobby Lee's offensive and defensive statistics were a pleasant surprise to the organization. He returned to Wheeling for a second season, but was assured a promotion to the Pirates' top farm club in Scranton at the midway point of the schedule if he continued his outstanding progress.

Everything seemed to go right for Bobby Lee from Opening Day. In the team's first game, he took the lead in home runs and runs batted in and kept expanding it during the first 45 games of the schedule. He was hitting .361 and leading the league in several categories when the Pirates accelerated the schedule they had in mind for him and sent him to Scranton. Bobby Lee continued putting big numbers up at the Triple-A level and became a crowd favorite. At the end of the season, the fans there chose him as the winner of the Tenth Player award, given to the player on the team who most exceeded their expectations by his performance during the year. At 21 years old, Bobby Lee was fast approaching the top of his game, and the Big Leagues were no more than a year away.

But he never got to put on a Pirates uniform and go to bat in Forbes Field. During the third week of play the following season, when the

Scranton ball club was entertaining the Rochester Tigers, Bobby Lee got hit in the face by a ball he never picked up when it left the pitcher's hand. It came at him out of the glare of the sunlight that still spilled across the mound, and disappeared from his sight for just the barest moment before entering the area of shadow around home plate. The ball's flight was redirected only slightly as it grazed the peak of his cap and smashed into the thin ring of soft flesh between his cheekbone and his right eye.

The two weeks Bobby Lee spent in the hospital were followed by a series of examinations in Pittsburgh. Finally, after several months, the doctors determined that the spots and floaters he continued seeing whenever he concentrated intently on an object and put pressure on the injured eye would probably keep reappearing under those conditions. He was told that an operation would be dangerous and that it offered no more than a 50-50 chance of remedying the problem. Three specialists tested him exhaustively and came to the same conclusion. It was their strong opinion that he should never again stand in a batter's box and try to hit a baseball coming in his direction at 90 miles an hour.

Bobby Lee had returned to the house in Tileston while recuperating, and stayed there between visits to the Pittsburgh ophthalmologists. When he got their final diagnosis and discussed his options with his mother, she sided with the doctors. She had come to believe strongly that what wasn't meant to be couldn't be changed. It was better, she felt, to take whatever life let you have, but not reach out dangerously far for what seemed, enticingly, almost within one's grasp. She played catch with Bobby Lee a couple of times and noticed that he moved his glove into place very late for some of her throws, instead of having it there waiting for the ball to arrive.

When Bobby Lee made the decision that ended his baseball career, he told Roselynn that he wanted to move back to the farm in Plainfield with his two uncles and earn his living that way. He said that he intended to take courses at an agricultural college and learn the most up-to-date methods of farming. Both brothers were married and had families, but were eager to have their nephew work along with them. They made plans for adding several more rooms to the house.

Roselynn knew he'd be happy doing what he liked, but regretted the fact that Bobby Lee would never be able to earn much more than he needed to get by, especially when he had a family of his own. She often thought about the tragedies in their lives and how differently things might have turned out. Sometimes, her reflections about the past were suddenly interrupted by the bursting of a large bubble she didn't even realize she had blown.

As the years passed, the cardboard box company where Roselynn was employed expanded. She was promoted several times until she reached the top clerical position as administrative assistant to the president. The Whitman Insurance Agency did very well also. Sarah and Neal asked Roselynn to head up another branch they wanted to open in Cushing, at the point of a triangle almost equidistant from Knoxville and Tileston, to the north. But she refused, and advised them to find another partner their own age instead.

Not long afterward, just before she turned 30, Sarah met a lawyer named Mark Bailey in Knoxville and fell in love with him. At first, she talked about a one-year engagement, but reduced it to four months when she began to have concerns about her biological clock. The reception, following the wedding in Tileston, was arranged by Roselynn and Sam's sister, Belle, from Chattanooga. The couple decided to move into Sarah's room in the house and save money for their own home. At the same time, Mark agreed to leave the firm he was with and open a law office in Cushing that would also offer insurance services through the Whitman agency.

Roselynn didn't make an appointment to see the doctor until the third time she felt a sudden stab of pain in her stomach within the space of two months. The blood tests and X rays that followed revealed a tumor in one of her kidneys, and the operation that took place about a week afterwards indicated that the cancer cells had spread too far to be controlled by any treatment. When Roselynn understood that her life was probably going to be measured in months, not years, she made a trip to Memphis to see Etta and to have a will drawn up by Mason, the wonderful lawyer Etta had married.

Back home, Roselynn gave up her job and spent the better part of a week on the farm she had once owned. While she was there, she intended to let Bobby Lee know what the doctors told her, but didn't want to dampen her son's happiness when she was introduced to the girl Bobby Lee said he was sure he was going to marry. Roselynn liked her very much, thinking that Kathy reminded her of herself at that age. She was content with the thought that his life was soon going to be a full one.

She asked Bobby Lee to drive her out to the cemetery so she could visit her husband's grave. She also wanted to look around at where she would soon be resting herself. Bobby Lee left her alone for a few minutes, long enough for Roselynn to bend down by the pink-shaded granite marker and whisper some thoughts to the man she had always loved.

"We've got a fine son, Bob, and he would have played for the Pittsburgh Pirates if he didn't get hurt. I told you he'd get all those good genes from us. Now he's farming the land we bought, with your two brothers, and you should see what they've done to it. It's beautiful, the kind of place you dreamed of making it."

Roselynn closed her eyes and could picture her husband, just 22 years old, turning her to the four points of the compass and telling her excitedly of his plans for the farm in each direction. "Today," she continued, "I met the girl Bobby Lee's in love with and she's everything we could hope for. I know just what I'm going to give them for a wedding present, Bob. You wouldn't believe it if I told you. In fact you'd laugh out loud and say I was either crazy or making it up, but it's going to do just fine. I know it will, and I'll be able to tell you all about it soon."

Roselynn died in her sleep, three weeks later, before the pain they warned her about began. Shortly after the funeral, Sarah and Neal decided to sell the Tileston house, each intending to use half the proceeds for another home in Knoxville. Neither one suggested that any of the money be given to Bobby Lee. They knew that he could sell the large diamond ring he'd be getting from his mother, the one Sam gave her when they got married. They also assumed that Roselynn left whatever money she had to her son.

Etta's husband, Mason Turner, drove in from Memphis a couple of weeks later to meet with the family and let them know what was in the will. They sat around the dining room table and listened to him read off each of the bequests. Roselynn had specified that whatever savings she had left after the payment of her bills and burial expenses be given to Bob's brothers, thanking them again for coming to the farm when Bob went off to war. She wanted Sarah to have her diamond ring, the gift from Sam, and expressed the hope that she would always wear it and pass it on to one of her children. "Your father would like that," she had written. And Neal was to receive Roselynn's Pontiac, only a year old and fully paid for.

Sarah and Neal looked at each other and then glanced at Bobby Lee. There wasn't anything left for Roselynn to leave him that either of them could think of. Bobby Lee sat with his hands folded, watching Mason Turner. He knew that there was still something more to be disposed of by his mother's will, something for him. He just had no idea what it was.

The lawyer continued reading: "And finally, to my son, Bobby Lee, the best twenty-year-old baseball player I ever saw, I leave all the baseball cards I've collected since I began chewing bubble gum. They are your inheritance and my wedding gift to you and your future bride. I hope they'll make you both very happy."

Sarah waited for Neal to stop staring at Bobby Lee and look back at her. She wondered now, in view of everything she had heard, whether Roselynn's illness had caused her to lose her senses before making out her will or whether she had some reason, unknown to them, for wanting to shame her son in this way.

Neal's thoughts were exactly the same. Of course, since neither of them knew anything about baseball, they had no idea that the collectors' market was suddenly assigning rapidly escalating values to such things as a 1935 card showing Babe Ruth in his Boston Braves uniform — his last year of play in the Major Leagues; or a series of Ted Williams cards that covered his entire career, from his rookie season in 1939 to his last in 1960; or those detailing Joe DiMaggio's rise to the pinnacle among outfielders, including the one from 1941 when he went on his incredible 56-game hitting streak and was voted the league's most valuable player.

The Ty Cobb card that Roselynn impulsively purchased at a flea market for $30 in 1947, when Sam told her to buy herself whatever she wanted to celebrate their first anniversary, was already worth 50 times more than she had paid for it. It was put out during one of the years Cobb hit over .400 and won the batting title. Roselynn's collection included the rookie cards of every player who made it to the Major Leagues between 1938 and 1967, the season that recently ended. And it was full of cards issued by Topps and competing companies that featured many of the game's greatest performers who had gone into baseball's Hall of Fame since the first induction at Cooperstown in 1939. All in all, there were a total of almost 4600 cards in the stack of shoeboxes in which they had been carefully put away.

Roselynn almost failed to mention the collection when Mason Turner questioned her about everything she owned and could give away when she died. She was surprised to find out that he was a baseball card enthusiast himself, and was astonished, to the point of joyful tears, at what he told her the cards she had saved for so many years were worth.

When Bobby Lee returned to the farm that day, he and Mason spent some time sorting through the collection. They discovered that almost every card was in mint condition, still inside the wrapping of the gum packages in which they came. Afterwards he went to his clothes closet and removed a cardboard box from one of the far corners. In it were the scrapbooks Roselynn had given him of his father and her. They were filled with stories and snapshots taken of them in baseball uniforms, some during the action in a game. Bobby Lee turned the pages of one of the books until he found what he remembered seeing many years earlier. It was a picture in black and white of a lovely Memphis Mudder, her eyes wide open in amazement, with bubble gum all over her nose and mouth. The bubble had burst an instant before the camera recorded the scene. Bobby Lee smiled. He intended to get the picture blown up as large as he could before it was framed.

THE KANSAS CITY KID

*"If I ever find a pitcher who has heat, a good curve and a slider,
I might seriously consider marrying him, or at least proposing."*

—Sparky Anderson

THE RESTAURANT WAS called "Sir Sirloin," and it was located on the west side of Kansas City, about a home run's distance from Missouri's border with neighboring Kansas. He had suggested meeting in the main dining room at the Crown Center or at the quieter Alameda Plaza Hotel which was walking distance from his condominium. She pushed for something away from the center of town where she thought the chances of him being recognized were less likely.

Gregg Talbot parked his car in an open lot on Independence Avenue and walked slowly down Jason's Crossing. It was a narrow side street, with no automobile traffic, allowing pedestrians to cut through to Nevada Avenue without having to walk all around the block. Many of those who took advantage of its convenient location were in no hurry, and stopped to window-shop at the boutiques that gave the alleyway its character. The pace reminded him of being a tourist on the main street of a small resort town.

At times, Talbot looked carefully through his designer sunglasses at the faces of people walking in the opposite direction to see whether he caught a glimmer of recognition in their eyes as they came closer. He had become a star attraction in the city during his thirteen years there, one of its best-known celebrities. Anyone who followed baseball knew that he had been the outstanding pitcher on the Royals staff for most of that time. This was only his first season of inactivity, of being out of the game. Damned if he'd say retirement, he thought, because he certainly hadn't quit on his own.

In just three weeks, on the Sunday before Labor Day, Talbot would be 39 years old. He was in excellent physical condition, although he'd put on about ten pounds since early April when the baseball season got under way. That's when his agent called with the discouraging news that no team had expressed any interest in signing him. He had given himself four months to see if things changed, hoping that a contender in either league would find itself short on pitching and come after him. But by July, when it was easy to see which ball clubs needed help, none of them called. So he had recently begun to think about what he wanted to do with the rest of his life.

Talbot was a bachelor and still enjoyed the singles scene. He was the prey of dinner party hostesses craving the presence of a well-known personality who was unattached and could be counted on to exhibit a lively and sometimes shocking sense of humor. Talbot had the looks that made hearts swoon. He was handsome, with a smile that punctuated the stories he told, and an athletic body that advertised his virility. The suntan he picked up in Florida during the winter, where he owned a condominium close to the Royals' spring training site in Vero Beach, stayed with him the rest of the year. Its color was an attractive complement to his wavy blond hair, which he no longer allowed to grow as long as he did when he was a player.

Inside the restaurant, the maitre d' told him that Ms. Edwards hadn't yet arrived, but invited him to have a seat at a table in the far corner.

Talbot preferred to wait in the small lounge adjacent to the entrance. He sat on a leather stool at the bar and ordered a glass of Perrier with a twist of lime. Two men sitting kitty-corner to him were talking about the game the Royals had blown the night before in the last inning. Talbot saw one whisper to the other and then pretended not to notice as the man's companion turned slightly around and tried to glance nonchalantly in his direction.

He still couldn't figure out why Michelle wanted to see him. "What's up?" he'd asked her when the call came three days earlier, but she made it clear that she didn't want to discuss the subject until they were together. He lost a good part of a night's sleep wondering whether the thing on her mind might possibly involve his return to the Royals' pitching staff before the season was over. The next morning he classified it under wishful thinking.

Talbot met Michelle Edwards during his first season in Kansas City, where he had been traded by the California Angels. In his first five years in the Big Leagues in Anaheim, he'd won 52 games. He had been called up from the minor leagues just after his twentieth birthday, and was often referred to in the Orange County press as the team's "pitcher of the future." But the Angels' management thought he was losing his skills when his record fell to nine wins and thirteen losses in what turned out to be his last year with that team.

Michelle was three years younger than he and had graduated from the University of Michigan the year before he arrived in Kansas City. Wayne Lancaster, the owner of the Royals, was her uncle, and had given her pretty much free rein around the ballpark. Talbot was attracted to her when they met and thought of asking her out on several occasions, but was afraid of upsetting Lancaster. Ballplayers did not have good reputations, especially those who, like Gregg, had not finished college. Besides, he noticed that she was often showing some male friend around the park while the team practiced in the afternoon, and he could see her holding hands with one or another of them at different times. He kept his feelings to himself, and began going out with some of the women whose names and telephone numbers showed up in the little black books of his new teammates.

Lancaster pushed hard for Michelle to go to business school and get an advanced degree. She resisted, but finally, two years after receiving her Bachelor of Arts, she returned to Michigan. But the competition was too overwhelming for her, and she withdrew shortly after the start of the second semester. Michelle returned to Kansas City and found work in a large public relations firm. Her appearances at the ballpark, even for the games themselves, were far less frequent over the next several years.

On one occasion, when she sat in the first row of box seats next to the Royals' dugout, Michelle complained to Gregg before the game about the excessive number of hours she was working at her firm. She was expected to be in the office for ten or more hours a day and to host dinner meetings at the city's best restaurants afterwards. There, the marketing strategy was to entertain prospective clients over a sumptuous meal and attempt to persuade them to switch their PR needs to Michelle's firm.

Another time, when Lancaster's wife, Loretta, passed away suddenly, Gregg had a chance to sit and talk with Michelle at the funeral home. He realized then, listening to her, that she was troubled by some of the work she did. She questioned the integrity of certain campaigns she handled, and was discouraged by the constant pressure to steal clients from the competition. He played the role of a good listener on both occasions and said very little. He was afraid of depressing her even further by the opinions he might offer. But he came away from the second conversation convinced that she would soon be doing something else.

And he was right. Several months later Wayne Lancaster brought Michelle to the Royals to oversee both public relations and the team's charitable activities. She was 27 at the time. Gregg didn't know whether she had gone after the job or whether Lancaster wanted his only niece to start learning the business so she could run the ball club herself when he retired. Talbot had overheard conversation in the Kansas City locker room years earlier about how Lancaster's son, his only child, had been killed in an automobile accident. It had occurred barely a month after getting his driver's license when he stopped to help a disabled car on the road.

A lot of Michelle's PR work for the club had involved getting Talbot to speak at various civic organization lunches, and to appear before groups of school children to warn them about drugs. He was welcomed everywhere because he had become the team's best pitcher, averaging twenty wins a season in his first six years in Kansas City. He was also one of its most popular players.

He was thinking about some of his best seasons with the Royals when he felt a hand on his shoulder.

"Hi, Gregg. I'm a little late, I guess. Sorry."

He got off the stool, smiled, and leaned forward to kiss her cheek. "No, no, I just got here a few minutes ago," he said, not realizing that almost half an hour had passed while he nursed his drink in the lounge.

She was wearing a smart canary-yellow jacket over a powder-blue blouse. They were the colors of the sun in the sky on a perfect summer day. Her black hair was cut shorter than he remembered it the last time he saw her, almost five months earlier, and he liked what it did for her. It certainly made him take notice of her long earrings, a string of differently shaped plastic pieces in an assortment of hues, held together by springy metal coils. Michelle's face, smiling back at him, showed that she had taken plenty of time getting ready for their meeting.

"You look terrific," he told her, giving the word the best sound he could, and meaning it.

"So do you," she replied. "Come on, it's my treat." Michelle turned toward the dining room and he followed her.

Lunch was fun. They reminisced about a number of things and laughed a lot. But when they began talking about Wayne Lancaster over the piece of chocolate mousse cake they shared for dessert, it turned serious.

"I liked Wayne. I played for the man for thirteen years and never once heard a bad word from him. Even when I didn't report for spring training last year because he wouldn't pay me what I wanted, he treated it like just another piece of business, nothing personal."

"If that's what you really think, Gregg, you didn't know my uncle at all."

"Why do you say that?"

"Because he hated you for disrupting the team the way you did."

"Then he should have been willing to give me what I was worth," he shot back.

"Wait a second. Let me finish," she said.

He told her to go ahead, and took the napkin from his lap to wipe the corners of his mouth.

"Wayne thought the Royals would be the best team in the division last year. When the season was over, he was convinced that we would have finished in first place if you'd been at training camp. You could have taken your time and worked yourself into shape the way you always did. But by the time you agreed to a contract, April was almost over and you'd already missed five starts."

"Four starts," he interrupted.

"Four or five, it doesn't matter," she said. "You probably hurt your arm because you rushed to get yourself in shape after you signed. You weren't ready to throw 125 pitches your second time out. So instead of giving the club the twelve to fifteen wins everyone was counting on, you wound up going eight and ten and the team finished four games out of first." Michelle put her palms up against the edge of the table and pushed her chair back to give herself more room.

"Are you finished?" he asked.

"For the moment."

"Well, it was his own fault. Wayne knew what other guys with my numbers were making around the league but he wouldn't pay it to me without a fight. If he had treated me right — "

"Please, Gregg." Michelle's eyes narrowed and she raised her voice slightly for the first time. "He couldn't guarantee you eleven million dollars for three years. This is Kansas City, for Chrissake, not New York. Your salary would have been thirteen percent of the payroll that was budgeted for the entire team."

"I was worth it. You're forgetting one little thing. I won 244 games for his club."

"That's right, you did. But you would have done a lot better with what he offered you at the beginning than with the one-year deal you finally took. You'd have been out there pitching this year and getting the last four victories you needed to be a 300-game winner. Instead, you're not playing for anyone. And I'm sure it's killing you inside."

Talbot began tapping his left foot against the rounded base of the table. Now he had to ask her the question he'd thought about many times. "Is that why Wayne released me in the winter?"

"Of course it is," she told him. "He could never forgive you for ruining the best chance he ever had of seeing the team win the American League pennant and playing in the World Series. Do you realize how long this town has gone without a winner?" Michelle didn't have to answer her question. It was enough that they both knew Gregg hadn't played on a first place team in his entire Kansas City career.

She looked hard into his eyes when she continued. "Wayne knew he didn't have a lot of time left to live. He understood that for him it was last year or never. He let you go after the season because he didn't want you to have a chance to reach 300."

"That doesn't make sense, Michelle. He knew that any other club could have picked me up."

She smiled at him, but didn't answer right away. She wanted his words to hang in the air, for him to think about what he had just said.

"Sure they could," she replied finally, "but they didn't, did they?"

Gregg picked up a teaspoon. He held the two ends between the thumb and forefinger of both his hands for several seconds, as if he were going to try and bend it. Instead, he let go of the bottom and rapped the spoon several times, easily, against the black-colored rim of his half-empty coffee cup.

"And do you know why they didn't?" she continued. "Do you really believe it's because you won only eight games last year? You're kidding yourself if you think your record had anything to do with it." She hesitated again, waiting for him to finish playing with the spoon and look straight at her. "It's because Wayne Lancaster asked every club in both leagues not to go near you. And Wayne had done too much for baseball and the other owners over the years for anyone to say 'no' to him on something like that. So here you are, having lunch with me, instead of in some ballpark getting ready for your next start."

Gregg put down the spoon, took a sip of coffee, and sat back in his chair. "Is that why we're here today, so you could let me know all this? Is it something Wayne made you promise to do on his deathbed?" Gregg realized he had raised his voice and that his remarks had caught the attention of the couple dining at the table closest to them. He waited for them to resume their own conversation and paused a few seconds longer before finishing his thought. "Revenge from beyond the grave, huh?"

"No," she answered, "this meeting isn't about you and Uncle Wayne. I just thought you should know the story once it came up. Maybe you've been blaming your agent for not finding you a spot on another club. But he never had a chance. No, this little soiree is all about Wayne Lancaster and his only niece, yours truly."

Her answer caught him off guard. He'd been prepared to continue defending himself, to reject the blame for what had happened to the team, when suddenly the attack was over. He felt as if there should be some sort of an interlude before going into what Michelle wanted to discuss, like having the waiter bring cool sorbet to the table between the appetizer and the main course. But that wasn't going to happen.

"Okay, what's the problem?" he asked.

"I'm tempted to give you the bottom line first, but it might scare you right out of here if I did, so I won't." She smiled at him, but he could sense how nervous she had suddenly become.

"After Wayne lost Loretta and I came to work for the team, he used to tell me every so often that he wanted me to have control of the Royals when he died or retired to his place in Arizona. He insisted that I work in every department and learn every little detail about how the club operates. And I did. Then he made me vice president."

Gregg interrupted. "I remember the party he threw for everyone on the club in the press room when that happened." he said. "I also remember that I kissed you on the cheek when I congratulated you. It was the first time."

Michelle could feel herself blushing, but continued talking. "The title was an excuse for his letting me sit in on meetings he had with his general manager, first Woody Marshall, and then Don Aikens when Woody moved to the Dodgers. Wayne wanted me to know what was going on when contract negotiations with the players were being discussed. And he took me with him whenever he attended an owners' meeting. He told me to smile at everyone and listen carefully to everything that was said. Afterwards, he'd ask me a lot of questions and make sure I understood where each of the club owners was coming from. Believe me, after all the training I got, I know how to run a ball club, even without a degree from business school. So when Wayne's illness became serious, I expected to take charge as soon as he died."

"I thought you *did*," Gregg said. "I thought you've been the boss since May."

"Most people think so, but the truth is that I'm *not*. That little detail has never been given out to the press."

"Then who *is* running things?" he asked.

"I'm getting to that, Gregg. It all happened in a certain order."

"Okay," he said. He nodded his head, waiting for her to go on.

"Right after the funeral, Wayne's lawyer met with me and showed me a letter Wayne had dictated and signed just a few weeks earlier."

He interrupted again. "Do you trust the guy?"

"Of course I do," she said immediately. "It's nothing like that. Herb Collins has handled all of Wayne's affairs for years. His firm is the third largest in the city and Collins is one of the main reasons for it. He's a marvelous person and the most distinguished-looking lawyer you've ever seen. Right out of central casting. Anyway, the letter said that three trustees would be responsible for actually running the club as soon as Wayne couldn't do it anymore, and that there were further instructions I would hear about as soon as his will was probated."

"Did you know the trustees?"

"Yes. He had simply chosen Herb Collins, plus his banker and his accountant."

Gregg waited to see if she was going to say anything negative about the men or the arrangement. He was satisfied from the silence that followed that she had no such intention. "What next?" he asked.

"What next is that a couple of months later Mr. Collins took me to lunch and read me the stuff in Wayne's will."

"And?"

"I'll get to that in a second. First, there's one other thing you've got to know to understand all this. Wayne was always teasing me about getting married. He wanted me to hurry up and find a husband and have kids. He was bigger on that subject than my own mother and father. I used to think that maybe my folks were telling him to keep up the pressure on me because they couldn't do it often enough from New Orleans, where they live." Michelle smiled. "Wayne made a point of introducing me to every eligible bachelor at the meetings we attended. He certainly tried to help me find a man."

Michelle excused herself and reached down next to her chair for her pocketbook. She took out a tissue, sniffled a couple of times, and dabbed at her nose. "And now we come to the bottom line. Are you ready?"

"I guess so," he answered. And then added quickly, "I hope so."

"Well, Uncle Wayne didn't want to tell me this himself while he was alive, but the will gives me exactly 30 months from the time he died to have a child or lose control of the team for good."

There was a short silence. Gregg mouthed his answer silently before speaking the word. "Wow," he said.

"The biggest 'wow' of my life," she answered. "But that's how strongly he felt about me having a family, and I guess he figured a 36-year-old woman needed a man-sized shove in the right direction. I'm still vice president, and I can give my advice on what ought to be done, but any decision that Wayne would have made before gets made by the three trustees right now."

Gregg looked puzzled. He continued staring at Michelle without saying anything, then picked up his cup and slowly sipped some coffee. As soon as he put it down, Michelle reached for her water glass. They each shifted position in their seats. Gregg cocked his head to the side when he finally spoke.

"And now you want to know if there's some guy I — "

"I want to know if you'd be willing to father my baby."

As soon as the words spilled out, Michelle rested both elbows on the table and put her hands together under her chin. It was almost as if she were saying a quick prayer. She looked at Gregg, waiting for him to answer.

"Did you just say what I think you said?"

His question moved her to sit up again, and she answered right away. Her voice was a little out of control.

"I've got to have a child, Gregg, because I'd be devastated if I lost the Royals. In all honesty, you're one of several good candidates I could ask, but you're the only one I can do a big favor for in return." She was talking very quickly, hoping she could finish what she had to say without crying. "There's two ways of doing it, you know. There's the regular way, or you could just give your sperm to my doctor at the right time and he'll do the rest. Either way is fine by me. Actually, the second way is probably better because I don't want you to think for a second that you'd have to be a father to the baby when it comes. No involvement necessary. I'm not trying to change your life, just mine."

A few tears began rolling down her cheeks. She wiped them away with the back of her hand. "I mean that," she went on. "You'd have no emotional or financial responsibility at all. We can put that in writing, and I'll pay for both lawyers. The baby never has to know who its father is. I'm asking a lot, and it's not easy for me to do, but at least you know why."

His first impulse, after taking it all in, was to get her to relax. He could see that the floodgates of her eyes were ready to open. "I've already got a pretty full schedule this afternoon," he said. "And tonight there's a James Bond doubleheader on TV I don't want to miss." He followed up with a sly grin.

It worked. Michelle took a deep breath and let herself ease back in her chair. "Thanks," she said. "I needed that."

"And I thought Wayne had been tough on me. I guess he saved his best for last."

"I can't be angry with him, Gregg. My mother was his only sibling and I don't have any sisters or brothers. When Randy died in the car accident, it was too late for Loretta to have any more children. So Wayne saw me as the only way of keeping the family going. I guess now I know why he teased me as much as he did and how strongly he felt about it."

"Look, Michelle, I'm flattered, or whatever the right word is, for your asking me. Let me have a couple of days to think it through. I'll either do it or I won't on just what you told me. You don't have to return any favors."

"Thanks," she whispered. "You were a terrific listener, Gregg."

"But just so I don't lose any sleep over it, what is it you had in mind?"

Michelle moved in close to the table and put her right hand on his. "Are you still interested in joining the 300 club?"

"Only if it won't cost me more than an arm and a leg."

She spoke slowly and deliberately. "If I run this team, and you can still pitch, you'll get the chance for those four more wins." Her words had an immediate effect. He smiled broadly, and she smiled back at him. "We could both be celebrating next season if we get started early enough," she said.

When Gregg agreed to father Michelle's baby — the natural way — he insisted that they start dating like any other couple and let nature take its course. If anything, the certainty of where they were heading in the relationship made each of them uncomfortable at the start. It wasn't until they had spent several more evenings together, at dinner, at a Lyric Theater production of "Hello Dolly," and dancing themselves into a sweat at "Nirvana," Kansas City's rock and roll palace, that they made love for the first time. After that, they looked forward to being together as often as they could.

Michelle watched carefully for any sign of pregnancy, but none appeared. She made certain to be with Gregg during her most fertile periods. The disappointment that followed the first three months of their courtship made her wonder whether her biological clock had simply wound down earlier than it should have. It was like setting the alarm to go off at six in the morning for the most important appointment of her life and then sleeping way past the time because the battery in the clock lost its power in the middle of the night.

And then suddenly, with Christmas just a week away, her body began letting her know that something was going on. She bought a home pregnancy kit at the drugstore and watched the patch of blue appear on the paper strip, giving its positive reading. She scheduled a hurry-up appointment with her doctor, had a blood test in his office that confirmed the results, and called Gregg with the good news early that evening.

"Hey, that's terrific," he hollered into the phone. "I'm going to be a daddy. I'll pick up a bottle of champagne and be right over."

Michelle wasn't sure whether there was some rule about not having any alcohol at all. Her doctor, escorting her out through a crowded waiting room, had promised to give her a whole list of "do's and don'ts" when he saw her again on the Monday morning after the holiday. She told Gregg to pour only a few drops in her glass. They toasted her new condition and kissed.

"When is it due?" he asked, joining her on the sofa.

"The doctor's not sure yet. Right now it looks like any time after September first." She gave him a big smile.

Gregg reached over and patted her stomach. "That could be a little late in the season for me to get a chance for those four big ones. You tell Junior here not to stall for time."

Michelle made a Greek salad and some scrambled eggs for dinner. Gregg had two more glasses of champagne while she ground up some decaf coffee beans and heated a half cup of milk for a cafe au lait. Later on, after they cleaned up in the kitchen, he suggested that their celebration include some lovemaking. Michelle declined.

"I'm just too tired from all the excitement," she said, "and I've got some things to do before I go to New Orleans on Thursday."

"Are you going to let your folks know you're pregnant?"

"And spoil Christmas for them? No way."

"When will you be back?"

"Sunday night."

"I'll pick you up at the airport."

"No, it's okay, Gregg. I've already arranged the round-trip with a cab. You'd just get stuck in a lot of traffic both ways."

He knew she was right. "Then I'll probably see you Monday." He leaned over and kissed her, first on the lips and then just above each eye. "You take good care of our little bundle."

Michelle waited more than a week after her return from New Orleans before letting Gregg know how she felt. When he called on the Monday before New Year's Day and wanted to come over, she told him she had picked up a cold while she was away and needed some rest. When he tried again on Wednesday, she said that she still had some last-minute paperwork to get ready for the club's accountant before the end of the year. Gregg wanted to have dinner with her, or at least spend some time together during the long holiday weekend, but Michelle informed him that two former roommates from college were going to be staying with her the entire time.

"What about New Year's Eve?"

"I can't leave them alone and go out with you. It wouldn't be right. They don't know anything about Kansas City. We're just going to have a girls' night together and watch Times Square on TV."

When the holiday had passed, they met at a small Italian restaurant just a block away from her high-rise condo building. That's when he learned that there was no paperwork for the accountant and that the one friend who visited had stayed for only a day.

"I'm sorry," she whispered, "but I couldn't see you until I was sure of what I wanted to say." As the tears rolled down her cheeks and she picked at her food every so often until it was cold, Michelle told Gregg that she didn't want to spend a lot of time with him before the baby was born. She could see how attached he would become to it if he was around while she grew bigger, and she was certain that would lead to problems after she gave birth.

"I told you that you didn't have to get emotionally involved and I meant it. You've done me a great big favor, Gregg, something I'll never be able to repay, but now I don't want you to make things harder for me or for the baby. I've got to bring it up my own way, without caring about whether you agree or not. That's going to be very tough for you to take if you keep thinking of yourself as the father. It's just best for you not to be involved anymore and to get on with your own life."

"Hold it right there." Gregg's arms flew up in the air as he spoke. "You don't seem to understand that what I want is to be with you. I got you pregnant because that's what you wanted, and I agreed to every word your lawyer wrote about waiving any rights I had toward the baby. I know that legally I'm simply the sperm donor, period. But that's got nothing to do with how I feel about you. If there was no baby thing going on here, I'd still feel the same way." He hesitated before going on. "What I'm trying to say is that I'm in love with you."

Before she could answer, the waiter was standing at the table. "Finished?" he asked uncertainly, seeing most of the food on their plates.

"Yes," they answered simultaneously. Michelle used the interruption to find some tissues in her pocketbook.

"Was everything all right?" He looked from one to the other.

"Yes," Gregg said. "We just weren't as hungry as we thought."

The waiter suggested some cappuccino and they agreed. He cleared the table and moved away.

Michelle picked up where Gregg had left off. "Listen, you're a wonderful man, and I've enjoyed being with you. But right now there just isn't enough room in my life for another person. I'm in love with having a baby, and knowing what that means for me. I don't think I'm ready to see if I'm in love with you, too."

Gregg waited until they were looking in each other's eyes. "You mean you wouldn't marry me if I asked?"

Michelle hesitated, turned away momentarily, and then looked at him again. "I wouldn't want you to ask, not now."

There was a long silence at the table before he spoke. Their eyes avoided each other. "So what are you saying?" he finally asked. "That we just break it off cold?"

He watched as she bit her lip, and he could see how close she was to crying. "No, I wouldn't want that either," Michelle said. "Call me on the phone. Let's see each other once in a while." She paused and managed a half smile, even as mist appeared in her eyes. "I've got to keep an eye on you every so often just to make sure you're in shape for your comeback. You've got those games to win."

Gregg realized that it was useless to try and change her mind. "Yeah, that's right," he answered, willing to change the subject. "What does your doctor say? Am I going to have the month of September to pitch?"

"He's still not sure. You may have to throw some games on just two days rest to get enough starts."

He laughed. "Well, in case that manager of yours ever asks, you tell Foxy I always thought three days between starts was more than I needed."

Early in February, Michelle attended the club owners' meeting in Sarasota. It felt strange, at first, not having Wayne Lancaster sitting next to her, but the long grind of the business that had to be discussed was enough to put her at ease. She fielded the questions that were asked of her directly and joined in the debate over various matters some of the more recalcitrant owners had on their agendas. When the formal sessions ended each day, she gave interviews to the media.

A number of owners brought their general managers with them to the four-day conference. Inevitably, there was a steady stream of trade talk in the lobby, in private suites, and over dinner at some of the fashionable, multi-star restaurants on Long Boat Key. Executives from other clubs tested Michelle's knowledge of baseball talent by proposing various player exchanges between their teams and the Royals. Don Aikens had not accompanied her to Florida, another consequence of the trustees' bottom line outlook on everything. Michelle made notes of every deal that was offered her, and led some of the other owners on, almost unconscionably, by feigning enthusiasm over how well some of their players would fit into the Royals' lineup. She promised to get back to all of them either before or during spring training.

"Whatever happened to Gregg Talbot?" a National League general manager asked her.

The question raised hairs on the back of her neck. Michelle hadn't spoken to Gregg recently, but on hearing his name she immediately pictured herself in his embrace. She also had a suddenly ominous feeling that the verbal agreement each of the owners had made with Wayne Lancaster to deny Talbot a spot on their rosters might not have survived her uncle's death. If that were the case, Michelle told herself, some of them might see him as a desirable free agent to sign and bring into spring training for a tryout. She realized that it would be a wonderful opportunity for Gregg to be able to go to another team and have a whole season to pick up the victories he needed. She also knew that she didn't want to see it happen.

"The last time I saw him he was eating Italian food and drinking cappuccino," she said. Then, hoping that her companion had immediately gotten a mental image of an athlete going to pot, she attempted to drive home the point, adding, "I'd say that he's put on a fair amount of weight." It was all true, she told herself, but she was ashamed of every word.

"Too bad," he replied. "Probably still had some good games left in that arm of his."

"Who knows?" Michelle said, and shrugged her shoulders.

The alarm raised by the question remained uppermost in Michelle's mind. As soon as she returned to Kansas City, she put in a conference call to the three trustees. She gave them her opinion of some of the trades that had been proposed to her at the meeting, along with her view of a number of free agents who were still unsigned.

"According to their agents, they're negotiating with different teams. We'll have to be ready to move fast if we want to go after any of them."

The trustees knew little about talent or value in comparing or assessing ballplayers. Still, they reminded her that they retained the final word on all trades, free agent signings, and contracts. She couldn't push any buttons in those areas unless at least two of them agreed with her and authorized the deal.

"By the way," she said, "I'd like to sign Gregg Talbot to a minor league contract before some other team grabs him. We may need some more pitching later on in the season and I think he could help us. It would be a relatively cheap investment."

Their negative response was immediate and unanimous. "Michelle, I think your Uncle Wayne would start spinning in his grave if we said 'okay' to that," Herb Collins told her. "Forget about Talbot. His career with the Royals is over."

In the middle of spring training Michelle got permission from the trustees to trade the veteran Royals third baseman, Eddie Waldiman, to the Baltimore Orioles. In return, Kansas City received Don Campbell, a second-year pitcher who had won only five games in his rookie season. The trustees saw the deal strictly as an opportunity to trade a seven-figure salary for one in the low sixes, and quickly approved. They didn't ask Michelle who was going to fill Waldiman's spot for the team, and she didn't tell them that she was very close to reaching agreement with Henry "Dutch" Alcorn, a Cardinals free agent, for that position.

Alcorn's own agent had been up front with her. He let Michelle know that the only other team bidding for the third baseman's services was San Diego. Although the offer from that club exceeded the numbers Michelle had been discussing by almost a million dollars over a three-year period, Alcorn would take less for the chance to play with a pennant contender. He didn't want to go to the Padres, and St. Louis had already decided to fill his position and one other with rookies in order to bring its payroll in line.

Michelle was enthusiastic about having Alcorn on the team. He was a long ball threat who had hit 27 home runs the year before, despite losing a month with a wrist injury. She felt that at 29 he was ready to blossom into a star. She was certain he would be even more productive on a steady diet of fastballs in the American League than he'd been against the National League's curveball pitchers with whom he had to contend. Moreover, Alcorn had a reputation for being an inspirational leader, and Michelle knew that was something the Royals needed. She was eager to wrap up the negotiations when she called and informed Herb Collins of all the advantages of adding Alcorn to the team. But she was shocked and angry when Collins reached her in Vero Beach the next day and told her the trustees had rejected the deal. Michelle had difficulty informing Alcorn's agent of her change of heart without revealing the truth about her limbo status with the Royals.

On the night before Opening Day in Kansas City, Michelle had dinner with Gregg at a Thai restaurant. She was glad to see him — it was the first time they'd been out together in almost three months — but unhappy about the fact that the Royals had lost their first two games of the season in Cleveland.

"Are you sure you're pregnant?" he asked. "You don't look it to me."

She was wearing a black suit, and had recently let out the skirt enough so that she was comfortable in it. Her initials, "MCE," were sewn onto the breast pocket of her lime-colored blouse, and a black pearl gave the pocket its buttoned-down look. A long necklace, made up of assorted wooden shapes and polished seashells, stopped just above her waist.

"It'll show pretty soon," she said.

"I just want to be sure I'm not putting in all that time in the gym for nothing. When I'm flat on my back holding those weights over my head, all I think about is being on the mound again. By September I'll either be the best-conditioned pitcher in baseball or a basket case."

They both laughed.

"Did your agent try and find anything for you?" she asked.

Gregg shook his head from side to side. "He called three or four clubs. But he said he could tell from the way they talked to him that nothing had changed. I was in Florida for two and a half weeks last month, just in case any managers had a sudden urge to watch me throw. But no one wants any part of Gregg Talbot. Good old Wayne did a great selling job."

"Don't forget, 'He who laughs last,'" she said. "Some of those teams will regret it when they see what you do for us."

He pointed his finger toward her stomach. "If that little package you're hiding gives me a chance. Anyway, how's that team of yours going to do this year?"

Michelle looked to the side a few moments before answering, as if gathering her thoughts. "I think we'll be right up there with a few other clubs all season because no one in our division is very strong. But if we had signed Dutch Alcorn, I think we would have had an easy time finishing first."

"You went after Alcorn?"

"I practically had his name on the dotted line for a million less than the Padres are paying him, but the three stooges nixed it." She emphasized her displeasure with them by banging her fist on the table. "I take that back. I shouldn't call them names. They're only concerned with the bottom line and making sure the Royals stay in the black. It's not like they checked out Alcorn and decided he wasn't worth the money."

Gregg nodded his head.

"But you didn't invite me to dinner to hear me talk about baseball, did you?" She gave him her biggest smile.

"I'll talk about baseball, Michael Jackson, or that whatchamacallit treaty we just signed with Mexico. Anything you like. I just wanted to be with you for a few hours and find out how you're doing."

His words made her feel wonderful and she realized how much she missed him. "Thanks, Gregg. I'm fine. I'm frustrated at the position Wayne's put me in, but that will end eventually. A week ago I felt the baby move for the first time. I was so excited I broke down and cried."

He could see tears come into her eyes when she spoke about it. "There have been days when I wished you were there, but I'm doing all right."

"I can be there any time you want," he said.

Michelle inhaled and let out a deep breath. She was trying hard to control herself. "I know it, and I wish you knew how reassuring that is to me. But I haven't changed my mind about what I told you last time. I still think it would be bad for you to get emotionally involved right now."

They talked about it for a few more minutes until Gregg saw that there was no point in pursuing the subject. He didn't want to make her regret accepting his invitation. They spoke about other things, but by the time they finished the chicken coconut soup, the half order of pad thai, the grilled beef in sesame sauce, and the mango ice cream, the conversation had returned to baseball several times. Gregg told her that he had a grandstand seat for the opener and predicted victory over the Twins.

"I'll drink to that," Michelle said. She touched his water glass with hers and took a sip.

"Can I take you home?" he asked. "I'm parked right outside."

"I don't think so," she said.

He reached across the table for her hand. "Listen, when we get to your building I'll pull up in front and just watch from the car until you get in the door, okay?"

She nodded her head up and down without saying a word. Then, quickly, before he could see it, she wiped the tear from just under her eye with the back of her hand.

Michelle's prediction held up for the first three months of the season. The Royals stayed in the race for the western division lead, never falling more than five games out of first place. When play ended on July 4th — the midway point of the season — the team's seven-game winning streak had brought it to within a half game of the Seattle Mariners. Still, Michelle realized that the ball club needed a strong cleanup hitter if it was going to remain in contention.

A week later, after what seemed to her like endless hours of discussion with Don Aikens and his follow-up negotiations with other teams, the Royals found themselves with the opportunity of obtaining Russ Middleton from the Houston Astros for cash and a minor league player. The Astros were going nowhere in their own league and wanted to unload Middleton's contract. Michelle was certain that his presence in the heart of Kansas City's lineup would supply the power the team had been missing. She also saw him as the key to improving their record in the tight one and two-run games played the rest of the season.

In the conference call that ensued, two of the three trustees came out against the deal. They wanted no part of Middleton's large salary, which was guaranteed for the next two years, and expressed confidence that the Royals could continue to fight for first place without him. Michelle knew their words were just wishful thinking. A week later, the Astros sold Middleton to the Toronto Blue Jays who were already four games ahead in the American League's eastern division. In the weeks that followed, Middleton's slugging pushed his new team to an insurmountable lead. At the same time, the Royals stumbled badly, losing a number of close games that could have gone in their favor with a hit at the right time. Michelle's team was leading the league in runners left on base.

On Friday, July 29th, Kansas City was in third place, behind Seattle and California.

That morning, the trustees arrived at Royals Stadium for their semi-annual review of the team's financial status with Michelle. Joining her in her office, they discovered that she was pregnant and approximately six weeks away from having her baby. None of them had seen her since their meeting in the same room at the end of January. They congratulated her on her impending motherhood and confessed that they were unaware she had gotten married.

"You must have eloped," Herb Collins said. "I wish at least one of my three daughters had done that. I could be retiring a lot sooner." His fellow trustees chuckled.

Michelle replied as casually as she could. "I don't have a husband. Actually, I intend to be a single parent, at least for a while."

They looked askance at each other, obviously surprised at hearing this, but didn't say anything. Michelle took a pile of papers off her desk and put them on the conference table. "Well, let's get to work," she said.

On the following Monday, Collins telephoned Michelle and said that it was urgent he see her again. He declined her invitation to meet over lunch and came to the ballpark that afternoon. As they sat in Michelle's office, he told her first that the trustees now regretted the decisions they had made about Dutch Alcorn and Russ Middleton. They were aware of recent newspaper stories by reporters covering the team that the Kansas City ownership appeared unwilling to spend the money to purchase either player. The fans were irate and beginning to express strong doubt that management was interested in doing whatever it could to help the Royals win.

"At this point," Collins told her, "we know it's our fault that the team is where it is. Alcorn's had an excellent year with San Diego so far, and Middleton's been hitting like a young Joe DiMaggio since Toronto acquired him. You were right on both of them. It's our stupidity that's to blame if the Royals don't at least win the division."

Collins caught himself slouching in the soft, leather chair and sat up straight. "We paid too much attention to the bottom line and never stopped to think about what a championship would mean for the city. You and Don Aikens should be able to call the shots on personnel in a pennant race. You're baseball people, we're not."

Michelle perked up as she listened to Collins. She and Aikens had had a number of recent conversations about other players who were becoming available as more teams dropped out of contention. The Royals still had the potential to win, she knew, especially with about

55 games remaining. She was convinced that one or two new faces could turn things around. And now it sounded as if Collins was about to tell her that the trustees wanted her to run the club as she saw fit from here on in.

Collins continued talking. "We had been hoping to turn over control of the team to you as soon as possible, even if it was just limited to letting you do what you wanted with the players. That's something we'd been discussing in the last week, so it was a pleasant surprise to come here and see that you were pregnant. I'm sure we would have agreed to let you handle some of these things even prior to your baby being born."

Before going on and speaking the words he had rehearsed several times that morning in his office, Collins clasped his hands over his belt buckle and tilted forward in the chair. His tongue moved slowly along the bottom of his silver mustache before he spoke again.

"But finding out that you're not married has changed everything." He paused, and his voice dropped to almost a whisper. "I have to tell you, Michelle, that the trustees have voted against giving you power to run the baseball team when your baby is born."

He watched the look of disbelief spread across her face and waited patiently until he sensed that she had regained her composure. "I hope you can understand where we're coming from. We honestly feel that we'd be degrading Wayne Lancaster's memory if we did anything else. Wayne was devoted to family. You know that. And he obviously intended to pressure you into getting married and raising one of your own if you wanted to succeed him. We think he'd be awfully unhappy if he knew your situation, and that he'd be directing us not to let you take over the team. I'm sorry, but we've got to respect what we believe he'd say about this."

Michelle felt sick to her stomach. It was like reading the single essay question on a final exam and realizing it was based on the one part of the course she hadn't studied. Recalling the meeting at which Collins had familiarized her with the stipulation in her uncle's will, she felt betrayed.

"But you told me last fall that the will provided for me to assume control when I had a baby. You never said a word about my having a husband."

Collins had prepared himself for that objection. "I may have put it that way, and frankly it is kind of loosely worded in the will. Still, we're sure Wayne had in mind the traditional way of going about it. You get married and then you have children."

"That's ridiculous," Michelle countered. "What if I married someone, became pregnant, and then got divorced before the baby was born? I'd still be a single parent."

"That's a different set of facts," he said. "We have to deal with the ones that exist."

Michelle got up and paced back and forth behind her desk. She stopped in front of the window in the corner of the room and looked out at the empty parking lot for a minute or so. Turning back to face him, she asked, "What if I marry the baby's father before it's born?"

Collins thought about it. Michelle was familiar with his habit of looking up and studying the ceiling above him while he pondered a difficult question.

"That might force us to look at it in another light," he said. "I think that if you assured us the marriage wasn't a sham, and if we retained the right to check on paternity if we thought it was necessary, that would be good enough. I guess you're saying that you know who the father is."

"Of *course* I do. I asked him to father the baby and he agreed."

Collins's legal experience guided his response. "Then why don't you write his name on a slip of paper, put it in an envelope, and seal it. I'll sign my name across the flap. If you get married, we'll open it together. If the name inside the envelope is the groom's, and subject to what I said a minute ago, I'm sure that would satisfy the three of us."

"Do I have your word on that?" she asked. "No changing your mind later on?"

He hesitated, eyeing the ceiling again while he considered her question. "You do," he said finally.

"Okay, that's fine," she said, and tore a piece of memo paper from the pad on her desk.

Gregg Talbot was smiling. "This has to be very significant," he said. "You've invited me to have lunch at the same place where you originally propositioned me. We're even sitting at the same corner table we had then. I want you to know that I cancelled all my plans for the rest of the day, just in case you had something special in mind." He winked at Michelle, and she smiled back at him.

They had spoken on the telephone fairly regularly since the start of the season. He called at night to give her an outlet after some ballgames that were either very encouraging or disheartening for the team. On occasion he played devil's advocate to the latest swap or purchase of players she and Don Aikens had in mind. They had also seen each other about once a month since having dinner the night before the Royals' first home game in April. Over Memorial Day, with the team playing on the east coast, Gregg talked Michelle into driving south to Lake of the Ozarks, and they spent the weekend together. It was the first time they had made love since December. She realized afterwards that if he had asked her to marry him at the time, she would have said "Yes." Now, back at "Sir Sirloin," Gregg felt he was about to find out when he'd be able to put on the Kansas City uniform again. He figured that was the only reason she had for coming back to this place.

"I want to make you an offer you can't refuse," Michelle said. She had on a long, loose-fitting cotton dress in a red, yellow, and blue floral pattern. Her hair was cut short for the summer and her lipstick matched the color of the roses in her dress.

Gregg had already told her several times how beautiful she looked. "And what could that be?" he asked, in a playful tone. He was certain he had guessed right.

"But seriously, Gregg, if you say 'No,' I'll understand."

Why the hell would she think he'd say "No," he wondered. "Okay, godmother," he teased, "let's hear what you've got."

"It's like the last time we were here," Michelle said. "You've got to be patient until I get to the end." She waited for him to agree, and then told him all about the conversation with Collins. "So here I am, needing you again," she concluded.

Gregg leaned his left elbow on the table as she spoke, covering his mouth with the curled fingers of his hand. He realized that she didn't have to tell him everything she was confiding. She could have simply said she'd been wrong about his relationship with the baby and her feelings about wanting to raise it on her own.

"You know how I feel about you, Michelle. You could have said just enough to get me to propose."

"I couldn't do that, Gregg. I wanted you to know the truth, to know what prompted this."

He thought about what she was telling him now and what she had said so often since the start of her pregnancy. There was no avoiding the question he asked. "Are you saying that you're ready to love both me and the baby right now?"

Michelle's eyes studied the face she knew she wanted to look at the rest of her life. "That's all I've thought about since my meeting with Herb. I wouldn't be here today if the answer wasn't 'Yes,' even if it meant that I'd never get to run the team."

He reached over and took her hand. "Have you thought about the fact that Collins and his friends could turn you down again when they find out I'm the baby's father? All they've got to do is say they're sure Wayne Lancaster wouldn't want you married to a bum like me and running his old empire."

"Yes, I've thought about it, but I don't think they will. Besides, I really don't have any other options."

"Of course you do. You could find yourself another guy and say it's his kid."

Michelle decided not to say anything about the slip of paper in the envelope, the one with his name on it. "Too late for that. Uncle Wayne always told me to marry for love," she said, "and that's what I'm going to do."

Gregg grinned. "Then let's sum up what we've got here. The offer I can't refuse is your proposal that we get married, right?"

"Wrong," she answered, and covered the hand holding hers with her other one. "The offer gives you the chance to ask me to marry you. A girl has got to have a proposal she can accept or turn down."

"What a broad," he whispered, smiling at her. "Okay, Michelle Edwards," he said, completing the union of their hands, "will you marry me and make me an honest father?"

"I will, Gregg Talbot, I absolutely will. Are you doing anything tomorrow?" They laughed, and their lips met halfway across the table.

★ ★ ★

Michelle would always look back on August 15th as the biggest day of that season for her baseball team. In the morning, she brought Gregg to the office and introduced him to Herb Collins when the lawyer arrived just after eleven o'clock.

"My husband, and father of our baby," she said.

If Collins was flabbergasted, he was too diplomatic to let it show. He offered Gregg his hand. "Congratulations," he said.

"And here's the envelope," Michelle added, retrieving it from the top drawer of her desk and handing it to him.

Collins glanced at his signature across the seal and slid the envelope into the inside breast pocket of his gray pinstriped suit jacket. He had no doubt that Gregg Talbot's name was written on the slip Michelle had inserted two weeks earlier, but he would open it and make certain later, in private.

"Well, Michelle," he said, settling himself in a chair as he spoke, "there's a month and a half left to the season. The trustees aren't sure whether you can pull off a miracle and get the team into first place, but it's in your hands as of right now. If you want to make any roster changes, just do it, and let us know. When the baby's born, you're in full control. We'll be there to give you any help you need until you're ready to handle it all yourself."

She thanked him, and they talked about the division race for a while before Collins got up to leave.

"What are you doing these days?" he asked Gregg as the two of them walked from Michelle's office toward the elevator.

"Thinking about winning four more games," Gregg answered.

Collins pushed the "Down" button, and the door opened immediately. "For whom?" he inquired, stepping into the elevator.

"I don't think the boss would let me do it for anyone else," Gregg replied. He gave the lawyer a big smile.

Signing Gregg to a contract was one of the two moves Michelle made that same August afternoon. The other was the purchase of Lance English, a 30-year-old power-hitting first baseman who was in his sixth year of playing for the Cubs Triple-A team in Chattanooga. He couldn't be used at any other position and had no chance of moving up to the parent club while Frank Casey played for Chicago. But Michelle and Aikens were convinced that English could hit at the major-league level and would make a difference in the Kansas City lineup as the designated hitter.

Talbot worked out with the Royals' minor league team in Vero Beach for twelve days, appearing in two games, before being called up to make his first start. He was limited to five innings against the Yankees at home, and left the ballgame trailing 4-3. But Kansas City won the game with a rally in the eighth inning, thanks to a clutch double by English. The victory allowed them to gain a full game on the league-leading Angels. Seattle had gone through a disastrous month of August, losing thirteen in a row at one point, and had fallen into fourth place in the division.

"We're only five games behind California now," Michelle told Gregg when he woke up the next day. He had learned that the first thing she did every morning was devour the sports pages.

"And the writers thought you looked great last night for someone who's been out of the game for so long. It looks like they're all pulling for you to reach 300."

On Labor Day, Gregg threw six innings against Seattle and left with a 3-2 lead. After the Mariners tied the score, Kansas City came back with a run in the ninth to win it, but Gregg's victory total remained at 296. Still, the fans calling the talk shows and the writers giving the Royals more ink in the newspapers every day were excited by the fact that the team won both of his starts. The gap with the Angels had been closed to four games.

There were 25 games left in the season and Kansas City had to play fourteen of them on the road. But the final eight contests would be in Royals Stadium and California would provide the opposition in a two-game series to close out the schedule.

While the team was on a five-game road trip out west, Gregg moved one game closer to the 300 mark with seven strong innings against Gene Autry's Angels. The big hit for the Royals was a three-run homer by Lance English. When the club returned to Kansas City for a series against Minnesota, it was still four games out of the lead and hoped to make up some ground with three games against the last place Twins. But they played sluggishly, losing twice, and were fortunate that California ran into the same problem against Seattle.

Michelle's doctor had calculated that September 20th would be her due date, but warned that the baby could come any time after the middle of the month. Since the Royals' final road trip of the season took them away for ten days, starting September 12th, Gregg insisted that Michelle have her mother come up from New Orleans and stay with her in his absence. He told her that he would call every day and he made her promise to let him know if she had to go to the hospital.

"I don't care whether I'm supposed to pitch that day or not," he said. "I'm going to be there with you when the baby's born."

The team played three games each in Texas, Seattle, and Minnesota. They got hot and won seven out of nine, including a sweep of the Twins before returning home. Both games Gregg started on the trip resulted in "W"s, although he got credit for the victory in only one. The excitement in Kansas City grew greater by the day as the Royals moved to within two games of the top.

Gregg got into bed at almost three o'clock in the morning after the plane ride from Minnesota.

"Two down, two to go," Michelle said.

He turned toward her and kissed her on the forehead. "What are you doing awake?" he asked. But before she could answer, he said, "And hopefully number 299 will come tonight against the Rangers. I may only get one more start after this one. How's the baby doing?"

"It never stops kicking, but I'm not sure it's interested in getting here in time to see who wins the division."

"That's because it already knows we're going to finish in first. It just wants to let you get out to the ballpark and watch me win those last two games."

In the first inning that night, the Royals made two errors behind Gregg. He opened the game by walking the first two batters, but then got three consecutive ground balls from the heart of the Texas lineup. Unfortunately, one was a seeing-eye single over second and the other two went through the legs of his infielders. The Rangers scored four runs before taking the field for the first time, and coasted to a 9-2 victory. Gregg was taken out of the game after five innings when "Foxy" Moore, the Royals manager, saw that the visiting pitcher had everything working for him that night. It was his first loss in his comeback. He and Michelle were back in their apartment before the seventh inning was over.

Texas won two out of three and knocked Kansas City three games off the lead. Several reporters covering the team wrote that it was almost impossible for the Royals to make up that kind of deficit with just five games left on the schedule. They felt the best the club could hope for would be a tie with California and a one-game playoff to decide the division championship. At a meeting in the office of the American League commissioner, a coin toss was held and the Angels won the right to host a playoff, if it was necessary.

Kansas City had a day off before Oakland came in for three games. During practice that afternoon, Ray Woodard, who was scheduled to throw the series opener against the A's, slipped on a wet spot while running in the outfield. The accident resulted in a mild groin pull. When "Foxy" Moore learned that Woodard couldn't throw for a couple of days, he asked Gregg if he thought he could step in and pitch on three days' rest.

"No problem," Gregg assured him. "I never liked hanging around four days between starts."

"I figured you'd say that," Moore answered. "Give us a win tomorrow and you get the ball again Sunday."

"You got it, Foxy."

And win he did. Career victory number 299 was a five-hit complete game 4-0 shutout that sent the team on its way to a sweep over the Athletics, with Woodard pitching the final game of the series. At the same time, California was having a ton of unexpected trouble in Seattle. It barely hung on for an 11-10 victory in the final game of the series after dropping the first twoslugfests as well — by wide margins. The Angels were reeling, just a game ahead of Kansas City, but had to win only one of the two weekend contests in Royals Stadium to capture the western division crown. Toronto, which had finished ten games ahead in the east, would have to wait and see whom it would face in the playoffs for the American League pennant.

On Saturday afternoon, after the off day on Friday, a nervous, standing-room-only crowd that had filled the park an hour before the playing of the National Anthem watched the game go into extra innings with the two contenders tied at 1-1. Both teams had their best pitchers on the mound. Strangely, each had lost his shutout on an unearned run in the first inning. After that, sixteen consecutive goose eggs had gone up on the scoreboard.

Gregg was sitting in the dugout, charting the pitches. His goal was to pick up anything he could about the tendencies of the California hitters. Before the game started, he blew a kiss to Michelle who was in the owner's box on the level occupied by the press corps. He had wanted her to watch the game on television from their apartment, especially since her doctor said that she could go into labor at any minute. But she insisted on being there. Gregg arranged for a limo to bring her to the park just before game time and to wait by the players' entrance in case Michelle felt the need to get to the hospital. During the sixth inning, she sent word to him that she was tired and was having the driver take her home.

In the last of the tenth, with two out and the bases empty, the Royals shortstop swung late at a fastball and looped it down the right field line for a double. The Angels manager decided against giving an intentional walk to Lance English who had looked bad, striking out three times that day. On the first pitch, a slider that was low and outside the strike zone, English golfed at the ball and sent it on a line just over the glove of the leaping second baseman. The winning run scored easily, without a play at the plate. English was mobbed by his teammates, and the 46,000 fans stood and cheered until every Royals player left the field. After 161 games spanning almost six months, the two teams found themselves in a dead heat, exactly where they had been on Opening Day.

"Are you awake?" Gregg asked, as Michelle turned from her right side to her left, facing him.

"Yes," she answered. She didn't tell him she was feeling some pain and that she thought the contractions might have begun. "What are you doing up in the middle of the night?"

"Pitching to the Angels," he told her.

She could see the digital clock on his night table. "It's three-thirty," she said. "You've got ten hours before the game starts. Get some sleep or you'll be throwing marshmallows out there tomorrow."

"Okay," he mumbled, at the end of a deep yawn. "I'll try."

While Gregg dressed and made breakfast for himself in the morning, Michelle pretended to be asleep. She knew for certain that she was in labor and would have to go to the hospital, but didn't want to worry him. It was his day to win the 300th game of his career and to bring a title to Kansas City.

She called to him when she sensed that he was ready to leave for the ballpark. Gregg sat down on her side of the bed. "Good luck, sweetheart," she said. "This is the day you've been waiting for."

"Thanks." He leaned over and brushed her lips with a kiss. "I suppose there's no way I can convince you to stay here and watch it on TV."

"No way is right," she answered, smiling. "In fact, I want to get there early and take care of some arrangements that have to be made for the playoffs with Toronto." She winked at him and he smiled. "If you don't see me in my box, I'll be in the office. Call the limo, honey, and tell them to pick me up at ten."

"It's already nine-fifteen. Aren't you going to eat something?"

"I'll have time. I'm getting up right now." She puckered her lips for him and raised her head off the pillow. He kissed her twice and then rested his cheek next to hers for a few seconds. When the limo arrived, the driver was disappointed to find out they weren't going to Royals Stadium. Instead, at Michelle's direction, he drove to Hospital Hill. She had already let her doctor know she was on the way.

During batting practice, Gregg loosened up in the outfield. He glanced toward the owner's box every few minutes but it was empty. He figured

Michelle was still in her office. As the starting time approached, some of the players stretched and did sprints while others were getting themselves ready in the clubhouse. Talbot left the dugout and looked up again for Michelle. He saw Don Aikens sitting in the box, talking to someone Gregg didn't recognize. Ten minutes later, Johnny Fall, his catcher, put an arm around Gregg's shoulder. "Let's go, old man," he said, "time to get loose."

In the bullpen, Talbot lobbed the ball to Fall nine times. He threw the first one from 30 feet away and the last from the full pitching distance. Michelle's continued absence from her seat bothered him. It was twenty minutes to game time.

"Hold on a minute, Johnny." Gregg picked up the wall telephone inside the covered area where the relief pitchers sat during the game. He waited until someone in the Royals' dugout answered. "It's Talbot," he said. "Let me speak to Foxy."

"Whatsamatter?" the manager hollered into the phone a few seconds later. He had no prior experience in being calm, cool, and collected for big games.

"Foxy, I want you to call upstairs and see if my wife's there. If anyone says she is, speak to her yourself just to make sure. If she's not there, tell them to try our apartment. Let me know right away."

"What's the difference…"

"Just do it," he said, and hung up.

Don Aikens told Foxy that he thought Michelle had decided not to come to the park. Two minutes later, Aikens rang the dugout and said she hadn't answered the phone at home. Moore dialed the bullpen and gave Talbot the information.

"Tell Aikens to call Memorial Hospital and see if she checked in. Hurry up, Foxy."

"Okay, okay, but keep throwin' out there."

As soon as he learned where Michelle was, Gregg ran in towards the dugout. He had his jacket over his shoulder. His manager saw him coming and met him out on the field. "What's goin' on?" he shouted, raising his hands in the air, next to his head.

"Michelle must be in labor. I've got to be with her."

"Are you crazy? This game's for the division. It could be hours before she delivers. It might be tonight or not even 'til tomorrow. Pitch the game and then go see her."

"Sorry, Foxy, I can't do it." Gregg didn't wait to hear the stream of profanities that flew out of his manager's mouth. He ran through the clubhouse, stopping just long enough to trade his spikes for his loafers. In the players' parking lot, he found the gate attendant.

"Get me a taxi, Freddy, fast," he hollered. The surprised young man ran into the street and stopped the first cab he saw. Gregg raced over and jumped into the back seat.

"Do you know who I am?" he asked the driver. He took off his Royals cap.

The driver turned around and looked. "Sure, you're Gregg Talbot. I had you in my cab a couple times when I drove for Black & White."

"Okay. Take me to Memorial Hospital." On the way, Gregg told him about Michelle and explained that he had no money on him to pay for the ride.

"No problem. It's an honor for me. I'm one of your biggest fans; have been for years. Wait'll I tell my wife and kids about this."

"Never mind the honor." Gregg looked at the name on the license posted in back. "This may be a round-trip, Solomon, and I'll see you get paid for it. I want you to wait for me in the cab as close as you can park to the main entrance. Don't leave unless someone comes out and tells you I said it was okay. You got it?"

"I hear you loud and clear."

"Okay. Now turn on the game."

By the time the taxi reached the hospital, the Angels had already scored twice in the first inning.

Gregg had to wait at the information desk for several minutes while the receptionist checked a patient's record and gave the information to someone who had phoned in. She then misspelled "Talbot" the first time she entered the letters on her keyboard and said that Michelle wasn't registered.

"I know she's here," he said. "Check it again."

"Is that "T-o-l-b-e-r-t?" she asked.

He corrected the spelling and moments later she told him that Michelle was on the seventh floor. All the while he was aware of people staring at him in his uniform and buzzing about who he was.

In the maternity ward, a heavyset nurse with a plain, round face and hair that was dyed closer to yellow than blonde, greeted him warmly. She confirmed that Michelle was in labor and pointed to the location of her room. When he went in, Gregg found the doctor standing by Michelle's bed, encouraging her progress. She smiled as soon as she saw him approach. He told the doctor who he was, pulled a chair up next to the bed, and took his wife's right hand in his.

The gynecologist looked to be about the same age as Gregg. "I'm Doctor Sanford," he said. "I thought you were pitching today."

"I thought so, too," Gregg chuckled, "but then my boss here changed the plan." He took one of the towels from the night table and wiped Michelle's forehead. "How's she doing?"

"Terrific," Sanford answered. "An hour at the most and I think it'll be over. She took her time getting here."

"What's the score, Gregg?" Michelle asked. "Who's pitching?"

"Woodard," he said. He didn't have to explain that Woodard was throwing on just two days' rest. She knew that. "Foxy probably just hopes to get a few innings out of him. There was no score when I got out of the cab," he lied.

Michelle started to say something but was interrupted by another long contraction. As soon as it subsided she told him that he should have stayed at the park. "The game's more important," she said.

"Wrong, honey. Being here with you is what counts. Besides, I'd have gotten creamed out there with you and the baby on my mind."

"If we lose, the fans won't ever forgive you," she said. She paused, then forced a smile. "I'd probably have to trade you to the National League."

A half hour later Sanford called for an attendant to take Michelle to the delivery room. "Do you want to come and watch the show?" he asked Gregg.

"No, he doesn't," Michelle said. "He'd faint if he were there."

"She's right," Gregg said. "Tell me where to wait."

Sanford told him exactly where to go and promised to bring him the news as soon as the baby was born. Gregg held on to Michelle's hand while the attendant wheeled the bed to the elevator. Just before the door opened, he wiped her forehead again and kissed her. "Do a good job," he said.

Gregg wasn't sure how long he had been pacing the corridor before Doctor Sanford was suddenly there, congratulating him, letting him know it was a boy. "Nine pounds, seven ounces," he said. "Michelle will be back in the room in about five minutes. You can go see her and the baby. She said to tell you she wants to know the score of the game."

He had tried to put the game out of his mind while he waited. There was a TV set in the small lounge at the end of the corridor. No one else was in there, but he hadn't turned it on. Now, he returned to the lounge and watched long enough to learn that the Angels were leading 4-3 and batting in the fifth inning.

Michelle was already in the room when Gregg got there. He couldn't hold back the tears when he saw her lying there, her head propped up on the pillows, holding their son. He kissed both of them. "You did terrific," he said.

She smiled. "He looks like a football player," she told him. "What about the game? Who's winning?"

"The Angels are up 4-3 in the fifth and threatening. Ray's still in there."

"Then you get out of here and go back to the ballpark. Foxy will need you, and I certainly don't. I'll be asleep in ten minutes."

He didn't argue with her. "You're right. I may still get a chance to pitch before it's over. Maybe even win it for little Wayne here."

Michelle looked at him and he could see the tears coming into her eyes. "We never once talked about naming him that," she said. "How did you know?"

"It couldn't be anything else. None of this would have happened if it weren't for your uncle. We both owe him an awful lot."

Solomon gave him the ride of his life back to Royals Stadium. Kansas City was at bat, in the fifth inning, when Gregg emerged from the clubhouse tunnel into the dugout. Foxy called time immediately and ordered him out to the bullpen. The fans stood and began clapping their hands as Gregg jogged across the outfield. A minute later, news of the baby's birth appeared on the giant scoreboard. Gregg's presence seemed to ignite a spark in the team, and two Royals came home with the runs that tied the score at five before the side was retired.

Ray Woodard had thrown 95 pitches in five innings and was exhausted. The Kansas City rally gave Gregg just enough time to get loose. Foxy Moore called the bullpen and told the coach to send Talbot in. Walking toward the mound, Gregg suddenly knew that this was the last chance he'd have to reach his goal. He was 40 years old, and new responsibilities had been thrust upon him. He was certain that he'd no longer have the desire to spend days or weeks playing baseball in other cities around the country, away from his new family. He realized that when the season was over he'd never play another major-league game again. This was it; do or die.

Foxy met him on the mound and handed him the ball. "How do you feel?"

"Like winning the division." Gregg began rubbing up the ball. "Sorry I had to run out on you like that."

The manager took off his cap and worked his fingers through the dark, sweaty hair that surrounded his expanding baldness.

"That's okay," he said. "You ain't the first guy to do it, though I never seen anyone take off in the middle of his warm-ups. Besides, if I got on your case for what you did, it wouldn't help me too much with the owner, would it?" Moore slapped Gregg on his butt. "Congratulations, old man. Now pitch like hell."

And he did. Gregg threw four perfect innings, retiring twelve Angels in a row, striking out five of them. With two out in the bottom of the eighth, Lance English paid the biggest dividend on the deal Michelle engineered to bring him to Kansas City, hitting his second home run of the game. It was a bullet that just cleared the left field wall and knocked in what proved to be the winning run.

In the ninth inning, the overflow crowd in the ballpark was on its feet even before Talbot left the dugout and walked to the mound. He knew what had to be done, and wouldn't allow the nervousness he felt when he started his warm-ups to take control. He was determined to keep the Angels from getting back into the game. The first two California hitters each bit on curve balls breaking inside to them and popped out to the infield. The fans throughout the stadium clapped their hands in a rhythmic tempo and roared on every pitch. Gregg thrived on their enthusiasm and ended it with a flourish, striking out the Angels' last hope on four pitches.

He had to see the sports coverage on TV that night to know for certain what happened when the game ended. They watched together from Michelle's hospital room and laughed at the sight of his jumping high into the air several times before he was mobbed by his teammates and hidden for minutes under a growing pile of ecstatic bodies. The cameras zoomed in on the scoreboard's message, spelled out in giant letters that seemed to rock back and forth while multi-colored fireworks burst all around them: ROYALS WIN — 300 FOR TALBOT.

"What a day," he said, turning to his wife.

Michelle moved her finger around his eyes and nose. "Who would have dreamed that we'd each get what we wanted on the same day?"

"Actually," he corrected her, "we each got both of the things we wanted on the same day; little Wayne and a big victory."

"You're right," she answered. She was quiet for a minute and then asked, "Do you think we'll beat Toronto, Gregg?"

"Of course we will. How else will I be able to tell this little Kansas City Kid when he grows up how it felt to pitch in the World Series?" He watched her face light up, seeing again how beautiful she was. "And we'll win that, too. I can't think of a better time to call it quits than after playing on a world championship ball club."

She reached for his pitching hand and held it in both of hers. "Is that a final decision, no matter what happens?"

"Absolutely. It's been on my mind a lot lately. This was it, whether or not I got number 300 today. I made the decision even before I almost suffocated at the bottom of that pile." He laughed. "Yup. it's time to find something else to do with the rest of my life."

"I think you're right," Michelle said. "And from the point of view of the owner and president of the Kansas City Royals who's going to have to spend a lot of time at home with her son, I'd like to interest you in the job of team vice president that I intend to fill." She squeezed his hand. "It's a good position," she continued. "I had it myself when Wayne was here. It doesn't pay anything like what a 300-game winner would get, but if he had to, a guy could support his wife and baby on it."

Gregg got up and walked to the foot of the bed. He folded his arms in front of him, bent forward slightly, and gave Michelle a very inquisitive look. "I'm almost afraid to ask," he said in a mock-serious tone of voice, "but what is it I have to do in return this time?"

He continued the act for several seconds, until Michelle began to laugh. And then he laughed uproariously himself, unable to stop, while he returned to the chair by her side.

THE SHORT END OF IMMORTALITY

"Statistics are used much like a drunk uses a lamppost: for support, not illumination."

—Vin Scully

YOU WANT TO know how I feel about it, Larry? Bottom line, I think it stinks. It's sure as hell depressing, I'll tell you that. All those sportswriters out there who supposedly know what they're talking about but can't see the big picture when it comes to voting for the Hall of Fame.

Some of them would give a ballplayer a free pass into the Hall if all he did was hit a lot of home runs in his time, as if nothing else counts. He could've been a big out in the clutch or the worst fielder in the league, but it wouldn't matter.

Then there are others who'll let a guy in if he happened to put together one or two career years and maybe carried his team to a pennant while he was hot. They forget the fact that he was nothing more than average all the rest of the time.

And you've got writers who'll vote for a guy just because he managed to hang around for twenty years and pile up a bunch of statistics. Big deal. Hell, any ballplayer can rack up a 150 hits a year even if he's batting at no better than a .270 clip. And what's fifteen homers in a season today? Nothing to write home about. But if some guy stays healthy and does it for eighteen or twenty years, he's suddenly Hall of Fame material in their eyes.

Come on, let's cut the crap and be objective. The trouble with some of these baseball scribes is that they really don't understand the game they're covering. They only see what's obvious and miss everything else. A home run that wins it in the ninth gets them all excited. They go into the clubhouse and drool all over the guy who hit it. Every word the big hero says is in the paper the next morning. But they can't appreciate the value of someone who goes out there day after day and makes all the plays his team needs without being the star of the game. Writers like that remind me of football fans who just watch the ball all the time. They don't see everything else that's going on while the quarterback is dropping back to pass or some speed merchant is trying to get around the corner.

I pushed as hard as I did for Charlie Garrison to get into Cooperstown because the man deserves to be there. This is the thirteenth time he's been on the ballot and the thirteenth time he's gotten jobbed. That means he's only got two chances left to walk in the front door. And you bet your ass I'll be going all out for him again on the next ballot the way I did this year. Why the hell shouldn't I?

In the first place, I've paid my dues. The rules say a writer becomes qualified to vote for the Hall of Fame once he's covered baseball for ten seasons. Last year was my tenth; so now I've got the chance to do something more than just write a column about who ought to get in and who wasn't good enough. I can vote too. And if I want to campaign for some ballplayer and try to get other writers out there to check his name off on their ballots, that's up to me. There's nothing that says I can't do it.

Ten years on the baseball beat means watching everything down on the field for close to 2000 games — I don't have to tell you that, Larry, you did the play-by-play on every one of them. When you're covering the home team in this town, you'd better have a damn good idea what's going on out there all the time. The fans around here know their baseball, and they won't put up with a reporter who doesn't. They can see for themselves when a shortstop doesn't have the gun to throw a guy out from deep in the hole, or when a power hitter keeps trying to pull everything in sight instead of going the other way when they're giving him half the field. Most of the folks who come out to see this team play don't need me to tell them those things, even though they expect me to, and a whole lot more. The point I'm trying to make is that I size up a ballplayer on his whole game. I know every which way he helps the club and how he puts himself out to try and get those "W"s, day by day, year after year. By the time he's through playing, it's no mystery to me whether he's Hall of Fame material or not.

In the second place, Charlie Garrison should've made it in before some of the guys who've been elected in the last ten or fifteen years. That's how I feel about it, and that's exactly what I wrote in my column every time Garrison had to swallow his disappointment and see someone get in who never did as much for the game as he did. I saw what he went through when that happened, and it broke my heart every time. I mean if you just compare his record with other second basemen who made the Hall, you can't help wondering why them and not him. I don't like to start naming names or making one-on-one comparisons. It sounds like sour grapes and it's a surefire way of getting some fans all hot and bothered. But I don't know how else I can wake people up to the fact that Garrison's total game was every bit as good as other players I could rattle off who've already been recognized as Hall of Famers.

Let's look at it and try to be objective. How many second basemen sitting in Cooperstown played the position in the big leagues for sixteen years? Charlie did, from when he broke in at 21 to when he hung up his spikes at 37. He was in the lineup for almost 2500 games, all for the same ball club. So if longevity's important to them, he's got it. And loyalty besides, because he was never interested in playing somewhere else for more money. He cared about this team and this town.

Playing second, remember, isn't like standing around in the outfield waiting for a fly ball and thinking about your next at bat or your golf game. You're involved in half the stuff that goes on: whether it's fielding a ground ball, turning the double play, or being the cutoff man and getting the ball in to the catcher for a play at the plate. You've got to be thinking ahead on every pitch in that position.

How many clubs have been able to win a pennant without a great second baseman? I mean someone who's always there to make the big defensive play when the game's on the line. You know the answer as well as I do. Very few. And he has to get the job done during the dog days of July and August, when it's a bitch to go out there and play every day. But let's face it, that's when any game you blow on an unearned run means another game you've got to win in September — under pressure — if you want to make the playoffs. So how can any writer with half a brain ignore the fact that Garrison was out there at second on six pennant winners during his time?

There just has to be more objectivity, Larry. The writers aren't supposed to let any personal feelings or prejudices get in the way. But how I see it, they're not living up to that when it comes to Garrison. Sure, the record books tell you some of the things he accomplished out there. You can read that he won five Gold Gloves in his sixteen years, three of them in a row, and that twice he had the fewest number of errors among second basemen in both leagues. But that's not the whole story. Great plays — I mean real game-saving kinds of plays — don't show up in the books. But the fans who were there when it happened remember it the rest of their lives.

Charlie had so many great ones. His club could've lost the pennant in '64, on the last day of the regular season, if he didn't make that grab over his shoulder in short right with the bases loaded in the eighth inning and everybody running. The right fielder had no chance to get there, and that play was the difference in the ball game.

Or how about game six of the World Series in '71? He must have dived almost ten feet to his right to backhand that liner off Toby Johnson in the webbing of his glove and save the game in the ninth. The guys up in the press box said that was the best defensive play on the team all year. There wasn't a reporter covering the Series who didn't agree that it may have been one of the greatest clutch plays ever made by a second baseman. Those are the kinds of things I'm talking about, stuff that a responsible writer is supposed to remember when he's got his ballot in his hand and ten players he can vote for.

It just makes me sick that so many guys turning out columns in other baseball towns won't take the time to study the case for Garrison and look at it objectively. Some of them either never knew or have just forgotten that he was one hell of an offensive player as well. Not with a lot of home runs or RBI's, I'll admit that, but that's not what's expected from his position anyway. There were three years he led the league in bunt singles, and four more that he put down more sacrifice bunts than anyone else. That tells you a lot about the guy. It says he was able to start a rally with his speed by getting on base, and that he could keep one going by moving a teammate over when the manager was playing a little small ball to win the game.

Don't forget about stolen bases. In his first nine years in the league, Garrison was in the top ten every time. It was only after he got his knee torn up that he slowed down a step and didn't have the green light to go on his own any more. I know how much he suffered with that knee. Some guys wouldn't want to think of stealing again after what he went through, but he'd do anything to help his club win.

Before he got hurt, Charlie also led the majors in stealing home four different years. He did it five times in '68, which was pretty unbelievable. Will anyone ever forget Mickey Coleman's no-hitter against Chicago that year? Garrison tripled with two out in the ninth, hobbled around for a few minutes like he was dying with pain after he got up from his slide, and then stole home on the next pitch! That was the only run of the game. What's-his-name, the manager, said afterwards there was no way he was going to let Mickey go out there for the tenth inning on a cold night like that with all the pitches he'd thrown. If Garrison hadn't won the game right then the way he did, you wouldn't see Coleman's name in the record books today.

Garrison also had four 30-30 years when he hit 30 doubles and stole 30 bases. Not a lot of ballplayers have pulled that one off. Some of the writers who don't think he belongs in the Hall point to his .265 lifetime batting average. But even most of them will admit he was always one of those guys you wanted to see up there in the late innings when the game was on the line. He didn't knock in a lot of runs for his career — I admitted that before — but he got more than his share of hits when it really counted. So why don't they take those things into consideration when they're voting?

That's what I'm talking about, Larry, when I keep saying that if you look at everything about Charlie Garrison objectively, there's no way you keep him out of the Hall of Fame. He was a terrific leadoff hitter. He got on base when you had to get something going. He was a threat to steal most of his career. He delivered the run you had to have when the game was up for grabs. And day in, day out, he was the spark plug on the club and did everything that was expected of him on the field.

With all he accomplished in his time, I had no problem making the pitch I did to everyone in the Association who had a vote, asking them to give Charlie their support. If I hadn't done it, I wouldn't have been able to look myself in the mirror. A few of them were offended by it, I know. Some told me to go easy, that he'd have no trouble getting put in by the Veterans Committee if the writers didn't elect him. But he shouldn't have to wait to go in the back door. Not, like I said, when you compare him with other players who are already there.

Sure, I had a long talk with Garrison before I started doing all that PR for him. He was afraid it might not look too good and could actually hurt his chances. But I reminded him that he'd already come up short in the balloting twelve times — the last time by 54 votes — so there wasn't much to lose. He finally gave me the okay, but made me promise that I'd just make the best case I could for him without twisting anyone's arm. That's the way he is, as much as getting into Cooperstown means to him. I told him all I'd do is try and get everyone to look at it as objectively as possible. I just wanted them to review the stuff I put together so they could see what he did when he played the game. Just leave their personal prejudices out of it when it was time to vote, that's all.

Now that the results are in, you can understand why I feel like this. We got a lot closer this time, missing out on the seventy-five percent he needed by just 28 votes. That means it's still going to take an awful lot of work to get him elected in his last two chances. I'm encouraged by bringing the number down like we did, but I don't know what else there is to tell those dummies who didn't vote for him. I guess I'll have to analyze his stats all over again and see if there's anything there I missed.

What I've thought about doing is getting some testimonials written up from the guys who played with him and against him during his sixteen years, especially the ones who already made it into the Hall. I'll let them put whatever they want to say in their own words. Maybe the Association members who see it will be more impressed by that. I'll do whatever I can, that's for sure. Anything at all to help the writers be as objective as possible.

But the hard part is coming tomorrow. Garrison's been out of the country, on vacation, so he doesn't know about the vote yet. His plane is due in about two in the afternoon, and he's expecting me to meet him at the airport. As soon as he sees me he's going to start grinning, grab on to my arms, and ask me what happened. Great, huh? How'd you like to pinch-hit for me on that one? I'm going to have to give him a hug and say, "Sorry, Pop, you didn't make it. You came up 28 votes short. Come on, let me help you with your suitcases and I'll get you and mom home. We'll talk about it in the car."

A FLARE FOR DAN NUGENT

"A baseball game is simply a nervous breakdown divided into nine innings."

—Earl Wilson

DAN NUGENT CLOSED his eyes for a few moments and took a deep breath as he waited in the slow-moving line for a taxicab. He had arrived at the airport in the middle of Boston's evening rush hour and knew that the ride into the city — especially getting through the tunnel — would be slow. Just relax, he told himself. Don't worry about anything. No one here's going to recognize you as an old Braves ballplayer. It's been too long.

Once Evelyn, his wife, had persuaded him to accept the invitation to the anniversary weekend and make the trip, he wanted everything to be positive. No qualms about seeing some old teammates for the first time in 40 years. No concern, when he took the field, about any boos or insults he might hear from fans who still remembered him. And no regrets about coming when, inevitably, the local papers recapped his play in the seventh and final game of the '48 World Series between his Boston Braves and the Cleveland Indians.

The cab ride to the new hotel in Kenmore Square was as slow as he'd expected. But when the driver finished cursing his way across several lanes of traffic, edging to the right each time, until he finally pulled up to the curb in front of The Grand Beacon, Nugent realized that he couldn't recall anything he had seen after leaving the airport. Once again, for the thousandth time, or was it the ten thousandth time, he had been replaying the ninth inning of that seventh game in his mind. It was always so clear.

The fans were on their feet, clapping their hands and cheering for the out that would make their team world champions. The Indians had runners on second and third, two out and Whitey Semanski at bat. Nugent remembered thinking that if he had been managing the team, he'd have put Semanski on base and pitched to Vic Walters, the lefty. Johnny Foster, the Braves ace, could handle lefties as easily as right-handers, and the infield could play for a force at any base. But Tommy Brenner, the manager, didn't see it that way.

As soon as Nugent stepped inside the open door to the hotel, the doorman reached out quickly and took his small overnight bag. It was as if two spies had met in the park and the transfer had been prearranged. "This way, sir," he said, "check-in is over there to the left."

Nugent followed him to the marble counter where a female clerk — wearing a black necktie over a pink shirt, the same uniform as the men around her — handled his registration and gave him the plastic keycard to his room. A bellhop, whom he hadn't noticed, snatched up the bag without asking as soon as the pretty clerk had wished Nugent a nice day. He resented the young man's forwardness, and in another time and place wouldn't have tipped anything after being shown to his room. But he reminded himself again to *stay cool*, as his grandson would say: "Go with the flow, be positive about everything."

The invitation had stated that there would be a dinner for players of both teams in the Charles River Room at seven o'clock. That gave Nugent a little more than an hour to rest, clean up, and get dressed.

He read the long distance dialing directions on a pad next to the telephone and called Evelyn, but gave up after seven rings. He arranged for a wakeup call in 30 minutes, just in case he fell asleep, then closed the drapes and got into bed.

Moments later Nugent was back in the ninth inning of the final game of the Series. *The count to Semanski was two balls and no strikes. Foster wanted to keep the ball outside, pitching to Semanski's weakness. The first pitch fastball had been high, and then the umpire made a bad call on the curve that painted the outside corner of the plate. Nugent thought the hitter's count would persuade Tommy Brenner to change his mind and give Semanski an intentional pass, but the Braves manager remained motionless in the near corner of the dugout. When the catcher called for the curve again, Nugent hid his face with his glove for a moment and hollered the word that let his shortstop know what the pitch would be. He inched a little closer to first base, reached down for a pebble he spotted on the infield and eased onto the balls of his feet as Foster went into his stretch.*

The dinner was enjoyable. There was an open bar for an hour, during which the players moved around the room greeting each other. They had been given nametags to wear, each with the player's name in large, easy-to-read letters and a picture in uniform taken at the World Series 40 years earlier. Aside from a barely noticeable set of love handles that partially hid his belt, Nugent had not changed very much since then. The years had been kind to him in comparison with many of the men in the room, and he was pleased to be recognized quite easily by a number of his former teammates. There was a lot of light banter about retirement, baldness, knee replacements, and especially golf games that were either improving with age or going to pot.

Each table at dinner was set for six. Nugent was seated with two former Braves players, one of whom was Frank May, his partner at shortstop for four years, the last of which was their World Series year. They were joined by three members of the Indians. The lenses of May's glasses were almost Coke-bottle thick, but he still had the same livewire energy he had shown both on and off the field years earlier. He kidded the Cleveland players about things that had happened in the Series, but didn't mention the play that had deprived Nugent of sleep on countless nights over the 40 years that had flown by. The tension that embraced Nugent's body while May had his fun didn't abate until the conversation at the table switched to a discussion of the modern day players. The emphasis was on their greater athleticism and record-breaking power statistics; but the talk returned several times, with undisguised envy, to the enormous salaries they were being paid as a result of free agency.

"Curt Simmons opened up a new world for all these guys," one of the Indians players said, "but I'll bet you can't find ten ballplayers in both leagues that can tell you who he was. The shame of it is that Simmons was near broke when he died."

As coffee and dessert were being served, the owner of the Red Sox, who was hosting the game in Fenway Park, welcomed them to Boston. He was younger than everyone in his audience and was someone whose name had been in the newspapers often as a candidate to be the next baseball commissioner. He joked about how much money it was costing his club in health insurance to have their group play three innings in the anniversary game, and gave them a preview of the activities that would take place at the ballpark the next day. "It was a sad day for the City of Boston back in 1952 when the Braves left here for Milwaukee," he said, "but unfortunately there didn't seem to be enough fans to support two ball clubs. The Red Sox are happy to have you play your anniversary game in our park and we look forward to seeing all you great old-timers on the field."

The owner was followed by the team's general manager, a very congenial man who had been in baseball for over 40 years himself — as long as some of them had been out of it, Nugent realized — but all of it in a front office role, never as a player. He recalled listening to the '48 World Series on radio and spoke nostalgically about some of its highlights as if they were games he could never forget.

"It's not often you have a Series that goes seven games and isn't decided until the ninth inning," he said. "But that's what you guys did, and it was a helluva Series from start to finish."

Nugent tensed up again at the sound of the words "ninth inning," but the GM then thanked them all for making the trip to Boston and said there would be a gift waiting for each of them after the game. One of the players hollered out that he'd have preferred to have his gift waiting for him in the bedroom when he got back from dinner. That brought a laugh from everyone, including the waitresses who had begun clearing off the tables. Minutes later the players were up and mingling again.

"Who's the guy who said that?" May asked as they were leaving the table.

"That's Whitey Semanski," one of the Cleveland players told him. "Now he's got the hair to go with the name. But he was always a joker."

When Nugent returned to his room, he saw that the telephone message light was on. Evelyn had told him on the way to the airport that she was joining several friends for dinner at a new restaurant that had opened on their side of Santa Fe, but would call as soon as she got home. She'd made sure he had the plastic container with his two-day supply of heart pills in his jacket pocket, and assured him again that he was doing the right thing by going to Boston. It was difficult, but she had done her best to convince him that no one would say a word about the play that had haunted him for so long. Her hope was that once he mingled with his teammates from that Series and had an inning or two of fun with them on the field, he'd be able to put the game behind him and let go of the guilt he had lived with all those years.

When he returned the call, she picked up the phone on the second ring, confident it was him. "Hello sweetheart."

"Hi Evy, how'd you know it was me? Oh, never mind, is everything okay there? Did you have a good time at dinner?"

"Yes, we all did. It's a lovely place. We'll have to go there sometime. How was your evening?"

"It was good. I talked to a bunch of the guys, mostly about what they're doing these days and how they try to stay healthy. Frankie May and Johnny Foster are both here, but a couple of the others I looked forward to seeing couldn't make it, especially Al Barilla, the relief pitcher we used to call 'Gorilla.' And I chose the fish instead of the steak."

"That's wonderful, Dan. Did you remember your pills at dinner without me there to remind you?"

"Yes, my love. I put them on the table in front of me as soon as I sat down. One of the Cleveland players sitting with me did the same thing, so we had a laugh over it."

"Good, and everything's all arranged for tomorrow?"

"Yup, our game starts at one o'clock, and then the Red Sox play at three."

"Well, remember what you promised me. Don't play more than you should and don't overexert yourself. You're 68, not 28. You know what Doctor O'Brien said when you had your last physical."

"Okay, Evy, okay, I know all that."

"Then get a good night's sleep and call me tomorrow when you get back to the hotel."

"I will. Good night, Evy. Love you."

"Love you too, Dan."

As soon as he switched off the light above his bed and found a comfortable spot for his head on the stiff pillow, Nugent was back in his World Series, 40 years earlier. *He saw himself crouching a little lower on the infield dirt, the back of his glove almost resting on his left knee as Johnny Foster got ready to throw the two and nothing pitch to Semanski. The curve fooled the Cleveland hitter again, but he had started into his swing at the fastball he was expecting and couldn't hold back. Nugent was certain that any contact with the ball would take place on the outside part of the plate, and he anticipated it coming in his direction. As he took a couple of quick steps to his left, the ball came off Semanski's bat as a flare heading into short right center field. Nugent turned and began racing into the outfield, looking back moments later to check the flight of the ball. He could see immediately that neither the right fielder nor the center fielder — both of whom had been playing the powerful Semanski deep — had a chance of reaching the ball before it dropped. It was his play to make, and the two Indians base runners were on their way home as he raced farther into the outfield. Another quick glance over his shoulder at the downward flight of the baseball let him see where it would land, and he knew he might not get there in time. Running at full speed, he stretched out his left hand and saw the ball kiss the tips of the leather fingers of his glove before continuing its fall onto the grass. Even as he picked it up and threw it home — too late for a play — Nugent was telling himself he'd have made the catch if he had dived for the ball.*

Foster returned to the mound from behind home plate where he had gone to back up the catcher. Brenner moved around in the dugout but showed no sign of taking Foster out of the game. Two pitches later, Vic Walters made the third out on a one-hopper to the first baseman. In the last of the ninth, Boston put a base runner on first, but then the overflow Braves Field crowd watched in stunned silence as a bunt — meant to advance the runner into scoring position — was turned into a double play. Moments later the third out was recorded and the Braves' marvelous season was over. The second run that scored for Cleveland on the bloop hit had given them a World Series victory.

In the clubhouse, as the players showered and dressed, some of his team-mates told Nugent he'd made a "nice try," or words to that effect, as they walked past his locker. He waited for someone to ask whether he thought he could have caught the ball with a dive, but no one did. Ballplayers were trained to forget the game that had just been played — win or lose — and start getting mentally prepared for the next one. But this game cost all of them a winner's share in the Series, and they wouldn't be putting on their uniforms again until the next season. Since he was already certain that leaving his feet would have given him that extra little extension he needed, Nugent was convinced that some of the players in the room blamed him for the loss they had just suffered. While his teammates were silent about it, several baseball writers from among the many sent from all over the country to cover the game speculated in their columns the next day that the ball might have been catchable if Nugent had only made a greater effort on the play.

There was a breakfast buffet in the dining room the following morning. Nugent waited for a vegetable omelet cooked to order on a mobile gas oven located just beyond the dessert display. He added two cups of black coffee to his tray, avoided looking toward the front of the room where he had seen a number of players eating, and found a table in the corner, beyond the buffet line. He was nervous and wanted to eat without having to converse with anyone. His call to Evelyn earlier had gone unanswered, which meant that she had chosen to attend the early mass that morning. He hadn't slept well; the thought of playing baseball again in front of a large crowd was giving him butterflies, and he felt the need for a fresh dose of his wife's encouragement. "Pray for me not to screw up," he'd thought to himself as he hung up the phone.

The schedule called for them all to board a bus at eleven o'clock for the short ride to the ballpark. Nugent lingered over breakfast so as to avoid having to join the players who he was sure were sitting or standing around in the lobby talking and joking with one another. He had considered taking a walk around Kenmore Square to see what changes had taken place in the area, but decided that it would be best to save all his energy for the game he'd be playing in shortly.

Moving down the aisle of the bus, Nugent nodded his head and smiled slightly at the players he passed before he found the first empty row and sat down. He turned his attention to the window and watched the flow of traffic make its way through Kenmore Square in both directions.

Minutes later, as the bus was moving, his reverie was interrupted by the voice of a player who had quietly slipped into the seat next to him.

"Hi, I'm Whitey Semanski. I don't think we've had the chance to talk to each other this weekend."

Nugent turned and offered his hand. "No, we haven't, though I got a laugh out of what you said to the Sox GM yesterday. I'm Dan Nugent."

"Nugent! You were the Braves second baseman." Semanski shook Nugent's hand as he spoke. "You're the guy who made a hero out of me when you didn't catch up with that bloop of mine in the ninth inning. I've been living off that hit for 40 years."

"Yeah, I came close, but no cigar," Nugent said.

"Foster was one tough pitcher. He scared me and I never did much off him. The truth is I was hoping back then they'd put me on and pitch to Walters."

Nugent was pleased to hear that strategy reaffirmed. "As it turned out, that would've been the right move for us," he replied. "I was thinking at the time we should've done it."

"Yeah, that story about the game in today's Globe said the Braves made a mistake not walking me. The guy who wrote it actually was there at the time. Egan, his name is. Did you read it?"

"No, I haven't seen a paper today." Nugent felt the tension coming on quickly, and was afraid of what Semanski might report next.

"And I remember Foster had me completely fooled on the pitch," Semanski said. "I was lucky to get the end of the bat on it."

As Semanski spoke, Nugent saw himself racing into the outfield for the ball, knowing he was going to come up inches short but more certain than ever of making the catch if he had dived for it. It hurt too much to think about the play at that moment. He had to move the conversation in another direction. "Yeah, anyway, so where do you live and what do you do now?"

"I'm in a little town just outside Orlando. Been selling used cars for the past twenty years. Beg your pardon, pre-owned cars we call them now. That's supposed to make you think they're in better shape than they are." Semanski smiled as he said it. "Maybe all us ballplayers ought to be called pre-owned or something, instead of old-timers." Semanski chuckled at that. "What about you? Still working?"

Nugent saw that the bus was pulling up in front of the players' entrance to Fenway Park. "Looks like we're here," he said. He waited a few moments as Semanski glanced out the window. "I live in the Santa Fe area," he continued. "We put some money in real estate there years ago and we've made out okay. So I take care of a bunch of rentals and keep my eyes open for any good deals that come along." After a pause, he added, "Keeps me busy and I enjoy it."

"Sounds good," Semanski said. He watched as the players in the rows in front of them got off the bus, then stepped into the aisle and winked at Nugent. "Well, see you on the field. Good luck today."

Nugent stayed in his seat. He'd wait until everyone else was off the bus, just as he always did whenever a plane he was flying on had landed. "Thanks. You too," he answered. The conversation with Semanski had gotten rid of his butterflies. He knew it was a lucky hit, he thought to himself.

Sandy Koufax, a close friend of Tommy Brenner, the pennant winning manager of the '48 club who had died about five years earlier, had agreed to drive down from his home in Maine and manage the Braves fortieth anniversary team. He confessed to the eighteen players who were there that he knew very little about them, and asked them to help him make out the lineup. As a result, Nugent was back at second base, batting eighth. Koufax wanted everyone who had made the trip to Boston to play in the game, and substituted freely as the Braves took a 3-2 lead after one inning and a 6-3 lead after two. He sent Charlie Banks, a pitcher, up to pinch-hit in the second inning, and told Banks to take Nugent's spot in the field when Cleveland batted in the third. But when Banks fell down, running to first on a ground ball to shortstop, he took himself out of the game and Nugent returned to play second for the Indians' last at bat.

The three-run lead was reduced to a single run very quickly. After the first Cleveland batter reached on a muffed popup by the third baseman, the next hitter lined a drive toward the "Green Monster" that split the distance between the left and the center fielders. Neither one was inspired to chase after the ball and each, with the clearest of Alphonse and Gaston hand signals, invited the other to retrieve it. As this went on, and as the crowd roared with delight, the two Indians players circled the bases. After they crossed the plate, the Braves pitcher got into the act by feigning a show of anger as he first pointed at his two outfielders, threw his glove down onto the mound, and stalked off the field.

With the fans on their feet, cheering and laughing at the scene, Koufax emerged from the dugout and signaled for a new pitcher from the bullpen. The only one still there to answer his call was Johnny Foster, about 100 pounds heavier than when he was the losing pitcher, 40 years earlier, in the seventh game of the Series.

Foster got the first two Indians he faced to swing late and hit easy ground balls to the right side of the infield, one to Nugent and one to the first baseman. The final out should have come just as easily except that the third baseman made quite a show of inspecting the baseball after he fielded it, and his hurried throw bounced in the dirt before hitting off the first baseman's glove. The next batter punched a soft line drive that landed directly on the chalk down the left field line and rolled slowly toward the corner. The runner on first, representing the tying run, made his way to third. Nugent, covering second base, called for the ball as the hitter rounded first and slowly chugged his way toward him. But the left fielder never heard him and tossed the ball into third instead.

As Nugent moved back into position and saw that Semanski was approaching the batter's box for the Indians, he suddenly realized that all the ingredients of the inning that had been haunting him for 40 years were back in place. Foster would again be attempting to preserve the victory by retiring Semanski without allowing either of the Cleveland base runners to score. There would be no thought of giving him an intentional walk to load the bases for a force play because it was understood that everyone there wanted the chance to hit in what may be their last opportunity to do so on a major-league field.

Nugent called for time and jogged over to the mound. As the catcher started toward them, Nugent waved him off. "Listen, Johnny," he said, "I rode next to Semanski coming over on the bus here today. He told me he's been living off that hit he got in the last game of the Series for 40 years. Don't let him beat us with another one now or he'll be in my nightmares the rest of my life."

Foster turned away from Nugent for a moment to spit and wiped his mouth with the back of his wrist. He looked grim, as if he were pitching again in the deciding World Series game. "You're forgetting, Danny boy, that I was the losing pitcher in that game. Today's supposed to be all for fun, but I still don't want that "L" next to my name in any box score, even if it's just for three innings. So if he hits it to you, don't disappoint me again."

The word "again" stung Nugent hard. It told him what Foster thought of the catch his second baseman didn't quite make four decades earlier. But it also revealed that he wasn't the only one who had carried the memory of that play with him over the years. He suddenly felt as bad for Foster as he always had for himself. He wanted to make amends, if he could. "You're right, Johnny," he said, "I should've had it. I cost us the game. You lost it on account of me." Nugent looked hard at his pitcher, who said nothing. He turned and went back to his position.

On the third pitch to Semanski, fate took hold of the proceedings and caused him to hit a flare into short right field. Nugent started back and realized at once that he was the only one with a chance to reach it. His heart pounded as he quickly grasped the drama into which he was again being thrown and as he willed his older body toward the spot where he thought the ball would land. Again, the fear of not quite reaching it overtook him, but then he saw a vision of himself diving for the ball at the last instant and having it drop into the pocket of his glove as his body slammed to earth. An instant later, he sucked in all the breath he could, threw himself in the air and stretched his gloved hand out over the grass. He heard a loud shout from the crowd at the moment of impact with the ground. He looked, and it was there. Nugent saw the beautiful white baseball nestled in the soft brown leather. He started to smile...

As the Red Sox came to bat in the third inning of the scheduled game with the Detroit Tigers that afternoon, the announcer informed the crowd that Dan Nugent, who had been taken off the field on a stretcher at the end of the exhibition game and rushed to the nearby Beth Israel hospital, had died of the heart attack he suffered while making the final play. The fans were asked to participate in a moment of silence in his memory.

STEALING AWAY

"A life is not important except in the impact it has on other lives."

—Jackie Robinson

Y OU KNOW, DAVE, you've gotta be at least the tenth writer who's asked me that already, and by God it's only the first damn day of spring training. All everyone seems to want to know is why Mo Fontaine didn't come back to play baseball this year.

Well, for the record, I'll tell you the same thing I told all the others. Mo just decided he'd be happier catching passes on a football field than playing this here game again. The simplest way I can put it is to say he'd rather score a touchdown than steal a base. He knows he's one of the fastest guys anywhere and there's big money to be made in the NFL today. I guess that's why he didn't see any sense in playing even part of the season anymore. If he did, he'd have to worry about 90-mile-an-hour fastballs coming at him or getting a knee torn up by some catcher blocking the plate. Too many ways a man can get hurt out there, especially when he's the fastest center fielder in the league, like Mo was. He had that habit of running into fences if that's what it took to make a catch. Mo knew he had to decide which sport meant more to him, and we lost out. No big story in that. A kid with so much talent just made the choice that was best for him.

Now put away your notebook, Dave, and I'll tell you what really happened. This is just between you, me, and the lamppost, understand? Not for publication any time, agreed? Okay, you're about the only writer out there I can trust to keep something like this to himself, and it's a hell of a tale. Sad thing is, it shows how a good ballplayer can go off the deep end over something that shouldn't mean spit.

What happened to Mo goes back to the first game of the Series last year, the one the Mets beat us 3-2. When you're playing for that big gold ring that says "World Champions" on it, you don't want to drop the opener like that. But anytime you're going up against Matt Saunders, you know you're not going to score a lot of runs.

It was the playoffs against Oakland, before we took on the Mets, that really messed us up. That's because they made us go the full seven games to win, and Jake had to pitch Tommy Gleeson the first five innings of the last one. We had just two days off when it was finally over, so Tommy couldn't start the Series for us. Don't forget, he'd already thrown 22 innings in nine days and beat the A's three times. Buddy Walker did a hell of a good job against the Mets in place of Tommy, but you always want to have your stopper to open the Series.

Do you remember how we got our two runs off the Mets in that game? On the first one, Fontaine walked, stole second, and scored on a hit by Brandon. Later on, he doubled to left on what would've been a single for anyone else, stole third, and came home on a fly ball to short center. That's the play he slid in headfirst and grabbed the edge of the plate with his fingernails just before the tag. So if it wasn't for Mo, we'd have gone into the top of the ninth down three-zip to Saunders, not just needing one run to tie.

Fontaine led off the inning for us and Jake told him in the dugout to be patient up there, see if he could work Saunders for another base on balls. But Saunders knew what Mo was after and hit the corners with smoke for strikes on his first two pitches. He wasted one and then tried to break a curve or a slider over the outside. You remember the bunt Mo laid down on that pitch with two strikes on him? Well, it was his own idea, not Jake's, and it was a thing of beauty. Even though Conlon was still playing in close at third, there was no way he could beat Mo going down the line. That man just flies.

I think Kippinger was out of the Mets dugout as soon as Mo crossed the bag at first. Old Kip must weigh about 60 pounds more than he did in his playing days, all in his gut, but he was out at the mound in nothing flat. He's got his ace working for him, but he knows that with that leg kick Saunders has, and being a right-hander, Mo can steal second off him in a breeze. Kip didn't want to see that happen with no outs and a one-run lead.

Saunders wasn't happy about leaving, you could see that, but Kip gave him the hook anyway and signaled for a southpaw to come in. We figured it meant Chico Hilton because he usually got the call late in the game. It was a big surprise when Judd Wheeler came walking across the outfield from the bullpen. Wheeler had been back with the Mets just over a month and they'd used him in relief about half a dozen times. He'd been on the DL the better part of two seasons after he blew out his rotator cuff the year before. Kippinger was working him in slowly, raising his pitch count each time, just to get a good look at him while he could. Remember that Wheeler had been a starter in the league for eleven years before the injury. I guess the Mets had to figure out whether he could come back for them or whether they'd think about dealing him over the winter.

I'd known Judd for a couple of years when we were both with the Giants, and I didn't like him personally. He was a tough redneck from Mississippi. He just had no shame about things he'd holler from the dugout to players on the other side during a game. It didn't bother him that pitchers had to bat in the National League. He'd say whatever he felt like saying without worrying about the consequences. And if he ever had to move out of the way of a fastball up at the plate, the other team knew that one of their guys was going to get the same treatment. A lot of the ballplayers called him "Johnny Rooster," which was their way of saying he had a foul mouth on him.

Jake had seen plenty of Wheeler over the years too, and knew what he liked to throw. I reminded him that Wheeler had a sneaky pickoff move to first. "That's why Kip's bringing him in," I said, "to try and keep Mo from taking off."

While Wheeler was getting loose, Jake sent word out to Fontaine to draw a few throws so he could get a good look at his motion before taking off for second. Mo had the green light all the time, so it was just a matter of what pitch he'd go on. That's why the whole damn infield came over to the mound after Wheeler finished his warm-ups. They were all reminding him that he had to keep Mo close at first.

You covered the game, so a lot of this ain't news to you. When he got set, Wheeler threw over to the bag a couple of times before his first pitch to the plate. His move didn't look anything special to me or to Jake either, though you can't always spot everything on a lefty from the third base side.

The pitch to Brandon was a strike so that gave Fontaine less time to fool around. He took a longer lead off the bag and drew a hard throw, but got back standing. Then he moved off another half foot or so, where he knew he had to start from if he was going down. Wheeler gunned another one over, but Mo slid back in, way ahead of the tag. "Sneaky move, shit," Jake said, "he must've lost it." He spit out some seeds as he got up off that seat pad he uses on the bench during the game.

We both knew that Fontaine would be moving on the next pitch. Heck, everyone in the ballpark was looking for it. Remember, Mo had already stolen second 58 times in 62 tries, counting the playoffs. That gave him over 100 for his two years in the big leagues. No one else had numbers like that, but he had the perfect body for it. He was lean, all muscle, and those long arms and legs of his were a hell of an advantage on a close play. The only times they caught him all season were on pitchouts, and he should've been called safe on two of those. But some of those damn umpires standing there at second are all set to give the "out" sign as soon as they see the catcher figured the steal was on. Most runners don't have a chance on a pitchout if the guy behind the plate has a decent arm. That's why the umps treat it like an automatic out. I'll tell you, Dave, sometimes the way they miss a call and screw up the game can break your heart.

Anyhow, Wheeler went into his stretch, stopped, and then came up high with his right leg so you'd swear he was throwing to the plate. Fontaine was leaning towards second, ready to turn on the burners, and all of a sudden that crafty bastard made a move to first that he hadn't shown before. It was a pisser. He'd been playing cat and mouse with Mo, giving him just one move all the time, setting him up for that one. Mo was dead in his tracks. He didn't have a prayer in either direction. He took off for second but they got him in a rundown. You know something? It was the first time in his two big league seasons he'd ever been picked off.

Jake was on the field like a bat out of hell, screaming "balk" at the umps. But he knew that Wheeler had put one over on us. He didn't want to get thrown out of the game, so he just bitched for a few minutes, making some moves with his body for the ump over at first. Problem was they didn't look anything like what Wheeler had done.

Fontaine had to wait out there while Jake pleaded his case with the umpires. Meanwhile, the big scoreboard out in center field replayed the pickoff twice. Every time the Mets fans saw Mo fooled again, they cheered the play and jeered him unmercifully. When Jake got through beefing, Mo began to cross the infield toward the dugout. I could see Wheeler smirk at him and say something, but I couldn't hear what it was.

I didn't know back then that while Mo was jogging in, he felt like he was in the middle of a nightmare. I found out later that all he could think of at the time was his last two years of high school in Louisiana when the black kids from his neighborhood got bused to a school in the white part of town. Fontaine was the star player there in three sports: football, baseball, and track. The crowds at his games used to cheer the things he did on the field. But that was it. In school and after class the white kids wanted nothing to do with him. It was like he didn't exist when he wasn't playing ball.

In his senior year Mo was nominated for captain of each of those teams. But the coaches always made sure there were more whites playing than blacks. So he always lost out when the vote was between him and a white kid. He had to come to grips with the fact that the treatment he was getting in school was just because of his color. Fontaine was real sensitive, and that made it very painful for him. The only way he could hang in there emotionally was by always telling himself he was a better athlete than his white teammates.

Near the end of his senior year Mo got into trouble. A couple of white guys on the track team kept harassing this girl he used to date. Whenever she came around to watch him practice, they'd give her a hard time. One afternoon a fight started and the coach had to pull Fontaine off one of those kids. He told his story, but they expelled him from school and just gave the other boys a slap on the wrist. The black parents raised a fuss, but the school wouldn't let Mo graduate with his class or attend the senior prom. Eventually, they backed down and gave him his diploma, but he'd missed out on all the fun.

One of our scouts saw Mo playing baseball that summer. We signed him and sent him to Single-A ball in the Gulf League. With that speed of his, he moved up fast through the minors, but always had a bad attitude toward whites. He didn't give his managers or coaches any trouble but never wanted to have a white player for a roommate. They let him have his way on that until Charlie Bromax got him at Richmond in Triple-A. Charlie wouldn't stand for it and told Fontaine he'd never see the inside of a major-league clubhouse if he didn't smarten up fast. So Mo roomed with white ballplayers after that whenever he was told to — we put him with Gerry Graboski on the road all the time — but I guess he could never let go of that feeling he had from everything that had happened.

Anyway, when he jogged off the field in Shea after the pickoff, the fans were already letting him have it. That was bad enough, I guess. Then, as he went by the mound, he heard Wheeler say, "Better luck next time, black boy." Those words brought that whole high school scene right back to him. This time, though, the white guy was better than he was, and had embarrassed him in front of 50,000 people.

Mo sat down on the bench and just stared out at the field while Wheeler got the last two outs. And that was the ball game.

No, that's not the end of the story. It's just the beginning. You wouldn't have known what went on the rest of the Series from watching the game in the press box. You had to be there in the dugout to see what was happening with Fontaine and how it was driving Jake up a wall.

Gleeson came back for us in the second game. Tommy was still a little sore from the playoffs with Oakland, but he gave us seven good innings. We led all the way, after Corcoran's three-run shot in the second. Morrison came in to finish up and we won it easy.

After the off day, we were home in our park for the next three games. I'll tell you, Davey boy, that was the thrill of my life, especially the first one when the crowd stood up and really let us hear it while we were getting introduced. That's the first World Series I was ever in, remember, and this here's my seventeenth year in the Big Leagues, playing and coaching. Even though we'd already had those two games in New York, it took me a couple of innings to settle down and get into what was happening.

Every one of those games at home was close, and we were damn fortunate to win two of them. Of course Gleeson showed them all goose eggs in game five to put us one up going back to Shea, but Jake was beginning to have a nervous breakdown on account of what Fontaine was doing out there. Actually, it was because of what he wasn't doing.

Go back to game three, for example. If you remember, we were tied 4-4 in the seventh. But at that point we'd blown a 4-1 lead and Jake had to lift Jimmy Ricci in the top of the inning to keep the Mets from going ahead. In our half he was hollering for the guys to get some runs on the board. If you remember, Fontaine walked with one out.

"Here we go, here we go," Jake was saying. He whistled out to Fontaine to get his attention and told him to go on any pitch. He hollered it loud enough for everyone in the infield to hear him. Jake figured Mo was going to take off anyway, but he wanted Cooper to start worrying about it on the mound. That way, maybe he'd groove a fastball for Brandon or McTigue while he's trying to give his catcher a chance to nail Mo when he went.

Cooper did everything he could to keep Mo close. For a right-hander, he's got a really sweet move over there. Before every pitch to Brandon, he made Mo dive back to the bag two or three times. The count to Brandon went to 2 and 2, and Mo was still standing on first.

"What the hell's he waiting for?" Jake kept asking, and I'm saying before every pitch, "This is it. He's taking off now." But I was wrong every time. I think the whole ballpark expected to see Fontaine on second already. The "Go, go, go" they were giving him kept getting louder all the time.

Well, Mo finally went on the next pitch and would have had the base stolen, but it was too late. Brandon swung at the ball and skied to right on a curve, deep enough so that Mo could have tagged and gone to third if he'd been on second at the time. But now he had to go back to first. By then, Jake was hot under the collar, and it got worse when McTigue smacked the first pitch into center for a single. Mo moved to third on it, but Jake knew we should have been up by a run already.

Cooper's an old hand at this stuff and he stayed cool as a cucumber. He got ahead of Browning two strikes with a couple of good sliders and then froze him with some inside heat that caught the corner. We came up empty. Jake cursed, pulled a bat out of the rack, and looked like he was ready to do a small number on the watercooler.

One of the guys brought Fontaine's glove out to him over by third, so Jake didn't have a chance to say anything to him right then. The Mets went down one-two-three in their eighth and then Graboski put us ahead with his homer leading off. Jake told me he was going to have a little heart-to-heart talk with Fontaine before his next at bat. But we shut down the Mets in the ninth to end it, so Mo didn't get up again.

There was a lot of stuff in the papers the next day about how it looked good for us to win three in a row at home and take the Series. If I remember right, you had a story like that yourself. The Mets didn't agree with you guys the way they handed us our lunch on the field. Saunders wasn't great for them that day but he had it when he needed it. They had ten runs across by the fifth inning and no one Jake sent out there could do the job.

Then it happened with Mo again. We were down 14-3 in the eighth and Kippinger brought in Wheeler to mop up. Maybe he needed a few more tosses to get loose, because he hit Fontaine, leading off, with his first pitch. Jake was happy about that. He figured that now Mo could get another good look at the guy's motion. Stealing a base wasn't going to help us, but Mo could do it to get his confidence back.

Brandon was up next. He got ahead on the count and then flied out to the warning track in left on the first strike Wheeler put over the plate. Before every pitch to Brandon, Mo was no more than two or three steps off the bag. Wheeler didn't even bother throwing over there.

Jake got up off his pad and went over to the watercooler for a drink. His face had started getting that beet color and I knew what was on his mind without him saying a word.

"Mo figures there's no sense taking a chance with the score what it is, Jake," I told him. "He knows that if he gets thrown out, the scribes will say you made a bonehead call sending him down."

That wasn't something my old double play partner on the Tigers wanted to hear. "I manage the game my way, not how the chicken-shit writers think I should do it," he said.

By this time, McTigue already watched a couple of pitches go by. Fontaine stayed so close to first it looked like someone was holding him there with a leash. I tried to keep Jake from boiling over and hollered out to Mo to take a good lead. He stepped off a little more but I could see he was leaning towards first when Wheeler delivered to the plate. The count was in McTigue's favor and Jake flashed the sign for Fontaine to steal on the next pitch.

"If he don't want to move on his own, we'll give him a push," Jake muttered in my direction. "He hasn't got a stolen base in three games."

Fletch went through all his motions in the third base coach's box and Fontaine knew what was on. It looked like he finally woke up. He took a good lead and began dancing back and forth with those bitsy little steps of his. He bent down lower and started shaking his hands. Wheeler saw that Mo had come to life out there, but with that kind of lead he just wanted to go after McTigue. He didn't bother keeping Mo close. He stretched, looked over to first, and pitched to the plate. But when the ball left his hand Mo was moving back toward first instead of the other way.

Now Jake was really hot. He grabbed a bat and slammed it down a couple of times on the top step of the dugout. He did it hard enough so that even the home plate umpire looked over to see what was going on. Jake sat down, still holding the bat, and gave Fletch the steal sign again. I was thinking to myself that if Mo didn't go on this next one, I'd better be ready to duck real fast in case Jake couldn't control himself.

Wheeler tried to give McTigue a Nolan Ryan fastball on the next delivery and threw it in the dirt about a foot outside the plate. The ball went to the backstop and Fontaine moved down to second easy. Jake and I could both see he got a late start on Wheeler's motion and would've been a dead duck on a good pitch. Jake didn't say anything, but he kept the bat in his hand the rest of the game and I knew he was burning up inside. The final score was 15-5. I was ready for some kind of explosion in the clubhouse, but Jake just slammed the door to his office and was still in there when I left the park.

Gleeson was close to perfect the next day, throwing the shutout and giving the Mets just three hits. He hadn't shaved since the Series started, and had that real mean look on his face all afternoon. I guess Jake figured he had to show Fontaine he didn't like what he was seeing out there because he dropped him from leadoff down to eighth in the order. He posted the lineup in the dugout without saying a word to Mo, and Mo didn't ask any questions. We won it 3-zip, on just five hits. Things stayed peaceful the whole game because Mo went for the collar in three at bats. He made two sensational grabs out in center, one of them on a dive at the warning track. Jake didn't say a word to him either time when he came back in.

We flew back to New York that night and worked out a couple of hours the next day. Afterwards, Jake reminded the guys that they had a chance to become world champs by winning one more game. He warned them that the Mets would be tough to beat at home unless everyone gave a 100% out on the field. You could see that he looked a little harder at Fontaine when he said it. I knew Jake was hoping to wind up the Series in six games because he didn't know who he'd pitch in the seventh if it got that far. There was no way he'd send Buddy Walker back out again after the way "Big W" got clobbered in game four.

Well, you saw how close Jake got to getting his wish the next night. We pulled ahead 4-3 in the sixth on another Graboski homer and hung tough. Then it came down to Morrison getting the last three outs for us in the bottom of the ninth.

He fanned Rivers leading off, and when he threw a couple of quick strikes past DiAngelo, it sure looked good. You could smell that championship. Everyone on the bench started moving toward the steps so we could run out on the field as soon as it was over. Then bang, bang, and it was over alright. But the Mets had pulled it out on DiAngelo's handle hit and Richie Ross's belt just inside the foul pole in left. It was a low fastball that Jake had called from the bench, and Ross got all of it. Morrison's eyes almost rolled out of his head when he saw the ball take off. He just stood there, staring out at the bleachers, while Ross rounded the bases. It looked like he was hoping the ground would open up and swallow him.

The fans went wild, and all of a sudden Jake had some tough decisions to make about the final game on Sunday.

Jake couldn't try to do anything with Fontaine that day. Mo reached twice, once on a perfect bunt when he was up there to sacrifice, and on a single in the fifth. That's when we loaded them up with two out but couldn't score. Mo had nowhere to go on the bases either time, with a runner on second ahead of him, so he still didn't have a steal to show since game one.

At seven o'clock Sunday morning Jake called me on the phone. He wanted to know what I thought of him starting Gleeson on two days' rest. I'd been awake most of the night with the same question and told him that if I was managing the ball club, that's the call I'd make.

"What about the lineup?" he asked.

Since I'd spent a few hours tossing and turning over that one too, I told Jake that if it was up to me I'd put Fontaine back at the top of the order. "He's still 58 for 63," I said, "and a stolen base might win this thing." He said he'd think about it and we could talk some more on the bus on the way over to Shea.

Everyone was a little edgy on the ride from the hotel over to the park. Jake never said a word to me. During batting practice he taped the lineup in the dugout and had Fontaine hitting eighth again. Then, just a couple minutes before I had to meet with the umps at the plate and give them our batting order, Jake called Fontaine over and asked him how he felt.

"Real good," Mo told him.

So Jake said he'd changed his mind and Mo's the leadoff hitter.

If Mo liked the idea, he didn't show it. "Okay" was all he said, and went back down to the other end of the dugout.

Well, you know what Gleeson did that day, Dave. Just pitched his heart out. Jake and I both figured the most he'd be able to give us was five good innings. But there he was in the bottom of the seventh with a 2-1 lead over Saunders who was looking for his third win of the Series too. Then, just like that, Tommy gave up a base on balls and a two-bagger with two out, and the Mets had runners on second and third. Jake had a couple of pitchers loosening every inning since the fourth, and he got up to go make a change. I should've kept my mouth shut, but instead I told him he ought to let Gleeson try to get the last out himself.

Jake took his time walking out to the mound. He talked things over with Tommy until the home plate ump moved out there to break it up. When Kippinger saw that Gleeson was staying in, he sent up Cody Bowman, his best lefty pinch hitter, to bat for the little second baseman. Jake looked at what we had on Bowman in the book, flipped a coin in his head and decided not to give him the intentional pass. Bowman missed on two swings and we figured Gleeson had him. Then, after a couple of teasers that Bowman wouldn't bite on, he got the handle of his bat on an inside fastball and poked it into left, just over the infield. Both runs scored and then suddenly we were losing 3-2.

Jake looked at me, shaking his head. I was expecting to catch hell, but all he said was, "Lucky son of a bitch, he didn't even see it." The pitcher was up next. Kip let him bat with the lead, so Gleeson stayed in the game and fanned him on three heaters.

If you remember, we caught a break in the eighth and tied the game with two out on a bad-hop grounder past the shortstop. Jake was all set to call Morrison in from the pen if we didn't score that inning. But now he asked Gleeson if he had anything left. Tommy took off his jacket right away and told Jake he could give him three more outs.

"Then go on out there," Jake says, and patted him on the rump. It took Gleeson ten pitches and the Mets went down one-two-three.

So there we were in the ninth inning of the last game and the Series was up for grabs. "Let's get some runs," Jake hollers down the bench. "Let's get Tommy a win and go home." He said it like it was just another ball game in July, not the biggest damn game of everyone's life.

Gleeson was scheduled to lead off, and Jake sent Wally Herman up to hit for him. The kid was the best hitter in the farm system all year and showed us a good bat in September when the club brought him up. But you could see he was a little nervous at the plate this time and got under a fastball. He showed the folks in Shea what a major-league popup looks like.

Fontaine was next and the whole bench was talking it up, telling him to get something started. Most of them had their caps turned around backwards on their heads, like little kids. Mo saw the first baseman playing back, guarding the line on him, and dragged the first pitch between the mound and the bag. By the time Saunders got over there and picked it up, it was too late to make a play.

Kippinger was out of the dugout like a shot. He was tapping two fingers against his left arm before he even got to the mound. The man knew a good thing when he saw it, and so far Wheeler had Fontaine's number. Kip didn't want to let Mo get into scoring position on a stolen base.

While Wheeler was on his way in, Jake hollered for Gibbons to come over to the dugout from his coach's box at first. He told him to pass the word to Fontaine that he was to go on either the first or second pitch to the plate, whichever one he wanted, but that Brandon wouldn't be swinging at the first one. Jake also wanted Mo to make Wheeler throw over there a few times so he could study his motion some more and get a good jump.

Gibbons went back and whispered in Fontaine's ear. As soon as Wheeler was set to pitch, Mo took a good lead and went into his back and forth routine. He looked ready to go, and Jake was whispering, "Watch him, Mo, watch him."

Wheeler threw over there, medium speed, and Fontaine hopped back to the bag. As soon as the left-hander put his foot back on the rubber, Fontaine moved off and stretched the lead a little more. He was challenging Wheeler to throw it again, and slid back in when the pitcher obliged. It was a close play, but Mo had learned exactly how far he could go. He took his lead and Wheeler gave him a long look out of the stretch before kicking and pitching to the plate. Mo didn't go, and Brandon took a ball up high.

Jake signaled for Brandon to lay off the next pitch too. Fletch went through his motions in the third base box, and Gibbons checked in again personally with Fontaine.

Wheeler gave Mo a couple of head fakes while his right leg was up in the air and fired a bullet over to first. Mo froze for an instant and then dived back to the bag. His fingers reached the outside corner just a split second before the first baseman's glove came down on his shoulder. It was so close it could've been called either way. Mo was up in a second, as soon as the ump gave the "safe" sign, and brushed himself off. He moved into his lead and then did the same dive all over again when Wheeler kicked his leg and Mo heard Gibbons yell "Back." But the throw over was almost a lob, and Mo knew he could have gotten back to the base easily.

This time he didn't bother brushing the dirt off his uniform when he got up. I figured he was embarrassed that he'd been fooled again. Wheeler was giving him that same smirk he'd shown him in game one when he picked him off.

"Watch him good, watch him good," Jake was humming, as Fontaine got off the base again. Wheeler got set, hesitated, and just as Jake hollered out, "Go!" threw the next one to Brandon that his catcher had to dig out of the dirt. The pitch was tailor-made for a stolen base. Trouble is Mo stayed right there on first. I didn't believe what I was seeing out there.

Jake was furious. He called for time, and waived Fontaine over to the dugout. When Mo got there, Jake sat him down in his own spot and turned his back to the field so the cameras couldn't pick up what he was saying. He told me to stand next to him and hide Mo from the other angle. That's the first time I'd ever seen something like that happening. I couldn't help wondering what the radio and TV guys upstairs were telling the fans about it.

"I told you to go on one of them two pitches," Jake said in a loud voice that's not quite a roar. "What the hell's wrong with you?"

Fontaine was trying to stay calm. "I was afraid of getting picked off," he said.

Jake was absolutely speechless for a couple of seconds. He wasn't even sure what Mo was telling him. He sputtered a little before he asked him, "What do you mean by that?"

"I don't want to be humiliated like the last time," Mo answered. "I can't handle it."

Of course, this means more to me now than it did when I first heard Mo say it. That stuff that happened to him in high school was something I knew nothing about at the time.

"This guy's motion has me all tied up," he told Jake. "I can't steal on him."

That would've been the end of it if Jake had anyone else on the bench who came close to Fontaine's speed. He'd have told Mo to go take a shower and sent in a runner for him. But there were no rabbits sitting around, and Jake also knew what he'd be giving up in center field if Mo wasn't out there. Pulling him out of the game wasn't an option. Jake looked at me, shook his head a couple of times and turned back to Mo. He lowered his voice to just a shade above normal.

"Listen, Mo, there's 24 other guys on this club who want to be world champs, plus a few coaches, and yours truly. That means I can't let you worry only about yourself, no matter how much it bothers you. The strategy right now is to get you on second so you can score on a hit. The next run will probably win the game and the Series. So I'm telling you again right now to go on the next pitch. Don't worry about getting picked off. Just keep your eye on that right leg of his, and as soon as you see it pointing toward the plate, take off! You hear what I'm saying?"

Just then the home plate umpire came over by the top step of the dugout and asked Jake if it was an official coffee break or what. Before Jake could answer, he shouted in at us, "Let's play ball," and started walking back.

Jake looked at Fontaine again. "This pitch," he said. "Have you got it straight?"

Mo didn't say a word. He just nodded his head up and down and got up off the bench. He started out of the dugout, then turned around and said to Jake, "This is the last time."

Jake sat back down and watched Mo jog out to first. "What the hell does that mean?" he asked, but he wasn't expecting me to say anything.

You know the rest, Dave. Mo started for second just a fraction too soon. Wheeler had him picked off dead to rights. But his cockiness must have caught up with him. Instead of just firing the ball, like he was ready to do, he tried to aim it over to first. Fortunately for us, he lost his rhythm and threw it wild past the bag.

Mo saw what happened and ran the fastest 270 feet in his life. The right fielder was playing over toward center for Brandon and had to go all the way to the stands, past the foul line, to get the ball. He made a good throw, and the play at the plate was close, but I don't think anything could have stopped Fontaine from scoring that run. He moved around the bases like his life depended on it, maybe like he knew it was the last chance he'd ever get to do it.

When he came into the dugout, everyone gave him a high five or a big hug. Even Jake got up and slapped Mo's shoulder a couple of times when he went by, but didn't say anything to him. We got just the one run. Then Morrison came in to close it and did what he gets paid all that money to do.

I was glad Mo caught the last out of the game on that ball up the alley no one else would have reached. Later on, after all the celebrating on the field and the champagne in the clubhouse, Mo brought the ball over to where I was dressing. He had already signed it and put the date on it.

"Give this to Jake for me," he said, "but hold onto it until the first day of spring training." He winked at me, and I had a feeling even then, without knowing what I know now, that we'd seen the last of him on the club.

A few months later, after Fontaine announced his decision to retire and concentrate on football, I got a call from his mother. I'd met her at one of our games earlier in the year. She had just learned the real reason from Mo herself and told me the whole story. She felt that someone in our organization ought to know what happened to him in high school — like I told you earlier — and what kind of scars it left. And the straw that broke the camel's back for Mo was Jake ordering him to steal off Wheeler after he told Jake he couldn't do it. In Mo's mind it was another white guy doing something to him he didn't deserve, ready to embarrass him again in front of a stadium full of people. He told his mother he wouldn't have to put up with anything like that in football, that it would just be him against whoever was covering him.

She made me promise not to tell the story to the press because Mo didn't want anyone's sympathy. I also think she was afraid most people wouldn't understand his feelings and would call him a quitter. This way, he went out as a hero and that's how they'll always remember him. I decided not to say a word to Jake at the time because I wasn't sure how he'd take it. I'm gonna give him that baseball today, but I'm still not sure whether I'll let him know what it was that kept Mo from trying to steal off Wheeler.

And you know what, Davey? When we had the breakup party a couple of days after the Series, Mo didn't show. He was the only one who missed it. I guess he'd already made up his mind what he was going to do. As far as I know, he left town without ever saying "Goodbye" to anyone on the club. Just stole away, you might say.

THE WAY THEY PLAY IS CRIMINAL

"It helps if the hitter thinks you're a little crazy."

—Nolan Ryan

WHAT I LIKE best about the baseball writers' dinners I get to take in during the off-season are the questions they ask me while we're standing around socializing and making a big hit out of the cash bar. Most of the fans who come around know I've done about everything there is in this game. I played fifteen years for the Dodgers in Brooklyn, coming up the same year DiMaggio did with the Yankees. When I couldn't hit anymore and was set to retire, the front office decided I had what it took to be a big league manager. I hadn't given it much thought before then, but I liked the idea when they threw it at me. First, though, I had to pay my dues down on the farm until the organization felt I could handle a major-league ball club and get respect from all the guys.

We won the Pennant the first year I took over the team, and then the World Series against the White Sox three years later. That came after O'Malley broke a lot of hearts and moved the team to LA. I ran the club for five seasons, which was more than enough for me. Then I got moved up to assistant general manager, which I was willing to try for a while, but being inside all day drove me nuts. I begged the team president, Bunny Durango, to get me into something else. He came up with a scouting job on the west coast and down into Mexico, and I grabbed it. That's what I did for the Dodgers the next eighteen years until I hit the big sixty-five and got out of the game for good.

Since then, the writers in town have been great, inviting me back every year and giving me a seat at the head table. I remember when this shindig used to cost 25 bucks and draw a couple hundred people. Now, they pull in over 700, which is about every seat they can squeeze into the Sheraton ballroom; and the price to come through the door is three times what it was back then. So I always get there early and start mixing with the crowd right away because I know there's lots of them who've got stuff they want to ask me about. And the truth is that's the part of the night I get the biggest kick out of.

People want to know things like, "How did the other Dodgers feel about Jackie Robinson when he first made the team?" or "How did Duke Snider stack up against Mays and Mantle in center field?" Another one I hear a lot is, "Was Sandy Koufax the best left-hander you ever saw?" That one's easy. I just say, "You tell me who was better."

Then there's folks who are big on details and ask things like did I ever see three triples in a row, or who hit the longest home run in Ebbets Field while I was there. I have to stop and think about questions like that, and sometimes I just say I don't know.

But at the dinner a week ago this guy came up to me, and he had half a dozen different Dodger buttons pinned on his jacket, including one with a picture of me and Peewee. We had a good laugh about how I only looked a couple of years older than in the picture, and then he threw this one at me: "With all the ball games you've seen in your career," he said, "is there one game that sticks out in your memory from all the others?"

That's something I knew I'd never been asked before, but I didn't have to think more than a few seconds before a certain game came right back to me. And it was like I'd just seen it played that afternoon. "Yup, there sure is," I told him, "and it'll probably surprise you to hear it wasn't even in the Big Leagues."

Well, a few other folks heard the question, and I guess they could tell from the way I answered that there was a good story there. So they moved in closer and I told them everything just as I remembered it.

It happened near the end of my first year scouting, while the wife and I were driving up and down the Pacific coast from Washington to Mexico nine months a year. I spent the day checking out ballplayers at the colleges and all the local parks while she stayed back at the motel watching her soaps and knitting something or other for the two grandkids we had. We were outside San Francisco on a trip, heading back to LA to rest up for a week or so, when I got a message at the motel to call my office. Harry Pidgin was the GM at the time, and that turned out to be the last year O'Malley kept him on the payroll because the club finished in the basement, too many games behind. He wasn't bringing in enough talent for the team to do any better.

Anyhow, Pidgin said he had an unusual assignment for me, and I found out he wasn't kidding. It had to do with this kid named Darnell Humboldt who'd been serving time in San Quentin for five years — since he was eighteen years old. He'd been sent up for killing the cashier in an all-night convenience store. It was one of those dumb early morning murders you read about where the guy usually gets away with all of 50 or 60 bucks for his trouble because the clerk who went home at midnight already dropped off the night's take in a bank deposit box just down the street. Humboldt's lawyer was pushing for a new trial, claiming some important new evidence had just turned up, and a story in the LA paper caught Pidgin's eye about how there was a chance the kid might go free.

The reason Harry got interested right away when he saw it was that Humboldt had been the best high school baseball player in LA for three years running. Everyone who'd seen the kid in action had said how he couldn't miss making it in the Big Leagues someday. He started playing for San Quentin when he got sent up, and every so often there was a blurb in one of the home town papers about something he did, like hitting three home runs in a game or finishing up with a .450 batting average.

What Pidgin told me was that San Quentin was going over to Alcatraz to play on Sunday and he wanted me to scout Humboldt in that one because the Alcatraz club had a great record and would be good competition. It wasn't anything I would have volunteered to do, so I hemmed and hawed a little when he came out with it, hoping he'd send someone else. But Harry said he'd already checked into the arrangements and I didn't have to worry about anything happening to me while I was there.

"It's part of the job, Joe,' he said. 'That's why you're getting paid to scout."

I didn't want him thinking I was getting lazy or anything so I tried to make a joke out of it and said he had me between the Rock and a hard place. He liked that one and laughed. Then he told me where I had to be at exactly ten o'clock that Sunday morning.

The boat that took us over to Alcatraz could probably hold about 50 people. It was what you'd more than likely be on if you were celebrating your anniversary and took the wife on one of those candlelight harbor cruises at night. I could see where a four or five piece band would set up and play at the back end and folks would be dancing, kind of squeezed together on a small floor, or sitting around with drinks in their hands.

When I first got on, there were three other guys up front, standing in the narrow passageway that leads to the bathrooms and the front deck. They were just staring out toward the Rock, sitting there in the middle of the bay. I figured they might have been the umpires for the game. Ordinarily, I would've gone over and asked, but Harry told me I was supposed to mind my own business and not try to get friendly with anyone.

There were five state cops on the boat, too, talking with each other along the side away from the dock. Every couple of minutes one of them looked over toward the pier to see if anything was happening. They were dressed in full uniform, like they were going to a parade, with their gray, baggy pants stuffed inside those tall brown boots they must have spit shined that morning. And all of them had on large, wire-framed sunglasses. There was a lot of laughing going on, but I thought they all looked kind of nervous.

At about ten-thirty a yellow school bus came down the wharf and pulled up alongside the boat. I don't know if they could see out the tinted windows from inside, but we couldn't look in. Maybe ten minutes went by before the front door opened and three prison guards stepped out. The cops moved over to my side of the boat to see what was going on.

The prisoners who came off the bus were all dressed the same, like a college football team traveling to another school for a game. They had on red sweatshirts, khaki pants, and baseball jackets that were silver and black, like the colors of the Oakland Raiders. Their black caps had silver lettering on the front — an "S" and a "Q" that were intertwined. I found out later it stood not only for San Quentin, but for SharQues, the team name.

The first two came down the steps, and I saw they were handcuffed together. Then, while they stood there, one of the guards opened a big duffle bag he'd pulled out of the storage area of the bus and spilled a pile of these metal shackles on the ground. He picked up a set and pinned one side around the right ankle of the first guy and the other around the left ankle of his buddy. The two other guards stood a few feet away, holding machine guns. It felt weird knowing the guys I'd be watching play ball in a couple of hours were dangerous convicts who had to be handled that way.

One guard helped the first two prisoners get on the boat and he walked them down to the end of the long fold-down bench that ran along the side next to the dock. At that point, the state cops got down to business and took positions opposite the bench, from one end of it to the other, about five feet apart. Each of them stood with his right hand on his pistol holster, and I could see that all the holsters were already unsnapped. Pidgin had told me that Humboldt weighed 200 pounds and was six foot three, but I couldn't pick him out by size as the guard kept bringing them on the boat in two's. Half of them looked big enough to go in the ring as heavyweights. I was sure that two of the smaller ones who came on together were twins. They both had big smiles on their faces as if they'd won free trips on a luxury cruise to Hawaii.

Eighteen guys in all were moved from the bus to the boat in the same way, and they all sat side by side on the bench. The guards pulled about twenty more duffel bags out of the baggage compartment and threw them on board. Then they brought over four folding chairs. The two guards that made the trip over with us took chairs for themselves and sat down across from the players at the two ends of the bench. They had their machine guns on their laps, and never said a word to the state cops, who went back to the other side of the boat as soon as we started heading across the bay.

When we got to the island, a few guys in civilian clothes were waiting for us. One of them recognized me from my Dodgers jacket, said his name was Dennis Renfro and asked me to go with him. Renfro was a small guy, no more than five-five, and thin, too. Both sides of the collar on his white shirt pointed way out toward his shoulders and the knot in his tie was fastened real loose. It was a strange-looking combination. But what surprised me was the leathery tan on his face, because that was something I didn't expect to see on anyone working at a prison. I figured I'd ask him about it if I ever got the right opening, but I never did. He gave me a short tour around the place in his minivan and took me to lunch in a small dining room that he said was used only by administrators who didn't wear uniforms. 'You can't eat here if you carry a gun,' he told me. It turned out he was an assistant warden.

"Were those three other guys on the boat with me the umpires?" I asked. He didn't say anything right away, like he had to think about his answer first.

"I'm not sure," he said. "Did you get to speak to them at all?"

I said I'd been told ahead of time not to talk to anyone and that they weren't acting too friendly anyhow.

"Well, the umps probably got here earlier this morning. Those guys might have been federal inspectors or a few of our own guards coming off vacation. I never noticed them. But look, the game's supposed to start at one-thirty, so let's get over to the field."

On the way there, Renfro told me he'd seen Humboldt play a few times and called him a "gifted" ballplayer. "If we kept statistics the way you do in the Major Leagues, I'm certain they'd show that Humboldt is both the leading hitter for average and home runs of any visiting prisoners we've seen here at Alcatraz. If he was a free man, he'd probably be making two or three million dollars a year."

"Does he do as well when your team plays at San Quentin?" I asked.

"He doesn't have that chance," Renfro answered. "The Rocks play only at home. No road trips for our boys."

When we got to the ballpark, guys on both teams were still doing sprints in the outfield or playing catch in front of the dugouts. Renfro pointed out Humboldt and then explained to me that the field at Alcatraz was regarded as neutral territory.

"Coming here to a game is definitely the biggest privilege these prisoners have," he said. "They can lose it if there's any kind of disturbance, even a fight among themselves. If one of them starts any trouble while he's here, he knows what he'd face from the others if they had to miss any games." As he spoke, Renfro slashed his throat with an imaginary knife. "So they stay on their best behavior while they're here. In return, we don't have any guards in the stands that they'd have to look at while they're watching the game. Makes it more enjoyable, you know. But if a riot ever started for any reason, there are a bunch of guards down in both locker rooms who can get onto the field through the tunnels the players use, and there are more on duty outside the entrances."

The ballpark was 320 feet down the foul lines and 375 to the deepest part of center field. The grass looked like professionals took care of it, and the infield was in great shape too. There was a 30-foot-high fence around the outfield, and a sentry box, with glass walls, was built right on top of the fence at each foul line. Both boxes were in fair territory.

Renfro saw me looking at them. "The guards in there are really supposed to be watching what's happening on the other side of the fence," he said. "Those are exercise areas down there. We've got guards in those sentry boxes all the time, even when no one's using this field. The glass is bulletproof all around, and if a Rocks player hits any part of it during a game, you'll hear a big cheer because then everyone gets a couple of candy bars with dinner."

The wooden grandstands ran just partway around the field, starting behind first base and going as far as third. The wall behind the stands was as high as the one in the outfield, but it dropped down to about twenty feet where it followed the foul lines. The first five rows were off-limits to the prisoners. Renfro said the reason was that once in a while the catcher or an infielder from the visiting team got beat up when he tried to reach inside the stands for a foul ball.

"Some of our boys had the idea that being a loyal fan was doing everything you could to help the team win." He thought that was pretty funny and flashed me a smile when he said it.

Renfro told me I could watch the game with him, from a seat behind either dugout, or sit with Humboldt and his teammates if that would help me do my job any better. "The two San Quentin guards are in there," he let me know. "Nothing to be nervous about."

I said I'd rather be in the stands, at least for a while, but that I'd like to meet Humboldt before the game started. Renfro said, "Sure thing," and took me over to the visitors' dugout on the first base side. Humboldt was sitting down, talking to the two players I thought were twins. Renfro called him and I could see him get interested real fast when he looked up and saw the name on the front of my windbreaker. He came over and Renfro told him who I was. Humboldt was a good-looking kid, with milky green eyes that caught your attention right away, and a short goatee that was trimmed just right. He seemed a lot bigger than Pidgin had said, and had arms that would have made Popeye look like the skinny kid on the beach. I told him I'd heard about his court appeal and that I was there to see what he could do in case he got out. He gave me a movie star grin and said he always wanted to play for the Dodgers, being from LA. I wished him luck and he said he'd remember we were the first team to show an interest.

"By the way, Darnell," I asked him, "are those two guys twins, the ones you were sitting with?"

He turned around to look at them in the dugout and smiled again. "Those are the Berry brothers," he said. "I call one of them 'Straw' and the other one 'Blue,' but unless I see the numbers on their backs I don't know who I'm talking to because they both got the same face. There's no way you can tell them apart, except that Straw's out at shortstop and Blue's over at second base."

Just then an older guy in uniform walked by, close to us. Renfro told me it was Buck Whiting, the San Quentin manager. When Humboldt said he had to go get ready, Renfro led me back to some seats on that side of the field.

"Whiting's been in San Quentin for almost 30 years. He's made the trip over here plenty of times and has friends in Alcatraz who came out of his same neighborhood. The story on him is that he got tired of his wife's nagging one day while he was watching TV and choked her to death with his bare hands. Then, when his in-laws dropped by for a surprise visit that afternoon and found out what happened, he did the same thing to them. He plea-bargained for life without parole. You ought to take a look at the size of his hands if you go in their dugout."

The game stayed close through the first five innings, but that's only because San Quentin had more talent in its lineup than Alcatraz. And they needed every bit of it. I couldn't believe the crap they had to take during the game: from the Rocks, the umpires, and even the prisoners who were watching. Let me give you an idea what I'm talking about.

First of all, I've been around the game long enough to know what a curveball, a slider, or any other breaking pitch is going to look like when it gets to the plate and does what it's supposed to do. And I've seen the tricks a pitcher can play if he cuts up the ball before he lets it go. So I didn't have to guess what was going on when I saw some of the SharQues swing and miss at balls that were falling off the table when they got to the batter's box. Whiting hollered out to the home plate umpire to look at the ball a few times, but the ump never took it out of play. When his own pitcher was out there, Whiting made a couple of trips to the mound to look at the baseball himself, but couldn't find anything wrong with it.

The thing is, though, Whiting kept missing something that I picked up on early. Whenever San Quentin's half of the inning was over, whoever had the ball for Alcatraz always jogged past the third base umpire on the way into the Rocks' dugout and flipped him the ball. Then that ump casually strolled down the line to the home plate umpire and gave it to him before the Rocks came up to bat. When the ump was back behind the plate, he put that ball in a separate pocket of his jacket and threw out a new one to Whiting's pitcher. Next inning, when it was San Quentin's turn to hit again, the ump made sure the ball with the cuts was back in the game. So I knew what was going on out there and realized that for some reason the umps were helping Alcatraz win. But I didn't say anything to Renfro who kept cupping his hands and booing every time Whiting showed his face on the field.

Here's something else. In the third or fourth inning, two unbelievable things happened while the cleanup hitter was at bat for the Rocks. They had a couple of men on base at the time. He fouled off an inside fastball and the bat flew out of his hands in two pieces. When the top half landed on the infield and Straw Berry picked it up at shortstop, about a pound of loose cork began spilling out of one end. I broke up laughing when I saw it. It was an open and shut case of a bat that had been hollowed out and corked up to give it more zip.

Whiting argued that the batter should be called out and given the old heave ho. But the umpire at home acted like he'd been hired to defend the guy. He said he might have been using someone else's bat and didn't know what was in it. So there was no reason to throw him out of the game or call an automatic out. I heard Whiting say "bullshit" a few times before giving up and going back to the bench.

But if Buck thought he was getting it tucked to him, then he was about to find out what a real screwing was like. On the next pitch the hitter put one out of the park down the left field line, foul by a good five feet. It would've hit the sentry box if it stayed fair. The third base umpire took about three baby steps toward the wall and signaled that it was a home run. This time Whiting raced across the diamond, screamed at the ump, and kicked dirt around the place like he was Billy Martin having one of his temper tantrums. Then he appealed the call to the home plate umpire, but that bozo said the same thing, and the three runs that scored brought Alcatraz back into the ball game.

"Looked foul as hell to me," I said to Renfro.

"From here, maybe, but we don't have a good angle on it like they do," he answered. He was still busy booing Whiting who took his time getting back to the dugout.

With the stuff that went on that inning, I knew the SharQues didn't have a chance unless they could keep scoring runs without the umpires having any decisions to make.

And the prisoners in the stands had their own way of helping out the team. There must have been over 200 of them there, and when the game started I noticed that almost all of them were holding onto oranges. I figured that was the Alcatraz substitute for hot dogs and beer and that the place would need a good cleaning when the game was over. But as soon as one of the Rocks hit a popup over near third base, in foul territory, the convicts on that side of the field got up and started throwing their oranges in the air. It was raining oranges all around the baseball. The third baseman kept his eye on it as long as he could, but then ducked out of the way when he saw a couple of oranges coming down where he was standing. The ball landed on the ground and there was a roar from the crowd. Whiting was waved back to the dugout by the umpire at home before he could get halfway there to protest. Then, as soon as the oranges were picked up off the field, the Rocks hitter doubled in another run with the new life he'd been given at the plate. You could say the SharQues got lucky after that because there were only two more infield popups by the Rocks the rest of the game. Both of them were out near second, so it was a much tougher throw from the stands. But that didn't stop the prisoners who still had oranges from trying.

I left Renfro and went into the SharQues dugout at the start of the sixth. At that point San Quentin was down by a run. I told Whiting who I was and got a chance to see his huge paws and feel his strong grip when he shook my hand. He had deep pockmarks on both cheeks and thick salt and pepper eyebrows that looked like inverted "V"s. He told me to take the seat next to him and I did.

The first two SharQues hitters in the inning fanned and Whiting was heating up. He banged his fist on the dugout wall a couple of times and then walked back and forth in front of me.

"He's doing *something* out there to make the ball dip like that," he said. "But I've been watching him every second and I can't figure it out. He's not hiding any Vaseline on his cap or anywhere else and he hasn't been rubbing the ball against his belt buckle. All I know is the movement he's getting on his pitches isn't natural. No one's that good."

Humboldt was up next. He stepped away from the on-deck circle and walked toward the batter's box.

"It's the catcher," I told Whiting.

"What do you mean?" he asked, turning to me quickly.

"An old trick, Buck. The catcher's got a few small nails, like thick thumbtacks, taped to his hand. The points of the nails stick out of the tape and go right through the leather inside his glove. Every time he catches the ball, he rubs it against those points before he throws it back to the pitcher. That's what's cutting it up. Go take a look for yourself."

Just then Humboldt swung and missed at a ball that landed in the dirt in front of the plate. In his first two at bats he'd had a strikeout and a fly ball to deep left field. There wasn't much I could say about him at that point except that he had a picture perfect swing and had shown a cannon for an arm on one throw from right field to third base.

Whiting called time and walked out to the plate. He started going at it with the umpire and I could see he was getting hotter by the second. He put his hands on his hips and was pushing his face right up close to the ump's mask, following him whichever way he turned. Finally, the ump waved to the pitcher and called for the ball. Instead of throwing it back, the pitcher rolled it in toward home, probably hoping it would pick up some dirt and hide the cuts.

Whiting scooped up the baseball, turned it around in his hands and showed it to the umpire. Then he began pointing to the catcher and hollering, "Look at his hands," over and over again. The umpire must have known what he'd find if he did because he kept stalling and trying to move away from Buck. But Buck wouldn't quit, and kept jawing until he finally convinced the ump he had no choice. When the catcher took off his glove, he had half a roll of tape around his hand, just as I'd said, and everyone near the plate could see the nails sticking out. All this time the prisoners in the stands were jeering at Whiting, throwing oranges up in the air around where he stood. The other two umps had come in to see what was going on, and one of them had an orange land with a squish on his shoulder.

I was sure the umpire would throw the catcher out of the game for something like that, but I was wrong again. He just walked part way to the Rocks' dugout, flipped the tape and nails in that direction, and hollered, "Play ball" as he went back to his position. He tossed a new baseball out to the mound, and Humboldt hit the very next pitch over the fence in dead center field.

Whiting thanked me when he got back to the dugout, but still couldn't understand why the ball hadn't done any tricks for his own pitcher. When I told him how the cut ball always got back to the umpire at home before the Alcatraz hitters batted, he picked up on the fact that the umps were trying to help the Rocks beat his team.

"Those bastards must be getting paid off," he said.

The game stayed tied for a couple of innings, but as soon as the Rocks couldn't doctor the ball anymore and lost that advantage, they pulled another trick out of their bag. Larry Laurel, the SharQues pitcher, had been getting stronger as the game moved along. But while he was working in the last of the seventh, he suddenly began sneezing and couldn't stop. He'd go ten or more sneezes, one right after the other, and then hurry to get a pitch off as soon as it let up for a few seconds. But he'd lose control in the middle of his delivery, sneeze again and be way out of the strike zone. Laurel walked two batters before Whiting went out to the mound. The kid seemed to be able to hold it back while Buck talked to him, but as soon as he dried his pitching hand with the rosin bag and put his foot on the rubber, it started all over again, even worse than before.

"The prisoners started clapping their hands and chanting, "Play ball! Play ball!" Laurel couldn't do anything but sneeze, and the noise from the stands got louder and louder. The home plate umpire came about halfway over to the San Quentin dugout. He shouted in to Whiting that unless Laurel was ready to throw in the next 30 seconds, the SharQues had to bring in a new pitcher. There was nothing Whiting could say, and Laurel's condition didn't get any better. He looked like a beaten man out there, bent halfway over at the waist, sneezing continuously, wiping his nose with the arm of his shirt and spitting all over the mound.

While this was going on, I noticed that some of the Rocks players were laughing up a storm in their dugout. I thought something smelled, and then it hit me all of a sudden. When Whiting started up the steps to go bring in a relief pitcher, I told him I wanted to see the rosin bag Laurel was using. When they came off the field, I said I thought I'd figured out what was going on but that Buck would have to sacrifice one guy on the bench that he was sure he wouldn't need later on in the game. He whistled one of the players over and I had the kid grab the bag in his hand and then rub his finger against his nose. A few seconds later the poor guy was doing a perfect imitation of Larry Laurel.

"It's certain kinds of pepper seeds they put in there," I told Whiting. "Jalapeno peppers and other hot stuff. It was a gag they used to pull in Single-A ball years ago. That's how they welcomed some new phenom pitcher into the league. They tortured the guy his first or second time out. It got so bad they made it unlawful, and a team would forfeit the game if it tried that crap."

Whiting was furious at losing his best pitcher that way. He grabbed the rosin bag with a towel, folded the towel over a few times until he could hold it in the palm of his hand, walked halfway across the infield, and flung it toward the Alcatraz dugout. His face was bright red, and I remember thinking that if someone had given him a hand grenade just then, he would have stuck it inside the towel, pulled the pin, and thrown the whole thing at the Rocks players on the bench.

The San Quentin relief pitcher was allowed to take as long as he wanted to warm up, but he stopped a little too soon. The first two batters he faced hit consecutive doubles and the Rocks took a three-run lead.

The SharQues came right back and got the hit from Humboldt that should have tied the score again in the eighth, but the umpires were still playing games. With two runners on, Darnell hit another blast, this time to left. It was over the sentry box, about six feet fair when it left the park, no doubt about it. But the third base ump, who had called the foul drive by the Alcatraz cleanup hitter a home run in one of the early innings, waved his arms away from the field, signaling that the ball was foul. Whiting couldn't believe it when he saw the home run being taken away from his team. He pulled off his cap, screamed out a few swear words he must have been saving for a call as bad as that, and was about to race out onto the field.

"Don't bother," I said. "It's a waste of time. The umps are in the bag. You said so yourself."

He banged the side of the dugout with both of his massive fists. "Sons of bitches," he hissed.

Humboldt walked back to the plate slowly, shaking his head in disbelief all the way. He got good wood on the next pitch but lined it straight to the center fielder, who caught the ball without having to move a step.

Alcatraz had a giant pitcher on the team; a right-hander. I'm not kidding when I tell you he was tall enough to play basketball up front for the Lakers, weighed close to 250 pounds, and looked as mean as they come. He had a heavy, black mustache, sideburns like Elvis Presley, and a growth of hair around his chin that was probably into its second week. It was a weird combination. The Rocks had a three-run lead after eight innings, and brought in this monster to try and close out San Quentin in the ninth. But it was a mistake, because the big guy had trouble finding the plate and wasn't all that hard to hit when he got it over. He could scare the crap out of you when he looked in from the mound. He was someone you wouldn't want to meet in a dark alley, but pitching wasn't his thing. Not that day, anyway.

Before the Rocks manager finally gave him the hook, San Quentin had two runs in, the bases loaded, and one out. The new pitcher who took over was a southpaw, and he must have been told to throw nothing but fastballs. He followed orders, and it took just four pitches for the umpire to call the next SharQues hitter out on strikes. The trouble was that three of the deliveries were so far off the plate that any manager would have chewed out his player, and maybe even fined him, for swinging at any of them. Whiting was absolutely boiling, but he knew that bitching about it was useless. His club was down to its last out.

The Berry brother who played shortstop began walking toward the plate. I'd seen during the game that the biggest difference between the twins was that Straw couldn't hit to save his life, but Blue, the second baseman, handled the bat like Pete Rose. He was already three for four in the game, with a double. At that point Buck must have figured he had one chance to get even with the Rocks and the umpires for everything they'd done to him and his team that day. He called Straw back to the dugout and hustled him into the tunnel that led down to the team's locker room. He sent Blue in there too, and told them to switch uniform shirts in a hurry.

"Get up there and hit," he told Blue, "and swing at it if it's anywhere near the plate. He's throwing all heat, no breaking stuff." Blue grinned and headed for the batter's box. When I looked down the bench to where Straw had taken a seat, his face was one big grin too.

On the second pitch, Blue nailed one into the gap in right center. Two runs scored, and the runner on first slid across the plate before the catcher tagged him, but the umpire pumped his fist and called him out. There was no holding Whiting back, and he ran out to argue the play. By the time he got there, the SharQues base runner had his face almost inside the umpire's mask, shouting to beat the band. I don't know if the runner intentionally spit during the argument or whether it was just an accident, but the umpire pulled off his mask to wipe his face with the sleeve of his jacket and then thumbed the guy out of the game as soon as he put it back on. Buck saw what happened, stared hard at the ump for a few seconds, and then jogged back to the bench without saying a word. I figured he was afraid of getting thrown out too if he did.

So now the SharQues had a one-run lead to try and hold onto in the last of the ninth, and I was tempted to tell Whiting to fasten his seatbelt. I was sure something bad had to be coming. The first Rocks batter hit an easy fly ball to right that Humboldt grabbed. The next guy up never took the bat off his shoulder and walked. Buck and I could both see that two of the pitches the ump called balls were right down the middle — perfect strikes. He turned to me and just shrugged his shoulders in disgust. I thought San Quentin had the game won when the cleanup man smashed a double play ball to the third baseman, but he took his eye off it for an instant and the ball bounced off his glove. That put runners on first and second. Then the Rocks center fielder surprised everyone with a gorgeous bunt and reached base without a throw.

As you could expect, there was one hell of a racket coming from the stands, especially when Alcatraz loaded the bases. It was the kind of mob eruption that would have had prison guards reaching for their guns in any other setting. Whiting ran out to the mound and called the whole infield around him for a conference.

"Anything up?" I asked, when he trotted back in.

"No, just a little pep talk. I told them there were still a few oranges left in the seats, so to get back in here quick when they made the last out."

The Rocks next batter fouled off the first pitch and then let three more go by without showing any interest. The SharQues battery thought they had him struck out twice, but the guy was still up there, with a count of 2-2, because the ump ignored two sensational curve balls that broke in over the plate. Buck's team got a break, though, when the Rocks hitter swung and missed at a low slider. He threw his bat on the ground, upset with himself, and started back toward the dugout. What happened next was unbelievable. The umpire called him back to the plate, indicating with his fingers that the count was 3-2. The SharQues catcher yanked off his mask and was so upset he began banging it against his thigh without realizing it while he moved in on the ump to get him to correct himself and call the strikeout. The pitcher ran in toward the plate. "That was strike three," he screamed. "It was 2-2 before that pitch. He's out of there."

"This has really gotten ugly," I said to Whiting. "And if the next one is down the pike, he'll call it ball four."

"I don't think so," he said. 'This bullshit is going to stop right here.'

Whiting waited for the argument at home to end. He heard the umpire telling his players they were wrong about the count. He was sure, the ump said, that he hadn't called any strikes after the foul ball, and told the pitcher to get back where he belonged or he'd be out of the game.

Then Buck left the dugout and walked very slowly out toward the plate. He stopped about ten feet short of home and stood there. I don't know if he said anything to the umpire just then because he had his back to me, but a few seconds later the ump walked over to where Buck was waiting. It looked to me like Whiting didn't want anyone else to hear what he had to say. He did all the talking when they were up close because I could see that the umpire didn't open his mouth. Then Buck called his catcher over, whispered something to him and came back to the dugout.

"Something tells me that SOB will start doing his job now," he said, and winked at me.

The noise in the park picked up again quickly. The runners at the three bases took their leads and tried to shake up the pitcher by calling him all kinds of names. The 3-2 pitch was a borderline strike. It could have been called either way and no one would have had a legitimate complaint. If it caught the outside edge of the plate, it was by the width of a toothpick. I couldn't believe it when the umpire's right arm shot up in the air and then in our direction while he hollered out the third strike. Buck just sat there calmly, but I could see a little bit of a smile on his lips. For the first time in the game the Alcatraz manager was out on the field raising a beef, but it got him nowhere.

"You must have said the right thing, whatever it was," I told Whiting, wondering what it could have been.

"I guess I did," he answered.

The game ended on a spectacular play. The Rocks catcher, who batted left-handed, was all that stood in the way of a victory by San Quentin. He found out that the umpire was suddenly calling a strike a strike, and he had two of them before going after the next pitch. He hit a screaming line drive into right center field that sent Humboldt moving to his right at the crack of the bat. Running as hard as he could with those long, loping strides of his, he dove for the ball at the last instant, stretching his body out as far as it could go, and backhanded it just before the ball hit the ground. His momentum forced him to roll over twice before he could jump up and show everyone that the ball was in his glove. If the first base umpire, who was closest to the play, had any thought of ruling that the ball had landed on the ground and that Humboldt had trapped it, he changed his mind fast when he heard the home plate umpire shouting from behind him that the batter was out.

Whiting had left the dugout and was out on the field an instant before Humboldt made the catch. When he heard the "out" call, he stopped, took a long look over at the Rocks' bench, and pointed the middle finger of his right hand in the air. Then he came back down the steps and shook my hand again. "Some game," he said, and headed for the tunnel to the locker room.

An hour later I was on the boat going back to San Francisco. Renfro had taken me to the dining room after the game and we talked about some of the plays over coffee and chocolate cake. I told him I thought the umpires had given Alcatraz most of the calls, but he disagreed and said they had no reason to favor one team over another.

"What really bothers me is the hit that beat us," he said. "I wouldn't mind if it had come from the Berry kid out at second, but his brother, the shortstop, is about the worst hitter I've ever seen." He took a deep breath and let out a sigh. "I guess that's what the damn law of averages is all about," he said. I wondered if he'd ever find out the truth. I hoped not, so that what happened would bother him for a long time.

Renfro asked me what I thought of Humboldt and I said I was sure the Dodgers would talk to him. I was already thinking to myself about Humboldt winning his case and word getting out around the league that I was the scout who signed him to a contract.

The San Quentin team, back in handcuffs and shackles, was already on board when Renfro dropped me off at the boat. They sat side by side on the same long bench, but now there was a lot of laughing and joking going on.

I figured that what I'd been told about not talking with anyone was the same on the return trip as it was going over, so I sat down by myself on the front deck to enjoy the scenery. I was surprised a little later on when one of the state cops came over and said that Buck Whiting wanted to see me. I went with him and he let me take the folding chair that was opposite Whiting's place on the bench.

"Like I said before, some game, huh?" Whiting said, in greeting me.

"It sure was," I told him. "One I'll never forget."

"I wanted to thank you for helping us out. Most of that shit the Rocks pulled was all new to me. They must have wanted to win that game awfully bad because we really beat up on them when we were out there last year. It was something like 15-3."

"Well, you found a good way to get even in the ninth," I said. "The assistant warden still can't believe your shortstop got a big hit in the clutch. It's driving him crazy."

Whiting laughed. "Yeah, Blue made a hero out of Straw, and Straw loves it. Everyone's going to say the shortstop won the game. But that assistant warden deserves it, man. I'll bet he was in on the umpire deal, too."

Buck had me confused. "What do you mean?" I asked.

"You remember how you were wondering what I said to the home plate umpire after he gave the Rocks hitter an extra strike in the ninth inning?"

"I sure do," I told him. Now I couldn't wait to hear.

"I'll tell you what it was. I never had a good look at that man all game because he kept his mask on all the time, even between innings. But then he took it off just that once in the ninth when our guy washed his face with some well-deserved saliva." Whiting laughed again, a lot harder this time. "You know, I never saw that happen to an umpire before," he said. The laughter brought tears to his eyes. "Anyhow, while he was wiping his cheek, I saw the scar he had on the left side of his face, going from the corner of his eye down under his chin. I knew I'd seen that face before, and then it hit me in the dugout who he was. His name's Cleon Townsend, but most of the time he's called "Candy.""

Whiting stopped. I kept staring at him until I realized he was waiting for me to ask the next question. "Who's Candy Townsend?"

"He's a prisoner, man, right there in Alcatraz. He's been there almost as long as I've been in San Quentin, and I remembered that he played against us for the Rocks once or twice when he first got there. That's when I knew that the umpires were ringers, not even regular umps who were getting paid off to help them steal the game from us. It was no wonder we'd been having every big call there was go against us. The home run they gave them and the one they took away from Humboldt made a difference of six runs right there."

Whiting stopped again. He seemed to be thinking about something. "Darnell is some ballplayer," he said. "You ought to sign that boy if he beats the rap."

"We'll try," I said. "Tell me more about Townsend."

"Yeah. So the next time I went out to the plate, when he said the count was three and two instead of it already being a strikeout, I told Candy I knew who he was. I gave him the names of a few close friends of mine at the Rock, guys with a heavy reputation, who'd be glad to stick a knife in his ribs if I asked them to. I told him he might be unpopular for a while if his team lost the game, but that if he made one more lousy call to help Alcatraz win, he was a dead man. I guess he believed what I said."

"What happened to the real umps?" I asked.

"I'm not sure," Buck said. "They probably got locked in their dressing room by accident, if you know what I mean. No one could find the key to let them out. That's what the warden or one of his boys would have taken care of so the ringers could call the game. I'll bet that's them sitting over there on the other side. Why don't you go ask?"

I told Buck I would, said goodbye, and wished him luck. I started to reach out to shake his hand, but then realized the guards might take it the wrong way. He saw what I had in mind and gave me a wink and a smile, nodding his head up and down. On the way back to my seat, I walked over to the three men, the same ones I'd seen on the ride over to the island. I asked them if they'd been involved in the baseball game at Alcatraz that afternoon. They looked at each other and then one of them surprised me when he said they had umpired it.

At first I didn't know what to say next. "Was it a good game?" I finally asked.

"Nothing special," he answered. "About what you'd expect from two teams that don't know how baseball ought to be played. Boring as hell."

I wondered whether he was too embarrassed to tell me the truth about why they had never made it onto the field. Perhaps there had been something else going on between them and certain officials on the Rock, something even Whiting didn't suspect. I knew there was no sense asking and that I'd never find out.

"Yeah," I said, "I've seen a lot of those games. You forget all about them as soon as you leave the ballpark. I was going to take it in while I was there, but I'm glad I didn't bother."

Two months later the papers ran a story about the fact that Humboldt's attempt to get another trial had been denied by the California Supreme Court. All of the so-called "new evidence" had been there all the time, the Court said. That's the last I ever heard of him. For all I know, he may still be hitting them over the walls for the SharQues and making those backhanded catches in right field. Too bad, though, he seemed like a good kid back then. And he might have saved Harry Pidgin's job.

ACKNOWLEDGMENTS

M Y M OST HEARTFELT thanks to Margot Hayward, whom I knew only as a SABR member when she answered my call to read and rank some of my stories. She has since become a dear friend over the years as many more have been written. She lives for her Mets, a love she once reserved for the Dodgers of Brooklyn, and when asked, she came up with the title for this book in her first at bat.

My gratitude goes out to the others who read these stories and gave me their helpful feedback, including Margot's husband Bob, Ray Anselmo, Chip Atkison, Tom Eckel, Steve Hoy, Marc Seror, Lisa Wrobel, and Jack Zerby.

Thanks to Sandy Lottor, my good friend for years, who always pushed me a little farther forward with his inspiration and suggestions. I owe much to my dear Brandeis University classmate, Myron Uhlberg, who, in those telephone calls that seemed to go on forever, encouraged me over the years to keep writing and offered wonderful insight into how a story could be improved. Another classmate, Bill McKenna, called periodically from Calgary to comment on a story I had sent him and to make sure I was still putting pen to paper. And Cliff Hauptman, a friend and great editor who took home a story or two to review whenever we met for lunch.

I also thank the terrific people at SABR, including John Zajc, Jim Charlton, and Ryan Chamberlain who were so generous with their time in answering a number of my questions and steering me in fruitful directions. My thanks also to Stan Rosenzweig for digging into his baseball encyclopedia whenever I called in need of another fact or two to help a story along. I am certainly most grateful to the distinguished baseball writers who read these stories at my request and honored me with what they have written about the book.

I am deeply indebted to my agent, Peter Riva, of International Transactions, Inc., who never let up in his determination to see these stories published.